A DUBIOUS LEGACY

Mary Wesley was born as Mary Farmar in 1912 to an upper-class family and grew up a rebel who believed that she was her mother's least favourite child. Like many girls of her background, she married for escape and her first marriage, to Lord Swinfen, was brief. In 1944, she met Eric Siepmann, an unsuccessful writer whom she adored. Their relationship, which was mercurial and bohemian, lasted until his death. Having taken the pen name Wesley from the family name of Wellesley she published her first novel when she was seventy years old and went on to write a subsequent nine dazzling bestsellers, including *The Camomile Lawn*. She was awarded the CBE in the 1995 New Years honours list and died in 2002.

ALSO BY MARY WESLEY

MARY WESLEY

A Dubious Legacy

VINTAGE BOOKS
London

Published by Vintage 2008

4 6 8 10 9 7 5

Copyright © Mary Wesley 1992

Mary Wesley has asserted her right under the Copyright, Designs and Patents Act 1988 to be identified as the author of this work

First published in Great Britain in 1992 by
Bantam Press

Random House, 20 Vauxhall Bridge Road,
London SW1V 2SA

www.vintage-books.co.uk

Addresses for companies within The Random House Group Limited can be found at: www.randomhouse.co.uk/offices.htm

The Random House Group Limited Reg. No. 954009

A CIP catalogue record for this book
is available from the British Library

ISBN 9780099513049

The Random House Group Limited supports the Forest Stewardship Council (FSC ®), the leading international forest certification organisation. Our books carrying the FSC label are printed on FSC® certified paper. FSC is the only forest certification scheme endorsed by the leading environmental organisations, including Greenpeace. Our paper procurement policy can be found at www.randomhouse.co.uk/environment

Printed and bound by CPI Group (UK) Ltd, Croydon, CR0 4YY

For Isobel

Part One

1944

1

'I thought you said you had a car?'

The horse, between the shafts of the dogcart, turned its head at the sound of the woman's voice. She was tall, with narrow shoulders and narrow feet; she had pale apricot hair and a white skin. The eyes noting the horse were green. She had painted her mouth pillar-box red. The horse, dark and polished as a conker, returned her stare, its startled eye fringed by straight lashes. It breathed out, expanding velvet nostrils and, shifting its weight, caused its harness to creak and jingle. Then, catching sight of the man behind the woman, it pricked its ears, raised its head, whinnied shrilly and lurched forward. The woman, stepping back, crushed a sharp heel onto the man's instep. She exclaimed, 'How horrible.'

The man said, 'Ouch! Hullo, my treasure, my beauty.' He stepped forward to stroke the animal's neck and breathe up its nostrils. 'This is Nellie,' he said, 'and there, where Trask is stashing our luggage, is her daughter. She is called Petronella, in honour of petrol rationing. The joke seemed apposite at the time of her birth.'

The woman said, '*Another* cart?'

'Well, yes. One for us and one for our bags. Trask thought it would be more comfortable for you if he brought both traps.'

'I thought you said you had a car.' She stood well back from the horse and looked round the station yard.

'A Bentley, you said. You said you had a Bentley.'

'I have. It was my father's.'

'Then where is it?'

'Up on blocks for the duration.'

'Not here to meet me?'

'No.'

'Why not?'

'An old Bentley only goes about ten miles to the gallon. Come on, now. Hop up.' He indicated the trap.

'No.'

'Why didn't you tell me you were afraid of horses?'

'I'm not.'

'Then hop up. Trask will follow with the luggage. It's eight miles; it will be dark if we don't start soon.'

'I don't *like* them.' Margaret Tillotson stared at her husband.

'Everything all right, Henry?' A slightly-built man wearing grey flannel trousers, an open-necked shirt and a sleeveless Fair Isle jersey came up from where he had been loading suitcases into the second trap. He was a servant, Margaret supposed, yet he called Henry Henry, not Mr Tillotson.

'Has madam mislaid something?' he enquired.

'Madam was expecting to be met by the Bentley,' said Henry evenly.

Trask said, 'Oh dear,' pursing his lips. He had a long upper lip and was clean-shaven.

Henry said, laughing, 'It *is*, Oh dear. This is Trask, on whom so much depends.'

Trask, smiling, said, 'Pleased, delighted, M—'

Margaret parted her red lips, showing excellent teeth, but said nothing.

Trask, glancing at Henry, said, 'What about the station taxi? It will be back in a minute. It's only taken the lady who lodges with the Watsons to the Post.'

Henry said, 'Mrs Watson is our postmistress.'

Margaret said, 'Oh yes?'

'Smells a bit?' said Henry, questioning the taxi.

'Combustion engine,' said Trask, straight-faced.

Henry said, 'True. All right, then, taxi it is. We'll wait,' on a cheerful note.

They stood looking at the empty station yard. From time to time one of the horses shook its head, stamped or blew gustily down its nose.

Trask said conversationally, 'Coming to meet you, Henry, I drove Petronella and Nellie followed on her own as sweet as pie.'

Henry said, 'The dear thing.' He caressed the horse's neck. 'And how are things?' he asked. 'Is all well?'

Trask said, 'Yes,' glancing sidelong at Margaret. 'Seemingly.'

'And Pilar and Ebro?'

'They are fine.'

'Pilar is the Spanish girl I told you about,' Henry told his wife. 'Ebro is her baby, quite a big boy now. Must be three or four.'

'Nearly six,' said Trask.

'Your Spanish maid.'

'Not exactly a maid, she's a refugee.'

'But she cleans?'

'Well, yes, but nobody asks her to.'

'*I* shall.'

Trask said, 'Here comes the taxi now,' jerking his chin towards the road. 'Name of Smith.' When the taxi drew up Henry walked across to speak to the driver. After a short discussion he beckoned to his wife and called, 'Come along, in you get.' He held open the car door. When Margaret was in, he closed it.

Alone on the seat, Margaret said, 'But aren't you—'

Henry said, 'No, I'm driving Nellie.'

Margaret and the taximan watched Henry swing himself up into the trap, pick up the reins and chirrup to the horse, who trotted off, followed by Trask in the second trap.

Margaret murmured, 'Bastard.'

The driver switched on his engine, let in the clutch and followed.

After watching the traps bowling merrily along for three-quarters of a mile, Margaret said, 'Can't you drive faster?'

'I don't know the way, madam,' said the driver.

Margaret said, 'You must be lying.'

The driver, who had lived in the neighbourhood for only three months and was chiefly employed driving children to school, thought of suitable ripostes but kept them to himself.

Although the horses kept up a spanking pace, inevitably, going uphill, they slowed to a walk. Rather than crawl after them in low gear, the taxi-driver amused himself by idling his engine while the horses toiled uphill, waiting a bit, then making a rush to the top, switching off the engine and coasting down. He excused his method. 'Saves petrol. Can't be too careful with my ration, have to stretch it. Though how you stretch an inflammable liquid, your guess is as good as mine.'

Margaret did not reply, but stared past him at Henry's back.

'My name is John Smith,' the driver volunteered. 'You must be Mrs Tillotson, new to these parts, like me. Very pretty country, of course. I'm a townsman, myself.'

Margaret was watching the progress of the vehicles ahead. From time to time her husband swung round to talk to Trask in the trap behind him. When the driver stilled his engine she could hear Henry's deep voice, but could not catch his words or Trask's, answering in a melodious tenor. After a while Henry stopped turning round and became absorbed by the view of the countryside.

From her seat in the taxi, Margaret took note of it also. They had left the main road immediately on leaving the station and negotiated a network of narrow lanes. In the taxi Margaret Tillotson felt enclosed, but the men driving ahead could from the high traps see over the hedges; they called out to each other when they caught sight of anything which attracted their attention. Presently, as they climbed, they reached more open country and crossed a stretch of moorland, before dipping into a valley of large fields bounded by thick hedges and surrounded by woods already turning copper and gold. Sheep grazed in the fields and several times the leading trap startled a pheasant, which flew up cack-cack-cacking. When a frightened hare bounded away Trask called out on a high eerie note and Henry laughed.

'Pretty.' John Smith stopped his car. 'Almost as nice as Kensington Gardens. Or maybe you prefer St James's Park? Or would you fancy Richmond? Lot of bushes with berries on them in Richmond. I'd say this is more like Richmond, but wilder.' His fare did not reply. 'Well, I guess we're nearly there,' he said. 'That will be the house. Those horses are trying to gallop, must want their tea. Is it as grand as you was expecting?' She had licked all the lipstick off her mouth, he noted as he watched her in the driving mirror; the only colour in her face was in her eyes. 'Nice house,' he said. 'I'd call it quite grand; just right, not too big and not too small.'

Ahead of them the horses had rattled up the last incline and come to a stop in front of the house. They now stretched their necks and snorted as Henry and Trask jumped down.

The house, built of honey-coloured stone, was

seventeeth century. Its walls played host to roses and honeysuckle. On one corner a late magnolia flowered; round another wisteria straggled. The paint on the front door was flaking and the paintwork of the windows was in need of attention; Margaret noted, too, as she sat waiting for the car door to be opened, that a young woman stood smiling on the front steps.

She was short, square and very dark; she had the parrot jaw often seen in southern Spain, black hair drawn back in a bun and small black eyes. The child dragging at her hand resembled her closely. They were a plain couple, but their evident joy on seeing Henry lit their faces with beauty.

'Pilar!' Henry jumped down from the trap, put his arm round her shoulders and hugged her. 'And Ebro! So big!' He fondled the child's head and patted the dogs, who had been waiting with Pilar as they moaned and wriggled for attention. 'Good to be home,' he said. 'Wonderful.'

'Your wife?' Pilar suggested.

'She preferred the taxi,' said Henry, smiling. 'Come and meet her. This is Pilar,' he said, opening the taxi door. 'Did you have an enjoyable drive?'

Margaret Tillotson stepped out of the car.

'Did he carry her over the threshold?' the landlord asked from behind the bar.

'Well, no.' Trask took a swallow of beer. 'He did not.'

'What then?'

'She'd bopped him one, hadn't she? Blacked his eye.'

'She *hit* him?' Normally taciturn and discreet, the landlord was incredulous. 'Whatever for? Why should she do that?'

'Wasn't for love.' Trask took another swallow. He was glad the bar was empty, felt he should not have

14

spoken, but the landlord was trustworthy. 'Seemed kind of irritated,' he said.

'You're having me on,' said the landlord.

'No.' Trask emptied his glass and watched the landlord refill it.

'So what happened?' asked the landlord.

'She said, "Show me my room, I am tired." '

'And?'

'Pilar takes her upstairs. I hear her telling that she has prepared all the rooms so madam has a choice. Pilar is a bit stumped, if you ask me, and little Ebro doesn't make things any nicer when he says to Henry in his piping voice – carries miles, that child's voice – "Henry, that lady hit you, why didn't you hit her back?" Henry says, "You don't hit ladies, Ebro." And Ebro asks, sharp that child is, "Was she really a lady?" He's never seen a lady that colour.'

'Has Henry brought back a blackie, then?'

'No. She's very pale, very white skin. I'd say beautiful, sort of translucent.'

'That's a long word for you, Traskie.'

'Tall and beautiful.'

'And translucent.' The landlord savoured the word as he polished a glass.

'Yes.'

The landlord pulled himself a half-pint and looked round the empty bar. Later it would fill up with people who would remain ignorant of Trask's revelations. 'So which room did she choose, then?'

'The best spare.'

'Ah.'

'Yes.'

'And?'

'She has Pilar unpack for her, light the fire, run and fill a hot bottle. She has Pilar on the trot: get me this, fetch me that, I want hot soup. Then she goes to bed.'

'And?'

'Stays there.'

'But that was twenty-four hours ago.'

'More—'

'She ill?'

'Not so's you'd notice, Pilar says.'

'And Henry?'

'Henry goes walking over the hills with his dogs. Came in about four o'clock this morning and goes to bed in the old room, the one that was his parents', that looks out across country. After an hour or two he comes down, Pilar says, drinks some coffee and goes out again.'

'He has to think,' said the landlord.

'It might have been all right if she had not hit the horse,' said Trask, sipping his beer, eyeing the landlord over the rim of his glass.

'She *never*!' The landlord set his glass down on the bar.

'Cross my heart,' said Trask.

The landlord whistled. 'Which horse?'

'Nellie. Swiped at the poor animal's nose with her bag and *then* bops Henry in the eye.'

Trask and the landlord exchanged troubled glances. 'Whatever shall us say to Henry when he comes in for his pint?' queried the landlord.

'Don't know when that'll be,' said Trask, setting down his empty glass. 'Henry has upsticked and gone back to the war. I put him on the train just now. He's had his think.'

'And madam?'

'Still in bed, looks so.'

'I don't know what to think,' sighed the landlord.

' 'Tisn't you as is called to,' said Trask.

2

Henry Tillotson watched the dogcart diminish as the mare, with ears pricked and head towards home, clattered down the road. Trask, mindful of possible damage to the young mare's legs on the hard road, had all he could do to prevent her breaking into a gallop; he neither looked back nor waved.

Henry carried his bag through the ticket office to the platform. He looked at his watch; his train was due in three minutes. Three minutes in which to kick his heels, chide himself for having no book to read on the journey, three minutes or less before the signal's arm clanged down and far down the line the train would come rumbling out of the cutting to charge into view and loom up, gasping and hissing. Already he could imagine the heavy brass handle of the carriage door, hear the clunk as he opened it, smell the dust and stale tobacco in the First Class carriage, recognize the width of the strap he would grasp to let down the window, to admit fresh air and be damned if other passengers complained of the cold as he found a seat and heaved his bag onto the rack. Henry scowled in anticipation and gritted his teeth.

The train would presently run parallel to the road and from the window he would see Trask.

'She's catching your mood,' Trask had said tetchily on the drive to the station. 'Look at her ears, laid back. Better let me drive. Look how she's sweating, she may damage her legs. Better let me drive,' he had repeated.

'At this rate she could slip on the tarmac and fall.'

Henry had said, 'No,' and held the reins tighter. 'No.'

Now, pacing the platform, he hoped Trask would have quietened the horse or turned off the road before the train overtook him.

Out of sight the train shrieked. In the station office a bell tinkled. Henry turned on his heel. The porter, coming out to meet the train, shouted, 'Sir?' He pointed at Henry's luggage. 'What about . . .'

'I'll catch a later train,' Henry called over his shoulder; the train was very close now.

'None till ten o'clock an' you have to change,' shouted the porter. 'Ain't no more through evening trains.'

If Henry heard, he made no sign. The porter picked up Henry's bag and put it aside. When the train had gone he would stow it in the left luggage, but now he must exchange a word with the guard and attend to passengers getting off the train. With a muttered 'Silly bugger,' he dismissed Henry from his mind.

Henry walked fast, cutting across the fields at an angle to the road along which he had lately driven in the dogcart, taking a path which led to a wood and through the wood to more fields, down a dip to a stream, along the stream to a footbridge which he crossed into an orchard.

There was a ladder propped against one of the trees; he stopped and looked up.

'We heard you were home but gathered you were *not* coming to see us,' said a voice from among the branches.

Henry said, 'I've come.'

'Too wrapped up in our newly-wed bride,' said the voice. 'Too absorbed, and honeymoony to bother about boring old chums,' it said, 'taken over by the lusts of the flesh and—' Henry shook the ladder. 'Don't *do* that!' said the voice. 'That's dangerous, I might fall and break a bone. You know how nervous I am of heights,' it said. 'For goodness' sake hold the thing steady while I come down.' A gumbooted foot reached for the top rung.

Henry said, 'Hand me down the basket and use both hands.' He reached up and took hold of a basket. 'What are you doing up there, anyway?'

'It's the war, my dear, what's called "doing your bit" and all that jazz. John says I must get used to it.'

'Always was a bully,' said Henry, guiding tentative feet down the ladder. 'Easy does it. You might have got stuck up there all night.'

'No, no, he's coming presently. Tip the basket into that barrow. We have so many apples we are feeding them to Hitler and Mussolini.'

'And how are they?' Henry watched the legs descending rung by rung until the whole man appeared to skip the last rungs and, risking a little jump, landed beside him.

'Terra firma,' exclaimed the man with relief. 'Ham and sides of bacon next week, pork chops, sausages, chitterlings, the lot. Sad when one knows them so well, but there it is and here you are. Oh, dear boy, it's good to see you!' Almost as tall as Henry, the man put his hands on Henry's shoulders and kissed him warmly on both cheeks. 'Oh dear,' he said, 'my appley hands have sullied your uniform.' He stood close, smiling at Henry, wiping his hands against his shirt as he scrutinized Henry's face at close range with warm brown eyes. He was a heavy-built man, older than Henry, hair brown where Henry's was black. His nose was longer than Henry's; his mouth, not so wide, showed excellent teeth. He was clean-shaven, with little tufts of hair on his cheekbones. He studied

Henry's face, whispering, 'You did come. It's a long time – we really thought – we—'

Henry smiled, saying nothing. Pleasure, seeping in, erased his ugly mood. They were silent in the orchard where the air was still. They could hear the soft thump as apples dropped from trees on to the wet grass.

Henry sighed. Then, aware that he was being scrutinized, he braced his shoulders as the other took stock of his tanned skin, face thinner than when last seen, older, sad.

Making no mention of Henry's bruised eye the man looked him up and down as he wiped sticky hands on his shirt, did up a button, tucked the tail into flannel trousers which had seen better days and said, 'Well. Shall we go up to the house and find John? It's his day for making scones.'

Henry said, 'Yes, Jonathan. All right, let's go and find him.' He threw the basket into the barrow. 'Let's go, then.'

Since Henry did not speak as they walked, Jonathan, too, kept silent, but now and again his lips pouted forward with an unspoken word, a throttled question, before pursing into silence. He ran his hands through his hair, absently teasing out a twig, discovering a leaf which he pinched before dropping it. Then he said, looking down at his feet, matching Henry's stride, 'We thought – well we – we heard, of course – and then when you wrote – but then nothing. And you didn't and – well – so.'

Henry, tacking away, said brusquely, 'You're now John and Jonathan? Not both Jonathan, as you were christened?'

'Well yes, yes.'

'You are the elder?' questioning.

'We suppose so.'

'You must know,' bullying.

'We do, it's a fact.'

'Really?' Henry mocked.

'Parish registers,' said the other, 'don't lie.'

'Oh ho! Parish registers.' Henry laughed.

'Of course.' The other was hurt. 'It's a matter of honour.'

'Oh,' said Henry, 'honour.' Then he said, 'Depends how you interpret honour.'

Jonathan said, 'No need to be sarcastic, it's what he wanted.'

'No proof of that.'

'No need to sneer. We both like the name, but I'm the oldest.'

They moved up the orchard in single file, Henry walking behind Jonathan. 'You've got flat feet,' he said, observing the other man's walk, large feet outwardly pointing in clumsy boots.

'Always have done. Haven't you ever noticed?'

'Can't say I have?'

'Quite an advantage these days; no good for marching.'

'Aren't you too old, anyway?'

'Verging on it,' Jonathan said, leading the way across an unkempt lawn. 'Mind the goose mess on your posh shoes,' he said as a group of geese hustled aside, hissing. 'They lay masses of eggs, which make wonderful omelettes. Here we are.' He led the way into a long cottage, kicking off his boots in a stone-flagged passage. He called out, 'Look who's here! Look who I found! He didn't go without seeing us after all.'

Wiping his feet on the mat, Henry breathed the smell of baking. He entered an airy kitchen. 'Just in time for tea,' exclaimed a man dressed also in grey flannels and white shirt, but wrapped around the waist by an apron which almost reached the floor. He was as tall as Jonathan but slim as a whippet, with thick dark red hair, immense brown eyes and a bristling moustache. 'Just in time for my scones,' he exclaimed. 'Oh, it is good to see you. Oh, dear boy, let me kiss – I won't touch – I'm all floury.' And, holding his arms back as though about to dive, he leaned forward and kissed Henry, saying, 'There. You are really here. You didn't forget us.'

Henry said, 'No. How could I? I wouldn't,' as he thought, But I almost did, I had to force myself. I had meant to get on the train.

The three stood close together. Jonathan and John smiled at Henry, their eyes glistening with pleasure, lips parted in joy. John said, 'Come, sit down, we are bursting to hear all about it. Come on, tell all.' His eye shied away from Henry's bruise. 'It's such an event. Such an excitement in our humdrum lives.'

Henry said, 'Those scones smell delicious, I am starving. Any tea?' The smiles faded as he remarked, 'Bugger all to tell.'

John said, 'Yes, of course, tea. Sit here between us. Get the butter, lovey, and there's honey. Or would you rather have jam?'

Henry said, 'Honey would be wonderful, but I won't eat your butter ration.'

'Oh my dear!' they said together. 'We've got lots.'

'Flourishing system of swap round here, black market to you,' said John. 'All the neighbours who are hoping for a slice of Hitler or Mussolini have been generous lately, afraid of being forgotten. Though they do say war brings out the best in people, don't they?' He let his eye linger on Henry's bruise. 'Got yourself quite a shiner,' he whispered into his moustache.

Henry sat at the table and watched his friends find cups, saucers, plates, knives, put honey and butter on the table, jostle the kettle to hurry it up, wash their hands at the sink, exchange worried and anxious glances. He did nothing to dispel the sense of unease which replaced their initial enthusiasm, but sat with teeth clenched and lower lip thrust out, waiting.

As though conscious of the change of atmosphere, several cats who had been asleep, balled up against the stove, detached themselves and slunk in a ripple of black and tabby out of the window.

Still Henry waited.

John poured tea and passed cups. 'You will stay the night?'

Henry said, 'I have to catch the late train. I go to France tomorrow.'

'France?' they said, interested. 'France?'

Henry said, 'The south-west.'

'My mother was French,' said the heavily-built older man.

'A French governess,' said the thin friend. 'She was only a governess.'

'French, nonetheless,' riposted the other. 'Your mother,' he said to Henry, 'was very fond of France.'

'Though not necessarily of the French,' said the other man, catching his friend's eye while concealing a smile under his moustache. 'One wonders,' he said conversationally, 'whether the French are really pleased to be liberated?'

His friend, seizing this lead, carried on. 'All that mess in the north; smashed villages, bridges blown up. There never was much love lost—'

'And the Americans! Bulls in china shops in the south; we hear they blew up the red light district in Marseilles. *That* won't be popular! You may have to do a lot of explaining.'

'You *are* perspicacious.' Henry helped himself to a scone, spread butter, dug his knife into the honey pot. 'No spoon,' he said. 'Standards slipping.'

The two friends laughed.

'Historical hatreds last,' said Jonathan. 'I don't mind betting that your average Frenchman, if neither a Jew nor a member of the Resistance, has been relatively comfortable under the Germans. My old ma, who liked the English, was hardly representative, and your mother, Henry, would have called the Liberation a misplaced act of kindness.'

What are these snide references to my parents leading up to? thought Henry. 'My mother is long dead,' he said.

'And your father,' said John. 'Our godfather, God bless him.'

'I thought we all agreed years ago,' said Henry, 'that my mother, after understandable initial doubts, accepted that neither of you is my half-brother?'

'We know that,' said John, 'but there was always the residue of doubt. We could have been his children; we could have been the results of wild oats. She never quite cured herself of sizing us up in that speculative way. She had a special way of looking at us.'

'I don't suppose,' said Henry, helping himself to more honey, 'that she ever really came to terms with Father's philanthropy.'

'Acting as our godfather? Paying for our education? Two little Jonathans.'

'One would be understandable, two an exaggeration,' said the larger man agreeably. 'His kindness brimmed.'

'I tried once,' said Henry, 'to get him to admit you were his younger brother's children. But he said no, the dates were all wrong, some friend had slipped up – twice, two friends actually. Can I have another cup?' He passed his cup to Jonathan. 'It's really absurd,' he now said, 'to have called you both Jonathan. It's idiotic—'

'Named for their godfather—' said the larger man, complacent, irritating.

Henry slammed his fist on the table, knocking a plate to the stone floor, where it broke. 'I'd like to break another,' he said angrily.

'Feel free, help yourself,' said the larger man, looking at the broken plate.

Henry said, 'I've come without a book to read in the train. Can one of you lend me something?'

'T. S. Eliot? Agatha Christie?' suggested the thin man. 'Why don't you grind the plate into the floor? It's past mending. They say bottling up rage is bad for you.' He spoke with concern and a trace of shame.

Henry thought, These two know something; it is making them feel awkward. There's something funny here.

'So you've come to tell us all about your marriage?' said the larger man courageously.

'Who is in a china shop now?' his friend murmured.

Henry, who had come to do precisely that, said, 'No. No, I haven't,' and leaned down to pick up pieces of broken plate. 'Tell me about your lives,' he said. 'Your pigs, geese, chickens. Are you still in the Observer Corps? Do you still do ARP?'

When, later, he had to catch his train, they walked with him in the dark to the station; they had lent him *The Screwtape Letters* and a Dorothy L. Sayers.

'We hear Aragon has written some wonderful poems,' they said. 'Will you send them to us?'

Henry said that he would.

Halfway to the station, he said, 'You neither of you liked my mother—'

'She used to say things like, "That man has Eton blue eyes—"' said the older man.

'Never pale blue,' said his friend.

25

'Snobbery is incurable when it's unconscious,' said Henry.

'Of course,' they said. 'Absolutely.' Then they said, 'We loved your father,' and one of them (Henry later could not remember which) said, 'He had the highest possible motives,' excusing the dead.

Just before they reached the station, Henry said, 'Will you go and meet my wife? Get to know her? See what you can do?'

They said that of course they would, they couldn't wait to meet her. Nothing they would enjoy more.

Henry said, 'Here's my train. I must run. Take care of yourselves. Goodbye,' and ran through the dark to the train.

The Jonathans waited outside the station until they heard the train leave.

In the train Henry sat alone in the dim light of a blacked-out carriage and reproached himself for being surly, for breaking their plate, a pretty plate. Minton, probably irreplaceable. Then he remembered the phrase 'a misplaced act of kindness' and mulled it over as it refuelled his suspicions.

Morosely he opened the books they had lent him, riffled through the pages, laid them aside, sat with head bent forward staring at his shoes; they had been his father's. I inherit my father's shoes and the results of his quixotic generosity, he thought wryly. The shoes fit, a lot of the rest pinches. Staring at his feet, he remembered his father's efforts to communicate, his own longing to reciprocate and their joint failure after his mother, seized by pneumonia, died.

He had been rushed from school, fetched by Trask just in time to see her die. She had struggled for breath. He had a miserable cold caught at school; when he kissed her, her breath smelled horrible. He had tried not to let her see his disgust. At the funeral his father had worn black. Friends and relations and all the village people had crowded the church, which reeked of lilies and chrysanthemums. The Jonathans singing in the choir had tried to catch his eye – they were his best friends – but he had stared at his feet. Back at the house the funeral guests crowded round the fires, warmed their hands, drank tea and whisky, ate cake; survivors.

He should have handed round plates of gentleman's relish sandwiches, been polite. But the Jonathans were looking for him; he did not want their sympathy, feared he would cry. He had escaped to the stables, where the dogs had been shut in for the afternoon, and in one of the loose-boxes he had wept with his face pressed against a horse's neck, gripping its mane with manic fingers.

That night his father said, 'I am taking you away. We will go to Italy; you can miss a term.' In the train his father had worn these brown shoes.

Together they had climbed up and down the cobbled mule tracks in the hills beyond Camogli, gazed down at the sea, boated round the cliffs to San Frutuoso, visited Portofino with its line of ill-used horses with drooping disconsolate heads in the long cab rank; eaten fried sardines and pasta in the piazza, drunk strong and bitter coffee. Communication was stilted and awkward; his mother had always bound them together. Could he have tried harder? She would have loved the flowers, long-stemmed, sweet-scented, purple-and-white violets, blue hepaticas, white anemones, pink cyclamen, sweet-scented narcissi, orchids, and the steady clop of the mules carrying their loads on the cobbled paths up through the olive groves. It was a relief to get back to school, and in the holidays his father talked more easily with the two

Jonathans, recounting to them in copious detail the course of his various acts of philanthropy, from which in advancing years he derived as much pleasure as he had from the girls he seduced in the company of the Jonathans' fathers in their pre-marital heyday.

'None so dangerous as a reformed rake.' Henry chuckled in affectionate recollection. 'I must get some new shoes,' he said out loud. 'These are past repair.'

Tramping back to their cottage, guided by a flickering torch, Jonathan said, 'I think somehow there's been a bit of a boomerang.'

'I didn't care for his tone of voice when he said "philanthropy",' said the other.

'And yet with Pilar—'

'But the old man saw Pilar, found her himself. This isn't the same thing; this was by proxy.'

'Seemed such a good idea.'

'Brilliant at the time.'

'I can't wait to meet her.' Jonathan burst out laughing. 'It's awful to laugh,' he said, chuckling. 'Awful. But I would have loved to have been there when she blacked his eye.'

The younger man joined in the laughter. 'What a mess! Let's go over as soon as we can.'

'Should we have meddled?' queried the older man.

'A bit late to ask that now,' said his friend.

It was years before the Jonathans spoke of their first visit to Margaret, and the subsequent visits which led to a relationship founded not on friendship but curiosity.

Henry had asked them to go, they told Calypso, when he left to go back to the war that autumn of 1944. (They had chosen Calypso for their saga in the knowledge that anything told went no further, not so much because she was discreet as that she had no interest in garbling. Gossip regaled to Calypso stopped there.)

They had dressed for the occasion, they told her, put on suits, shambled round by the road rather than cut across the fields, carried roses bought from a florist.

Margaret had received them in bed. They were impressed by her beauty, impressed that she was neither ill nor trying to keep warm. This was before Margaret and bed became synonymous. Searching for a subject, they asked whether she liked Cotteshaw, liked the bedroom she had chosen. She had said, 'It will do well enough,' dampingly. They enthused that they loved the place, had known it all their lives, had had happy times, been befriended by Henry's parents, loved Henry. Margaret had said, 'Really?' as though this was surprising, suspect even. It had been hard to find anything to chat about until they hit on her wish to have her room other than it was. They had offered then to help redecorate, told her they were interested 'in style', 'in matters of taste'. She said so had her ex-husband been interested; he was the same sort of person, 'a queer'. She used the appellation as an insult. Even so, they told Calypso, they rallied; had not Henry asked them to befriend his wife?

They had helped rearrange the room, brought mirrors and chairs from other parts of the house (Henry's mother had had many lovely mirrors), found wallpaper and paint, scarce for ages after the war. It was something they could do for Henry, they told Calypso – and, they readily admitted, an interest for themselves. And, too, it helped Pilar, who did not find Margaret easy, and of course it helped Ebro. But that all came later when a rapport had been established, when she knew that they knew – she had let it slip – that she had money of her own. Not that she used it to pay for decorations; only to buy clothes by mail order.

They had never expected Margaret to stay in bed; they had supposed she would get up, take an interest in the house. They had supposed that she would play the role of wife. These suppositions, hopes, if truth were told, died on their first visit. In Margaret's mind there was no question of love, sex or friendship; she made this clear. At first they thought this was some sort of act. 'We laughed,' they told Calypso. 'We thought she was having us on.'

Jonathan corrected this. 'Not so. We laughed because we were so shocked – we never expected Henry to get caught in such a terrible trap.'

Calypso was startled to see that he had begun to weep. 'It was so sad,' he said. 'She sneered at love; she thinks it disgusting. We came away blaming ourselves.'

To cheer him, Calypso said, 'But you have befriended the woman, done what Henry asked. How could you be to blame?' and she handed him a tissue, she being one of the first to give up the use of handkerchiefs and blow her nose on paper.

Jonathan said, 'Oh! A tissue! What a sensible idea!'

Calypso said, 'Saves laundry,' and as he ceased to weep she said jokingly, 'Come now, admit, you have had a lot of entertainment over the years. You arranged for her facials and massage as well as the redecorations. It's not all gloom.'

'Of course not,' they agreed. The unravelling of Margaret's past was a constant delight; she was such a liar. One week she would have been born in the Levant, the next it would be Bexhill-on-Sea. Her stories about her ex-husband were a joy. By then they had lost the temptation to bare their soul.

'One day,' they said, laughing, 'this husband was a brute, a Hercules who wrested her from her family and ravished her. On another she was raised by nuns in an orphanage and found a situation as a servant to a priest. Or conversely the ex-husband was a mouse, or again a burly homosexual who only cared for the rough trade. She makes up her past as she goes along,' they said, happy again, forgetting the tears.

It was all much more interesting than the truth, they told Calypso; they were almost sure from titbits she had let slip that she had been a manicurist at the Ghezira Palace Hotel, picked up by the German husband who needed a wife for cover.

When they had gone Calypso wondered why they had lost their nerve and not told her what they intended. Then, since gossip did not interest her, she forgot.

Part Two

1954

3

James Martineau and Matthew Stephenson, meeting in the Fulham Road and exchanging the time of day, discovered that they were both invited to Cotteshaw for the coming weekend.

'Henry suggested I should bring a girl,' said Matthew. 'Wants to make it something of a house party. You bringing a girl?'

'I was thinking of asking Barbara,' said James. 'Who shall you bring?'

'I have asked Antonia,' said Matthew, 'but she's being difficult. Says she wouldn't know anybody, and that anyway she's been invited by the Grants and would rather go there.'

'That's a tiny untruth,' said James, a kind man unwilling to call a lie a lie. 'Hector and Calypso are in Italy, I happen to know. Tell Antonia that if she comes, she will know Barbara.'

'That might do the trick,' said Matthew, 'they are great chums. Naughty of her to lie,' he said uneasily.

'Oh, girls!' said James indulgently. 'Why don't I give you a lift down? My car is roomier than yours.'

'I think I'll stick to mine, thanks all the same,' said Matthew, who hoped to be alone with Antonia. 'I like to be independent. If we find the atmosphere too difficult we might want to push off before you and Barbara.'

'Oh, the atmosphere!' said James.

'What was it like when you were there last?' asked Matthew. 'Dire?'

'I wouldn't say dire,' said James kindly, as he sought for another word, but failing to find one pursed his lips and said, 'Not exactly.'

'Is this house party of Henry's supposed to jolly things up?' Matthew enquired, grinning.

'I gather it is. Henry's father used to give dinner parties every June; Henry wants to revive them. Long tables on the grass, backed by tulip beds and yew hedges, lilac in bloom, good nosh and lots of booze. Candlelit, of course, and a full moon. Sounds fun.'

'Supposing it rains?' suggested Matthew.

'It never rained for Henry's parents.'

'But that was before the war,' said Matthew.

'The war has changed much, but not the climate. Gosh, look at the time! I must fly, see you there—' James broke into a run to catch a bus thundering towards the bus stop.

'Hoffentlich,' said Matthew, who had recently spent a week in Dusseldorf on business. 'One must give old Henry full marks for trying,' he shouted as James leapt on to his bus.

'I hear you are coming to Henry Tillotson's bash,' said Antonia on the telephone.

'Oh, so Matthew persuaded you.' Barbara's voice was muffled by a mouthful of marmalade and toast. 'Look, I'm in the middle of breakfast – got up late.'

'I *was* going to the Grants,' said Antonia, 'but—'

'They are in Italy, darling.' Barbara swallowed her toast and reached for her coffee cup. 'You couldn't go to the Grants. Are you playing hard to get?' she asked, not expecting an answer. 'They don't ever seem worried by currency restrictions.' She gulped her coffee. 'Nice to be rich.'

'I thought all that was over,' said Antonia. 'Anyway, a little thing like currency restrictions wouldn't worry Calypso. My mother says she stuffs her bra with fivers. I admire her panache.'

'She rather intimidates me,' said Barbara. 'Look, love, I must fly or I shall again be late at the grindstone. Oh! Do you suppose Matthew will make you change your mind?'

'He might,' said Antonia. 'And what about James?'

'Ah,' said Barbara, 'James—'

'Their being such friends would be nice for us,' said Antonia.

'I am mulling it over,' said Barbara.

'Actually, between ourselves, I loathe earning my living,' said Antonia.

'Me too,' said Barbara. 'This early morning rush, coming home exhausted to unwashed breakfast things, ugh!'

'It's the parents who think independence and not marrying until we are mature will stop us messing up our lives. I can't see any compensations in honest toil,' said Antonia.

'You're going to be late. I'm going to be late,' cried Barbara. 'See you at the weekend, then. Oh! Do you suppose we shall be allowed to meet the mystery wife?'

'I rather gathered that was the idea,' said Antonia. 'That's why I'm coming. What shall you wear? Got anything new I can borrow? I'll lend you my blue—'

'We are late, we'll get the sack—' Barbara rang off.

Antonia Lowther checked the contents of her bag and, slamming the door, raced out into the street. Hurrying towards the tube she wondered, not for the first time since she had set up on her own in a one-room flatlet, whether earning her keep and indulging in independence was the rosy experience her parents had envisaged for her. One week in her job had undeceived her as to the interest of work; an occupation such as hers would be dull if her bosses dealt in diamonds or international art. The fact that the company of which she was a minute cog dealt in oil was of little import. Typing and filing was typing and filing, and making tea was exactly that; she was unqualified for anything better.

There was no question of returning to the comforts of home, much as she missed the automatic meals, free laundry, bath soap, shampoo, lavatory paper, postage stamps, and messages noted by her mother or the daily lady; there was no going back. Her mother, Antonia knew, had with the connivance of her father eased her out.

My mother, thought Antonia, descending the steps of South Kensington tube station, would make a far better secretary than I ever shall. My mother, she thought as she elbowed an old woman aside at the ticket office, has taught herself to be efficient. It is the only protection she has from Father. My mother, Antonia told herself as she scampered onto the platform in time to miss a departing train, should have left Father years ago. She does not stay with him for the sake of us children, but because she deludes herself that he loves her.

How can she? Antonia asked herself. I cannot bear, Antonia thought as she felt the warm draught of an oncoming train seep up her skirt, I cannot bear the way he treats her. Considerate and thoughtful in public, offensive and rude in private.

The train doors slid open and she squeezed in among the strap-hanging bodies. Among the swaying bodies Antonia enumerated the remarks her father voiced in the privacy of home. His references to a crêpey neck, greying hair, double chin, veiny legs and yellowing teeth make me sick, she thought. The remarks about teeth are particularly vile.

His teeth glisten whitely since the accident Mother is never allowed to forget, thought Antonia, as she swayed with the crowd. Mother would not have been driving if he had not had so many drinks; it is when he has had a few drinks that he says these hurtful things. I, Antonia swore to herself, shall never allow myself to have too many drinks and endanger my marital relations.

Curse this brute, she muttered to herself as she tried to edge away from a strap-hanging man, he smells of persp. When I marry, she thought, for she was a girl determined on marriage, I shall not allow my husband to smell, nor shall I be a doormat. My children, if I have children, will live to boast of the sweetness of connubial bliss; no child of mine will risk the snub I got from Mother when I complained of Father's nastiness.

Antonia remembered her mother's laugh. 'Don't be ridiculous,' her mother had said. 'We love each other! He doesn't mean it; family life gets on his nerves. He is working too hard. He will be much happier when you have all left home.'

Ruefully Antonia remembered those words. I have been ejected from the nest, she told herself. I must marry. Perhaps Matthew Stephenson will do? Why not? I don't think he is all that exciting, but I would never want to be rude to him or unkind. I really think he might do quite well.

And Barbara? For Antonia always included her best friend in her plans. Barbara could do worse than James Martineau. He might lack the romantic zip Barbara yearned for, but by and large he would do. It was time

Barbara grew up. Antonia, under the impression that she herself had reached that stage, decided for her friend. And both lots of parents will probably approve. She snorted with laughter as she skipped out of the tube and hurried towards her boring labours.

'This is better than breaking my back planting trees in Hector Grant's wood.' Antonia sat beside Matthew.

'Now then,' said Matthew, his eyes on the road ahead, his hands tightening on the wheel.

'Only joking,' said Antonia, 'trying it on, teasing. I am not a mythomaniac, promise.'

'Better not be,' said Matthew, glancing sideways at his passenger. Sleek fair hair hid half her face. He approved the pert nose and full mouth which, the evening before, he had kissed, sliding his tongue between the slightly irregular teeth, which had nipped quite sharply. Matthew felt a frisson of pleasurable recollection. He was glad he had confronted Antonia with her lie; she had had the grace to apologize. She had lunched once with the Grants, she explained, and she hoped to be invited again. Her father had known Hector in the war and Calypso was the sort of woman she would like to be herself in her thirties, a pretty futile sort of ambition, she had said modestly.

Matthew had said, 'Rubbish, you underrate yourself absurdly,' and kissed her. He was looking forward to the weekend.

'What is Henry's wife like?' she asked.

'I hardly know. I have been to Cotteshaw several times and she hasn't appeared, or one hasn't been invited up. One knows she's there in her room but one rarely sees her.'

'But you have seen her?'

'Yes. Beautiful in a weird way.'

'When did they marry?'

'Some time in the war. It's said they met in the Middle East. I suppose Henry told somebody about it, but he's never told me. Her name, by the way, is Margaret. Towards the middle or end of the war they married, Henry brought her back to England and she went to bed.'

'What was wrong with her?'

'She wasn't ill.'

'Goodness! And she lives in bed?'

'Yes.'

'Isn't she bored?'

'Perhaps, if you met her, you could ask her.'

'I shall,' said Antonia. 'And if I don't, Barbara can.'

'I was joking,' said Matthew hastily. 'The whole situation is fraught. Not only does one *not* ask Henry's wife why she lives in bed, one doesn't ask Henry either. One just tries to behave naturally. I hope you will make it clear to Barbara, if James hasn't, that one keeps mum.'

'Ho!' said Antonia. 'I see. One is mum, is one.'

Not liking her tone, Matthew said, 'Yes,' and they drove in silence for several miles. Then Matthew said, 'It's more than probable that you won't meet her at all. I only met her once for about five minutes.'

'What was she wearing?' asked Antonia, whose mind had divagated to what dress she would wear at the party; she had brought two dresses. The choice was further complicated by the possibility of borrowing one from Barbara.

Matthew said, 'A nightdress, of course,' and was irritated when Antonia laughed.

Regretting his irritation, Antonia said, 'I really am looking forward to this party. I have never been to an outdoor dinner; if this weather lasts, it should be fun.'

Mollified by Antonia's enthusiasm, Matthew said,

'The forecast is propitious,' and, sensing that she smiled, asked, 'Do you find me a touch pompous?'

He was pleased when, laughingly, she answered, 'I do, but I love it.'

Just before they reached Cotteshaw they caught up with James and Barbara, who had left their car and stood leaning over a gate into a hayfield. When they saw Antonia and Matthew they turned to greet them.

'What are you two up to?' called Antonia.

'Stopped for a pee,' said James sedately.

'Good idea,' said Matthew, getting out of his car.

'Liar,' said Barbara. 'He stopped the car to ask me to marry him.'

'And shall you?' asked Matthew, vaulting the gate into the field.

'Don't piss on the hay,' said James, 'it's Henry's. No! She refused me.'

'But it was a sweet hay-scented proposal,' volunteered Barbara, smiling.

'And I am not altogether discouraged,' said James cheerfully.

'Antonia?' Matthew, returning from the field, caught her eye.

'Hay makes me sneeze,' said Antonia.

'Then I shall wait to pick a more esoterically-scented location,' said Matthew, 'and one where we are not crowded by eavesdropping friends. Come on, my dears, let us arrive *chez* Henry *en masse*.'

James followed Matthew's car. 'What a nice house,' said Barbara as they crunched up the drive. 'Pity it's so shabby.'

'We seem to be expected, the front door is open.' James braked to a halt behind Matthew.

While Matthew and James unloaded the luggage Antonia and Barbara wandered up to the front door and stood, hesitating, on the threshold. After the dazzling sunshine the interior of the house was dark; they sniffed the cool air of a flagstoned hall.

Barbara murmured, 'Something smells delicious. Lilies?'

Antonia said, 'Lilac, I think,' in a low voice and groped childishly for her friend's hand. 'There doesn't seem to be anybody here.' She dropped her voice to a whisper. 'Should we ring?'

'No need,' said a man's voice. 'Bell's out of order. Do come in. I am Henry; you must be Antonia and Barbara. So glad you could come. These are my dogs,' he said as two shaggy animals, appearing from nowhere, began sniffing and nudging round the girls' legs. 'Don't let them bother you,' he said, but made no attempt to dissuade the creatures from their intrusive attentions.

'It's all right, we both like dogs,' said Antonia, letting go of Barbara's hand. 'How do you do? I am Antonia.'

She held out her hand, hoping that Barbara's grasp had not made it sticky, but instead of shaking Henry's hand she had to push away one of the dogs who, venturing more boldly than the other, was thrusting his nose up her skirt. She stood beside Barbara, looking up at Henry.

Henry Tillotson was taller than either James or Matthew, both tall men; he towered above the girls, smiling down at their upturned faces.

Eager faces, he thought, unmarked but not innocent, two determined little beauties. The one dark, the other fair, hungry but not avaricious, neither would be likely to commit an uncalculated folly. They were probably aware that, posed against the light in the doorway, their summer dresses transparently revealed their legs (excellent legs, both).

'Ah,' he said, looking past them, 'James and Matthew. Good to see you.' He went down the steps at a trot to relieve them of their loads. 'Come along in,' he said, 'you must see your rooms. Then Pilar ordains that we should have tea on the terrace; she recently read that tea on the terrace of a country house is *de rigueur* in a *Homes and Gardens* magazine.'

The girls took note of Henry. Disproportionately long legs in corduroy trousers, a thin torso in a shabby sweater, long arms. 'Needs a haircut,' murmured Antonia.

'But what hair!' Barbara approved. 'I like the colour, almost black.'

'And gypsy eyes. Isn't his nose too big?' Antonia wondered.

Barbara opined that she liked large noses; James, too, had a large nose and Matthew's was not small.

'So he's rather dishy,' murmured Antonia as the men approached the house.

'Pity he's so old,' whispered Barbara. 'Must be middle thirties.'

'I like older men,' muttered Antonia.

'Me too,' said her friend.

'Share?' suggested Antonia slyly, and they laughed.

'Share what?' asked James, coming up the steps.

'We were wondering whether we are to share a room,' said Antonia smoothly.

'There is no need unless you want to,' said Henry. 'Ah, here is Pilar. This is Pilar,' he said to Barbara and Antonia. 'James and Matthew know her, of course. Pilar, this is Antonia, and this is Barbara.'

Pilar shook hands with the girls, her black eyes taking them in. She smiled, showing her large teeth. 'I show you your rooms,' she said. 'Come, please. No, Matthew, leave the bags, Ebro will bring.' She turned towards the stairs and Barbara and Antonia followed.

As they mounted the stairs they exchanged a smile at Pilar's remarkable shape. A tiny head on narrow shoulders sloped geometrically towards vast hips supported by very short legs which dwindled to tiny feet. Dressed in black, Pilar's triangular shape merged into the darkness of the landing at the top of the stairs. The house was silent; their feet made no sound on the carpeted stair. Matthew and James had moved away from the hall with their host.

Somewhere up there, thought Barbara, looking up, is Henry's bedridden wife. The idea of Henry's bedridden wife was suddenly creepy; she wondered whether she wanted to meet her and, should she do so, what she would be like? There was something white up there on the banisters, something white looking down. A face? Barbara drew closer to Antonia.

The girls jumped when they heard the screech. Barbara clutched Antonia's hand. As the screecher came towards them they backed away from the banisters and pressed themselves against the wall to let it pass, then gasped with amusement. Pilar, leaning over the rail and screeching too, yelled, 'Ebro! You catch animal or tell Henry. 'E teach it wicked tricks, the ladies are not amuse.'

'Gosh,' said Antonia, letting go of Barbara. 'Did you see it?'

'Look at it now!' Barbara pointed as a white cockatoo dropped from the banisters and waddled and hopped towards the open front door. 'It's going out!' she exclaimed. 'It will get lost.'

'No, no,' said Pilar, ' 'E go out, 'e come in this slide, it 'is latest amusement. You frightened?'

'Oh no,' said Barbara. 'Surprised, that's all. I wasn't expecting a cockatoo to slide down the banisters.'

'Happens in all the best houses,' said Antonia. 'Should be written up in *Homes and Gardens*.'

'Shut up,' said Barbara. 'Don't be tactless.' But Pilar was calling down to Ebro, who had appeared in the

45

hall and was loading himself with their suitcases.

Like his mother, Ebro was short, dark and very strong; he came up the stairs smiling. He had the same parrot jaw and outsize teeth.

'Which rooms?' he asked his mother. 'For which cases? I am Ebro,' he introduced himself.

'Hullo,' said Barbara. 'I thought that Ebro was a river.'

'Where my father died fighting Franco,' said Ebro cheerfully. 'I am named for it. This room?' He deposited the cases. 'And this?'

The girls' rooms were next to each other with a bathroom between. The sun, streaming through open windows, made rooms already pretty charming.

'When you are ready there will be tea on the terrace,' said Pilar. 'You find your way down?'

'Oh yes,' said Barbara, 'thanks.' But presently, as they descended the stairs, she whispered, 'In that half-light looking up I thought that white thing was a face. Just for a moment—'

'Your imagination,' mocked Antonia. 'Mistaking a cockatoo for a face. Honestly! But I must admit it made me jump.'

'Half out of your skin,' said her friend.

They crossed the hall into a drawing room, whose windows opened on to a terrace where the young men sat by a table laid for tea. Noting the starched white table-cloth, silver tea set, pretty china and plates of cakes, Antonia said, 'How lovely,' pausing in the doorway beside her friend.

Henry's dogs, lying by his chair, raised watchful heads. Henry, seeing the girls, thought that they paired very well with his friends; they were pretty, uncomplex, nice-mannered girls. He was generously pleased for Matthew and James. Yet with part of his mind he wondered which of the two would be most fun in bed, a speculation that was academic since both were bespoke.

'Come along,' he said, getting to his feet. 'Sit down.' He indicated chairs. 'We are waiting for the cucumber sandwiches, Pilar has pulled out all the stops.' The girls sat together, facing the garden. 'Pilar tells me my wife's cockatoo gave you a fright.'

'Oh *no*, not at all.' 'We thought it was your *wife*.'

The girls spoke together. Matthew frowned and James looked uneasy but Henry, watching the girls blush, said easily. 'There may well be a similarity; I had not thought. Actually, although I gave her the bird, they don't get on.'

'Does it always live loose?' James hoped to cover the girls' gaffe. 'I don't remember him when I came before.'

'He lived in Trask's part of the house, but now he honours me. Ah, here come the cucumber sandwiches.' Henry smiled at Pilar. 'Sit down, Pilar.' He made room for her beside him and she, placing the plate of sandwiches on the table, viewed her oeuvre with satisfaction. 'Shall I pour?' she asked.

'Please do,' said Henry. 'Where is Ebro?'

'Gone with Trask to fetch the tables for the party. Milk?' she asked Antonia. 'Sugar?' she asked Barbara.

Annoyed with herself, Barbara avoided James's eye, drank her tea and looked at the view.

'How beautiful,' she said, 'how lovely,' taking in the lawn which sloped from the terrace to a lily pond, the beds of iris which bordered it and the spring green of the woods beyond. 'There's a cuckoo,' she said, 'the first I've heard this year.'

They listened to the cuckoo.

Henry passed the sandwiches. Pilar watched them eat. One of the dogs pushed himself up into a sitting position and stared at Barbara as she ate. A thin stream of saliva slipped from his mouth to swing like a spider's thread. Matthew, unable to endure this spectacle, gave the animal a piece of cake.

James passed his empty cup to Pilar for more tea. Antonia searched her mind for a safe subject. Nobody seemed prepared to speak. She wondered whether one of the windows in the house behind them was the window of Henry's bedridden wife; whether Henry's wife, lying in bed, could hear the chink of cups and the absence of talk. Or was she, too, listening to the cuckoo?

James, angry with himself for minding Barbara's tactlessness, studied the dogs sprawling round Henry's feet. They smelt a big gamey, he thought, and wondered whether anyone bothered to bath them. One dog in particular, which was scratching its ribs, its lip curled in an agony of appreciation, could do with a wash. He watched it stop scratching, prick its ears and, following its eye, he saw the cockatoo approach along the terrace in a sort of nautical roll. The cockatoo said, 'Hullo,' its voice high, vulgar and feminine. Then, 'Have some tea?'

Everyone laughed. Matthew offered it a sandwich, which it ignored. Barbara had more success with cake; they stopped listening to the cuckoo.

'What's its name?' asked Antonia. 'Did your wife give it a name?' It was ridiculous, she thought, to ignore Henry's wife; she was somewhere in the house. She didn't care what Matthew thought, it was better to bring things – like a bedridden wife, for instance – into the open.

'I don't think she did,' said Henry. 'She had it removed p.d.q. There would not have been time to consider a name for it. Why don't you ask her? I was wondering whether you would like to meet her; she doesn't meet many people.'

'Of course we would,' said Antonia.

'Love to,' said Barbara, 'any time.'

Henry smiled in a way they would remember afterwards. 'Come on, then,' he said. 'There's no time like the present.'

They followed him into the house and up the stairs. Henry walked fast; they had to hurry to keep up. At the end of a corridor he knocked at a door and opened it immediately. 'Here are our visitors, Margaret. Antonia and Barbara,' he said and stood aside to let the girls go in.

'Come in, do,' said Margaret. 'An expected treat. Sit down.'

Henry closed the door and they heard his footsteps retreating.

4

As Henry's footsteps padded rapidly away, the girls stood for a moment, silent and dazzled.

It was an extraordinary room, a bright, light room, a golden room silvered by mirrors. Gold wallpaper, pale gold carpet, gold curtains and blinds, a gold bed with gold satin sheets and gold silk pillows. Neither Antonia nor Barbara had ever seen anything like it. They gaped.

Antonia's eye, seeking relief, was rebuffed by gold chairs, a golden sofa and gold hangings round the bed. She was tempted, she told Matthew later, to bolt back to the congenial shabbiness of the rest of the house.

Beside her Barbara, startled by a superfluity of mirrors, surprised her own reflection and Antonia's and beyond them the occupant of the bed, full face and in profile watching them. With an effort she turned towards the bed and said, 'Hello. I am Barbara and this is Antonia. How do you do?'

Margaret Tillotson lifted an arm from the counterpane and extended pale fingers. 'Barbara,' she said, 'and Antonia. Clement weather. Sit down,' and let her arm drop.

Obediently Antonia and Barbara sat on a sofa facing the bed and affected not to stare. It she had not moved, Barbara said later, it might have been supposed that Margaret Tillotson was part of the décor. Pale red-gold hair toned with the wallpaper, white arms and shoulders reflected the sheets, silvery eyes glittered palely, as did the mirrors. Why had they not been warned?

'How do you like it?' Margaret Tillotson had a pleasant husky voice as she quizzed her visitors.

'It's – er – it's extraordinary.' Antonia found her voice. 'So different from the rest of the house.'

'Oh, *that*.' Margaret Tillotson watched them. Antonia felt Barbara stiffen. 'I have just had it done up,' said Margaret. 'I got people from London. It is amusing watching them work.'

'Watching?'

'They have to work round me, I can't get out of bed.'

Barbara shifted uneasily. Was the woman a cripple? Nobody had prepared them for a cripple.

'Before this,' said Margaret Tillotson, 'the room was elegant, but I tired of it.'

Thinking how nice it would be to get back to her shabby guest room, Antonia asked, 'Was it like the rest of the house before you, er—?'

'God, no! It had black walls, the carpet and ceiling were white and the bed and sofas striped black and white. The mirrors were the same, of course. I like my mirrors.'

Barbara murmured, 'Ah, the mirrors.'

'Such dear liars.' Margaret laughed a small breathy laugh. 'I can see you don't like my room,' she said. 'Two ordinary healthy girls.'

Antonia might have let this pass, but Barbara could not. 'You look pretty healthy to me,' she said.

'I am,' said Margaret coolly, 'but not ordinary.' She waited for her visitors to assess this fact.

Antonia, dodging, asked, 'Before the black-and-white, how was the room then?' She had scented a game.

'Every shade of fuchsia. Not a success. I found it tiring.'

51

'What does your husband think of it?' Barbara tried to fit Henry into the colour scheme.

'I wouldn't know. I have not asked.' Margaret waited for the girls to make the next move.

'It is wonderfully feminine,' ventured Antonia. 'Shall you wear a gold dress at the party?'

Margaret narrowed her eyes. 'What party?'

'The party tomorrow. Dinner by moonlight in the garden—' said Antonia. 'Your father-in-law used to have these parties.'

'I know nothing about it,' said Margaret.

'Your husband must have been planning a surprise for you. We have blown the gaffe,' said Barbara, distressed, yet volunteering to share the blame with her friend. 'We did not know it was a secret,' she stumbled on. 'How awful of us, now his surprise is spoiled. How could we be so stupid?'

Margaret Tillotson watched her. 'I would say,' she said, measuring her words, 'that you take to stupidity like ducks to water.'

Antonia let out a shout of laughter.

'What have I said that's so funny? If you look over there on my dressing table, you will see a bottle of nail varnish. You can paint my nails for me.' Margaret's tone implied that Antonia's entertainment value was spent and that, this being so, she might as well make herself useful. She held out her hand. Antonia took it.

'Your nails are too long,' she said, and dropped it.

'They are not. Paint them.'

'Gold?' asked Barbara, getting to her feet. 'Paint them yourself,' she said bravely. 'You have nothing else to do.'

Margaret Tillotson let her hand drop and for a minute none of them spoke.

Then Antonia, mindful of her manners, asked, 'What shall you wear at the party?'

'If I come.'

'Is there any doubt?' Antonia was prepared to forgive. 'I mean,' she said, 'you do not look ill. What is there to prevent you?'

Barbara felt a mist of negative thought emanate from Margaret. She shifted uneasily, wishing James was beside her to give moral support.

'I have had nothing new since I married,' said Margaret. 'Other than nightdresses, of course.'

Hearing an explosion of girlish laughter, Henry Tillotson, on the terrace, glanced up. James, lolling in a deck-chair, said, 'At least she has not swallowed them whole.'

Henry said, 'If I warn people – well, you know what happens. You got nowhere.'

'Only so far as to be told that her previous husband's friends were of a higher intellectual standard than yours,' remarked Matthew. 'Bit sad for one's ego.'

'Listen, they are laughing again.' James sat up.

'Could Margaret have cracked a joke?' murmured Henry.

'It sounds as though they have found something in common,' said James.

'That would be stretching it too far,' Henry demurred. 'They are gutsy girls, though,' he said cheerfully. 'Look, you two, I have things to discuss with Trask. Will you stand guard? Stay within earshot?' Without waiting for James or Matthew to answer, Henry walked off, followed by his dogs.

'What are we supposed to stand guard against?' questioned James uneasily.

'No idea,' said Matthew. 'You've met her; what did she do to you?'

'Told me I bored her, asked me to open the window to clear the room of my odour. Odour was the word she used.'

'So you fared no better than me?'

'Worse, I'd say,' said James modestly. 'To smell bad and bore must be worse than to compare unfavourably with a divorced husband's cronies.'

'Oh, so she divorced, did she? I had the idea that she'd killed him off.'

'It was divorce. I definitely remember Henry's father telling me that Henry was marrying a divorcée.'

'Henry's father is dead,' said Matthew.

'Patently,' James, anxious for his girl-friend, snapped. 'Can't hear a thing,' he said. 'We'd better shut up and listen.'

They listened, Matthew with his head tilted sideways, eyes squinting along his nose, James with his head thrown back. In the woods behind the house the cuckoo called.

Matthew whispered, 'I don't like this.' Leaving his chair, he climbed on to the seat Henry had vacated. 'Hush,' he said, motioning James to keep quiet. 'I can hear someone talking.'

'?'

'It's not Antonia.'

'Barbara?' James whispered.

'No.'

'M—?'

'You all right?' Pilar came through the french windows. 'I take away tea things. Found a bird's nest, Matthew? Henry say is flycatcher nest in the vine.' She began stacking cups and saucers on to a tray. 'All cucumber sandwiches gone,' she said with satisfaction.

'They were delicious, Pilar,' Matthew stepped awkwardly down from the seat. 'Can I give you a hand?'

'No, no.' Pilar picked up the tray. 'Is all right.' As she walked away with the tray, she called over her shoulder, 'When you hear window shut, audience is over. The girls escape.' She pushed the french windows open with her foot and sidled through them.

'Escape?' asked James.

'She's making fun of us.' Matthew got back on the seat. 'It's Margaret,' he whispered presently, 'it must be. It isn't Antonia or Barbara, I know their voices.'

'Well, sit down,' said James, 'before Pilar catches you snooping.' Then, when Matthew resumed his seat, he said, 'Does anyone know the origin of Pilar? Was she Henry's, well, you know? Was she?'

'I can tell you *that*,' said Matthew. 'Nothing to do with Henry; his father got embroiled in the Spanish War succouring refugees. It was he brought Pilar and her baby to Cotteshaw. It was supposed to be for a few weeks, to get over the death of her husband, but the old man got ill and eventually died—'

'When?' asked James.

'A year or two into the war. Pilar nursed him, Henry told me. The old man was very idealistic, I believe; anyway, she took root and Ebro, too, I rather gathered when Henry told me that he had committed himself to looking after them. I remember Henry saying, "My father's ideals could turn into tripwires." Funny thing to say. And it wasn't to do with Pilar.'

'Oh.'

Matthew and James sat on in the late afternoon sun, ears cocked for sounds from the room above. Once Matthew glanced at his watch and whispered, 'They've been there nearly an hour.'

James whispered back, 'Still talking, I can just hear. Can't make out any words.'

And Matthew, growing impatient, said, 'And that bloody bird is still cuckooing.'

In the field beyond the garden Henry reappeared, his body casting an exaggerated shadow in the evening light. He waved and one of the dogs keeping him company barked.

James asked, 'How well do you know Henry?'

'As well as Henry allows.' Matthew smiled. 'I suspect his dogs know him a lot better than we do,' he said.

'And Margaret?' James asked.

'Oh, I shouldn't think *she* knows him at all.'

'Do you suppose the girls are getting to know her?'

'That would be rather interesting,' said Matthew thoughtfully. 'And do you suppose they will tell us what they know?'

'Of course they will,' said James. 'Barbara tells me practically everything now, and when we are married she will tell me the lot.'

'What an optimist you are,' said Matthew. 'Do I take it that she accepted you in the hayfield?'

'As good as,' said James.

Matthew said, 'Um.' Above them a sash window slammed shut. He said, 'Ah!'

Henry, approaching across the lawn, waved an arm. He jumped up the steps onto the terrace as Barbara and Antonia came out through the french windows. Antonia wore a bemused expression; Barbara looked slightly stunned. When they saw Henry the girls' expressions changed to cautious doubt. Antonia slid her arm through Matthew's; Barbara barely resisted taking hold of James's hand.

Henry said, 'Well now, who is for a drink before supper? I bet you girls could do with a resuscitating swig.' He looked at them quizzically. 'What do you two virgins think of my wife's brothel décor?' he asked.

'A drink would be splendid,' said Matthew.

'Excellent idea,' said James.

Barbara looked down her nose, displeased at being called a virgin.

As they moved into the house Antonia said in Matthew's ear, 'It *is* like a brothel. I've never been in one, but it's exactly what I would imagine a brothel to be.'

James, accepting Barbara's hand sliding into his as they followed the others into the house, said, 'Tell me what happened; I can't wait to hear.'

Barbara said, 'Not now. Later, when we're alone.'

5

Matthew had allocated the weekend at Cotteshaw as propitious for his proposal. Antonia was the kind of girl he had always intended marrying. Pretty without being too pretty, able to make a joke as well as see one, intelligent but not brainy, she could hold her own in conversation and was a good listener. Among the girls of his acquaintance he had marked her out as the most likely to suit when he realized that her father, John Lowther, was the John Lowther of Lowthers Steel. John Lowther had sent his sons to Eton and Antonia to a good but unflashy school. The Lowther ménage was exemplary; there was no observable hint of discord or divorce, no suggestion of financial scandal. The Lowthers, having noticed a loosening of morals during and since the war among their contemporaries, wished time for their daughter so that she could avoid making mistakes. They had insisted, as had the parents of Antonia's friend Barbara O'Malley, that Antonia, now grown-up, should earn her living at a worthwhile job before binding herself into marriage and motherhood. There was plenty of time, they thought, no need to rush; she was very young and certainly virgin.

Allowing himself to fall in love with Antonia, Matthew was not as sanguine as her parents that Antonia would observe the status quo. Thinking things over while on his business trip to Dusseldorf, he had decided that her youth was no barrier and that he would charge himself with her virginity before it slipped to someone else. Watching Antonia at supper on their first evening at Cotteshaw, he decided not to risk delay. Whatever her parents might think, Antonia – in his opinion – was not in need of time.

They had eaten supper in the kitchen sitting at the kitchen table, Pilar at its head with a space between herself and Ebro, Matthew and James opposite their girls. Henry, taking his place next to Pilar, glanced at the empty space and asked, 'Is Trask not coming?'

Ebro said, 'He took the supper tray up, but he wanted to go owling. I will fetch it presently.'

Henry said, 'All the more for us, then. That soup smells good, Pilar. My wife' – he let his eyes rest on the girls – 'has her meals in bed.'

Matthew observed Antonia cast a quick glance at Barbara before looking down, her cheeks flushing.

Henry went on, 'I must thank you two for making my wife laugh. We heard your laughter from the terrace. I supposed,' he said, his eyes travelling from Barbara to Antonia, 'that since you laughed, my wife laughed with you?' His remark took the form of a question.

Antonia ate a spoonful of soup and remained mute. Barbara, barely audible, muttered, 'She hasn't much to laugh about.'

Henry smiled, watching the girls. Pilar, holding up a ladle, suggested, 'More soup?'

Henry said, 'Yes, please,' and passed his plate. Matthew and Ebro had second helpings too. Henry was heard to murmur, 'Forget my wife,' between mouthfuls of soup.

James, who had finished his soup and regretted not accepting a second helping, asked, 'What is this about owls?'

'Barn owls,' said Henry. 'Trask is mad about birds. He is watching a pair who are nesting in one of my barns. He is also rather keen,' Henry began to laugh, 'on my investing in more cockatoos; he says our one and only is solitary and bored. In the wild they live in flocks. You met him, I think?' he addressed the girls.

Antonia looked up from her plate. 'Yes, he made us jump.' She stared at Henry.

'Made us both jump,' said Barbara, staring too. 'Then it slid down the banisters.'

'He is amused when he does that,' said Henry. 'Frightening you must have been a bonus.' He looked from Barbara to Antonia, sizing them up. 'He is not liked by my wife,' he said. 'It is difficult, when choosing presents for her, to know what, other than bed, she does like.' James, who had been looking vaguely uncomfortable, gave a barking laugh. Henry ignored James. 'And she can only occupy one bed at a time, so she is bored and solitary. But it was good,' he said, resting his eyes on Antonia, 'that you made her laugh.'

'We laughed. She didn't,' said Barbara.

Everyone sat in silence for some moments.

It had not been a happy meal, Matthew thought, as he managed to separate Antonia from the others and walk her out into the garden. Pilar had kept up some sort of chat as they ate roast duck, green peas and new potatoes and the girls, remembering their manners, had discussed the cinema with Ebro while they ate raspberries and cream. Once off, Ebro showed himself to be a considerable chatterer. Henry, having made everyone uncomfortable by his snide references to his wife, had sat watchful and silent. James, one of those rare people born with an upturned, perpetually smiling mouth, had chipped into the cinema talk with obvious half-heartedness and I, thought Matthew, taking Antonia's arm, found myself feeling bloody angry for some unknown reason.

'You seem,' he said to Antonia, 'you and Barbara, to have developed an instant rapport with our host.'

'Rapport?' said Antonia. 'What do you mean?'

'I mean,' said Matthew, 'that you kept staring at him and if you caught his eye, you certainly, I can't speak for Barbara, blushed.'

'It was the wine,' said Antonia. 'I really shouldn't drink; some wines make me go red and I did *not* stare. I cannot, of course, speak for Barbara.'

Matthew said, 'Don't be like that.'

Antonia said, 'Like what?'

Matthew said, 'You *did* stare, I was watching you.'

Antonia said, 'Feel my cheeks.'

They were now well away from the house. Matthew took Antonia's face between his hands. 'Oh, Antonia.' He was moved; her skin had the texture of fresh mushrooms. He said, 'I apologize.'

'So I didn't stare?'

'You didn't stare.' He held her face lightly. 'Are you still affected by the wine?'

'Don't think so. Why?'

'Will you marry me? Now don't answer if you are at all squiffy.'

'I am not. Yes, I will.' Antonia put her arms round Matthew's neck. 'Gladly,' she said.

In the tree above them the cockatoo raised its crest and shrieked, shifting its weight from one foot to the other.

Matthew said, 'Christ! And Henry talks of buying more of them.'

'I think Henry must be mad.' Antonia doubled up laughing.

'What makes you think that?' Matthew did not want to discuss Henry. Henry had no place in this proposal of marriage. He kissed Antonia's open mouth, slid his fingers over her ears to feel the texture of her hair.

'Let's go and sit on that seat over there,' he said, 'and talk about us.' He led Antonia across the grass and sat her on a garden seat. 'I have never asked anyone else to marry me,' he said.

'I should hope not. I am unique,' said Antonia.

'Henry may be a bit eccentric,' said Matthew, circling his arm round Antonia until his hand covered a breast, 'but he's got his head screwed on. Why d'you suggest he's mad?' He tried to decide whether Antonia's nipple had hardened.

Antonia covered his hand with her own, cupping her breast more conclusively in his grasp. 'Put the other one in your other hand,' she said.

Matthew complied. Antonia's breasts were just the right size, he thought. He said, 'Darling, I am so happy.'

Antonia said, 'Me too,' turning her face sideways to kiss his neck. 'You smell nice,' she said.

Across the lawn the cockatoo screeched again.

'It sounds as though it's screaming, "cuckoo, cuckoo",' said Matthew.

'You have a vivid imagination,' said Antonia. 'It screeches, that's all.' She leaned back against Matthew. 'Look,' she said. The cockatoo was scrambling slowly down the trunk of the tree; six feet from the ground it let itself drop. They watched it waddle and hop towards the house. 'What a creepy present to give his wife,' said Antonia. 'It sort of glows in the dark.'

'Henry tries his best,' said Matthew.

'Ho,' said Antonia.

'What d'you mean, ho?'

'You should have heard what she told us about him.'

Matthew said, 'And what was that?'

'The story of their marriage and courtship.'

'I am courting *you*.' Matthew was sick of Henry, sick

of Henry's wife. He kissed the back of Antonia's neck, nuzzling under her hair.

'Have you ever been to a brothel?' Antonia asked.

Matthew stiffened. 'Certainly not. Why d'you ask?'

'Have you seen Henry's wife's room? I think your friend Henry is a Bluebeard who keeps Margaret shut in there for his personal use, his – er – pleasure, when he feels like it.'

Matthew, feeling that Henry would be with them until Antonia got him off her mind, said, 'You'd better tell me what she told you. I've only met her once. She was pretty offensive.'

'She seems to have plenty to be offensive about.' Antonia snuggled against Matthew. 'I am so glad I am marrying you,' she said.

'Oh, darling, darling, I am more than happy, I am – well, everything that's wonderful.'

'More than can be said for that poor woman up there in her private brothel—'

'Oh, *God*,' said Matthew, sitting up straight. 'This is a unique occasion between you and me. Do we have to include the Tillotsons?' His mind went back to Antonia's covert glances at supper, swift looks at Henry under her lashes between spoonfuls of soup. 'Perhaps,' he said, 'you had better tell me about Margaret; your visit to her seems to be preying on your mind. Get it off your chest.'

'You seem to like my chest.'

'Get cracking.'

Antonia giggled. 'Very well, I will. She was very rude at first. We nearly walked out. Then she told us how she has her room redecorated; she gets a firm down from London. It's really weird. From that she started in on marriage, hers. Apparently she was married to some fiend who beat her, before she met Henry. She managed to divorce him and then, coming

63

across Henry, she befriended him.' In the dusk Matthew raised his eyebrows. 'And Henry fell arse over tip in love with her—'

'Where did you hear that expression?' asked Matthew, displeased.

'One of my brothers.'

'Well, don't use it. Go on.'

'Ho,' said Antonia.

'Go on.'

'All right. Well, Henry pestered her and pestered her to marry him and she finally gave in. He brought her here and expected her to like horses and so on. He never lets her buy clothes, only nightdresses. She exists by ordering things by mail. The room is full of catalogues. Her only amusement is having her room redecorated; she's got pretty awful taste, poor thing. She even paints her nails gold; the whole room is gold. She asked me to paint her nails. I jibbed at that. She never sees anybody apart from the daily lady and Pilar and Ebro and Trask.'

'Does she read?'

'I didn't see any books. She has a radio. Honestly, Matthew, it's the cruellest set-up I've ever heard of.'

'She has bed and board,' said Matthew, 'and a husband.'

'A husband who presumably comes in when he feels like it and, and, you know.'

'I don't think there is any question of that,' said Matthew.

'Gosh.'

'Yes – well.'

'And she hadn't heard a whisper about the dinner party in the garden and if she had she still would have nothing to wear.'

'What a gullible little darling you are.' Matthew hugged her.

'I am not.'

'If you believe all that, you'll believe anything.'

'Barbara did.'

'That makes two.'

'Brute, I shall give you back your ring.'

'I haven't given you one yet.'

'Are you suggesting I—'

'I don't know, darling. I don't know Henry all that well. I've stayed a couple of weekends; I've met his wife once. I don't believe she is ill. The only thing I happen to know is that Ebro does all the redecorating; he is training to be an interior decorator.'

'In London?'

'I suppose so.'

'So that wasn't a lie.'

'Half.'

'Oh.' Antonia was thoughtful.

'I suggest,' said Matthew, 'that if you girls are all that interested, you ask Henry for the truth of it.'

'Maybe I will,' said Antonia.

Matthew wished he had not made this suggestion. 'Can we get back to you and me?' he asked. 'When shall we marry? Where shall we spend our honeymoon? Where shall we live? How many children shall we have—?'

'Steady on,' said Antonia. 'Let's start with the engagement ring. I like rubies.'

'And you are virtuous,' Matthew ventured.

'Of course I am.' Antonia hugged him. 'Darling, darling Matthew.' There's a trousseau to choose, she thought. A house to find. What fun! I can stop going to my office and all that rush in the mornings and the horrible journey home on the tube. 'I shall try and make you happy,' she said.

'That will be no problem,' said Matthew. 'I am happy now. It will only get more so.'

6

James Martineau had enjoyed his supper. Pilar was a good cook. Eating the roast duck, he compared the meal with previous meals at Cotteshaw, each in its way excellent. As he ate the duck and watched Barbara, he remembered the weekend a year ago when he had brought Valerie with him. There had still been some small possibility that she would stop messing about and make up her mind.

Valerie had stopped messing about and she had made up her mind. Putting paid to any residue of hope he might have had, she had married a man richer, more intelligent and better-looking than himself. Savouring the peas, James remembered Valerie: he had been so very much in love!

During that weekend Valerie had chatted and joked, made herself interesting, drawn Henry out. Yet Valerie had not been invited upstairs to meet Margaret. Remembering Valerie, and the awful pain of disappointment, James determined, as he ate his pudding, never again to allow himself to be so vulnerable. Spooning fruit into his mouth, he watched Henry watching the girls and the girls' responsive glances, and Matthew watching Antonia. Helping himself to more cream, James tried to remember what exactly he had said to Barbara when they stopped on their way to Cotteshaw. Had he or had he not committed himself? Certainly Barbara had said neither yes nor no. The episode had been on a jokey plane. Remembering this, James thought that he need not necessarily follow it up, and that anyway Barbara was, and would always be, second best.

When supper was over Matthew and Antonia had strolled out into the garden, while Barbara helped Pilar clear the table. Ebro went to fetch Margaret's tray. Henry suggested, 'Like a walk? Come on, Barbara – and James.'

Pilar said, 'You go, Barbara, it's a lovely night, I finish this easy.'

Barbara said, 'Right then, thank you,' and put down the glass cloth and the plate she had been drying. 'Come on, James.'

Henry led them across the lawn through a gate to a path which ran across a hayfield. His dogs padded ahead, snuffling the night smells. Halfway across the field, Henry said, 'I must see to something in the wood. I'll catch you up,' and disappeared with his dogs into the half-dark. James and Barbara followed the footpath; haycocks, ghostly in the moonlight, stretched in geometric rows to the hedges.

'James?' Barbara slid her hand into his.

'Yes?' He held her hand, thrusting his thumb against her palm, as he used to do with Valerie. Barbara had a narrower hand than Valerie.

'Did you mean what you said this afternoon?' Barbara flinched closer to James as a hunting bat whispered and dived after moths.

'When I suggested that we get married?' James did not look at her. 'Yes, I did.'

'If you still mean it, I'd like to.'

'Of course I mean it,' James answered violently. Why did she say 'like to', not 'love to'?

They stopped walking and stood facing each other. James took Barbara's other hand and held both against his chest. 'Sealed with a kiss?' he suggested, and bent to kiss her.

Returning the kiss, Barbara was surprised by an incomprehensible sense of loss and disillusion which she quickly dismissed. 'It's such a wonderful night,' she said, kissing him again. 'A full midsummer moon.'

'Full moon tomorrow,' James corrected her, 'for the dinner party.'

She said, 'Ah yes, the dinner party.'

Presently they sat leaning against a haycock and listened to the night sounds. A tawny owl in the wood, a fieldmouse rustling in the hay, the loud cack-cack of a disturbed pheasant, sheep munching in the next field. James thought, I've done it now, let myself in for it. Then he thought, She will never be able to hurt me as Valerie did, I shall be far more comfortable with Barbara. Smiling to himself, he murmured, 'The doctrine of second best.'

Barbara, with her head on his shoulder, said, 'What?'

James said, 'Nothing, Barbara, nothing.'

She said, 'So you love me?'

James said, 'Of course I do.'

'Desperately?'

James said, 'That word would apply,' and kissed the top of her head.

Barbara said, 'Our marriage will not be like Henry's.'

James said, 'I should damn well hope not. What did you think of her – Margaret?'

'Strange.' Barbara laughed uneasily. 'Very odd. She told us that Henry pestered her and pestered her to marry him, he would not take No. Would you have taken No?'

James said, 'Of course not.'

'I am not convinced,' Barbara wheedled.

'Then be convinced. I am,' James said, lying. 'Totally,' he said, compounding his untruth.

'To spend your life in bed! It *is* peculiar. Does she

68

never get up? I am thinking of Margaret,' said Barbara.

'She must, if only to go to the loo or have a bath.' They giggled, leaning against the haycock and each other.

'Hullo, you two.' Henry reappeared from behind them, walking softly. One of his dogs panted in Barbara's face and tried to lick her. Pushing the dog away, Barbara said, 'Get off, you smell,' and 'Oh Henry, hullo. We are going to get married; James would not take No.'

Henry said, 'Felicitations. I hope you will be very happy. May I join you or would you rather be alone?'

Barbara said, 'Of course, sit with us. It's lovely here in the sweet-smelling hay by the light of the moon. We have the rest of our lives to be alone.'

As Henry lowered himself to sit with them, James thought bitterly of Valerie and wished her dead, but since he was essentially a kind man he immediately rescinded this wish. Taking Barbara's hand, he kissed her palm and folded her fingers over it. 'Barbara—'

Barbara said, 'M-m-m, that's nice, who taught you to do that?' and when James failed to answer she turned to Henry. 'Did you propose to Margaret by moonlight?'

Henry said, 'No. It was in Egypt.'

'But the same moon—'

'So?'

'The moon is even larger in Egypt, I've read. Did you ask—'

'In a bar, I think. Yes, it was in a bar.'

'Often?'

'What d'you mean?'

'I mean, how often did you propose? James asked me several times.'

'Just the once,' Henry answered shortly.

Barbara said, 'Oh,' and after a pause, 'Did you have a wonderful wedding?'

'A civil ceremony.'

'Don't let her bother you,' said James.

'Pester was the word Margaret used,' said Barbara. 'She said you absolutely pestered her to marry you.'

Henry said, 'I think I'll go in. My arse is getting damp and I have a lot to do tomorrow.' He jumped upright from his sitting position and, when Barbara held up her hand to him, pulled her to her feet and smacked her bottom. 'That's for nosiness.'

James, younger but less spry, scrambling to his feet felt excluded. To rectify this feeling he put his arm around Barbara as they walked back to the house. There they found Matthew and Antonia on the terrace, arms entwined. Antonia called out as they crossed the lawn, 'I allowed Matthew to talk me into marriage under a lilac bush. I shall for ever associate its intoxicating scent with—'

'Happiness?' suggested Henry. Then, 'Well now, isn't that nice? Two future tangles. This merits a bottle of champagne,' and he went away into the house to fetch it.

Antonia murmured, or it might have been Barbara, or again in later years, when memories played false, one or other thought Matthew or James had remarked, 'Some people's idea of wit is a trifle warped.' What they all remembered was the harsh screech of the cockatoo perched in the vine, and Henry calling up, 'Come down, my pretty,' as he set the bottle and the glasses on a table. Then he stretched his arm up for the bird to sidle on to his wrist.

Antonia had asked, 'Where did you find him?' and Henry, stroking the bird's yellow crest, had said, 'Caged in a pet shop. I cannot endure the thought of imprisonment for wild creatures.' And he had added, 'Or for any live creature.'

Then Antonia and Barbara had exchanged a

disbelieving look which was noted by the men, Henry in particular, and Henry, opening the champagne with a soft pop, had murmured as he filled the glasses, 'You are thinking of my caged wife,' and chuckled. The cockatoo screeched again and climbed up his arm to sit on his shoulder.

Sipping her champagne, Barbara said, 'And is she not caged? Don't you keep her prisoner?'

James had made as though to hush her, but Henry answered her seriously, 'I cannot interfere with my wife's liberty,' and watched Barbara's face. Then he said, 'Shall we drink to you and James? And Antonia and Matthew? To your – er – collective liberties.' When they had drunk the toast he had said, still amused but friendly, 'I see you girls as the prototypes for post-war women.'

Matthew had said, 'The war has been over for some years.'

Henry said, 'True, but we are still finding our collective feet, don't you agree?' Then he said, 'Time for bed, I think. Tomorrow will be a long day,' and led the way into the house.

In the hall he had settled the cockatoo on its perch before bidding them good night. 'I hope you all come again often,' he said, 'and when you have children that you will bring them too. This is a good place for children. Good night, all of you.'

Watching Antonia mount the stairs ahead of him, Matthew congratulated himself on a job well done, a sensible step. Beside him James suppressed a disconsolate pang, remembering the weekend he had brought Valerie, when he had shared her bed.

In the bathroom Antonia squeezed paste on to her toothbrush. 'Antonia Stephenson,' she said. 'How does it sound to you?'

71

In the act of brushing her teeth, Barbara gargled inarticulately, rinsed and countered, 'Barbara Martineau? I like both.' She made room for Antonia at the basin.

Antonia brushed her teeth briskly then rinsed, rolling the water around before spitting. 'Names matter,' she said. 'I feel sorry to give up Lowther but Stephenson will do, and your Martineau has a fine Huguenot ring.'

'Tillotson,' said Barbara.

'What makes you say Tillotson?' asked Antonia, startled.

Barbara picked up her hairbrush and began brushing her hair. 'It it just that since we sat in that weird room listening to our hostess, I suppose she *is* our hostess, I can't get her out of my mind.' Barbara sat on the rim of the bath and stared at her friend. 'I'm not a bit sleepy,' she said. 'Shall we discuss?'

They moved into Antonia's room. Barbara sat on the end of the bed while Antonia got in and propped herself with pillows.

Antonia said, 'It's not so much her as him, Henry. Were you able to talk to James about him?'

'We were too busy getting engaged,' said Barbara.

Antonia said, 'So were we.'

Barbara said, 'Henry seemed to be there with us. He went off, leaving us alone, but when he came back it was as though he had been there all the time—'

'In your thoughts,' said Antonia.

'Yes,' said Barbara.

'He was in mine too,' Antonia admitted. 'Why don't you get in with me, it's a double bed. You might catch a chill out there.'

Barbara said, 'Thanks, I will,' and joined Antonia in the bed.

Antonia said, 'Did you tell James what she said about Henry?'

'I told him that she told us he pestered her to marry him, and that I thought her very odd, but—'

'Not about his being impotent?' Antonia queried.

'No.'

'Not about him being homosexual?'

Barbara said, 'No.'

'Or only able to do it with *horses*?' Antonia pressed her friend.

'I was afraid James would laugh. It's not the sort of thing I could tell James. We were getting engaged. James would be shocked. How could Henry – with a *horse*?'

'Work it out for yourself,' said Antonia.

'I've tried,' said Barbara. 'Did *you* tell Matthew?'

'Of course not,' said Antonia. 'So all the time James was proposing and you were accepting you were thinking of Henry Tillotson?'

'Not all the time, of course not, but just a bit. You said you were thinking of him too.'

'Well,' said Antonia, 'how could one *not*?' and she pushed a propping pillow aside and stretched her legs down the bed.

Barbara, taking the hint, got out of bed. 'But you do love Matthew?' she asked as she moved towards her own room.

'Of course,' said Antonia firmly. 'Do you love James?'

'Yes,' said Barbara, 'of course – er – desperately.' She remembered James voicing this word in the hayfield.

'So why are we discussing Henry?' Antonia murmured, but not expecting an answer she called, 'Good night.'

Barbara said, 'Good night,' and closed the communicating door.

7

When Barbara woke she heard sounds in the garden. It was very early. She went to the window and looked out. Her room was at the side of the house looking onto a lawn, which stretched down to a gate leading into a walled garden; craning her neck, she could see the tops of fruit trees and rows of vegetables. Flanking the lawn were clipped yew hedges and, along the hedges, borders of yellow tulips. There was activity on the lawn: Ebro and Trask were putting up trestle tables, directed by Pilar. 'This way,' said Pilar, and, 'Is not straight. Is not in the middle. Yes, better so. Don't make a noise,' she said, gesturing up at the house. 'The ladies a-sleeping.'

Antonia, yawning, came into her room and joined Barbara at the window. 'What's going on?' she whispered.

'They are getting ready for the party.'

'Aha, here comes Henry with chairs—'

'And attendant dogs.'

They watched Henry unstacking chairs. He spoke quietly to Pilar. 'Leave the table-cloths till later,' and, 'Thank you, Trask. This table here, I think, for the buffet and that one for drinks.'

'How many people?'

'Lay for a dozen, some may not turn up. It doesn't matter—'

Barbara whispered, 'Bones.'

'Bones?'

'The bones of the party, the bones of our lives.'

74

'Getting engaged has made you poetic, you must keep your head,' Antonia teased. On the far side of the yew hedge a mistlethrush burst into song, to be answered by a rival in the distance.

'I feel so much older,' whispered Barbara.

'You are a prototype; we are both prototypes,' Henry said. Do you know what a prototype is?' Antonia teased.

'I know what a tangle is.' Barbara watched Henry. 'Why did he suggest tangle?'

'Because his marriage is a tangle,' hissed Antonia. 'It doesn't mean yours will be – or mine.'

'Perhaps not,' Barbara whispered, then, 'Of course not,' more robustly. 'Listen to that bird, and the cuckoo is nearer this morning.'

'Do you want children, Barbara?'

'Not much.'

'Me neither. But it's another way to earn a living and a better way than working in a boring office. I loathe typewriters. Anyway,' said Antonia, 'if I can't have a nanny, if Matthew can't afford one, I shall have an au pair.'

'Antonia, you think of everything.'

'I am not going to allow myself to be blocked,' Antonia muttered between gritted teeth. 'My mother,' she said, 'gives in to my father in everything. I don't want to be like her.'

'No need for you to worry. Matthew isn't masterful, like your pa.'

'Of course he's masterful—' Antonia protested.

'Not like your pa, that's all I meant.'

'Oh. And James?'

'Not so's you'd notice.' The girls giggled, leaning shoulder to shoulder, elbows on the windowsill, blond hair brushing against brown as they watched the activity below.

'The best silver,' said Pilar. 'I clean the chandeliers. Tall white candles.'

'Chandeliers!' whispered Barbara. 'Candle-light.'

'Don't go overboard.'

Standing immediately below the girls' window, Henry surveyed the scene. They heard him murmur, 'Flowers?'

'A beautiful setting for beautiful people,' said Pilar, hands on hips. 'They have the best.'

'Beautiful girls.' Ebro steadied a table. 'Eh, Trask?'

Trask, who had not spoken, smiled, shrugged and walked away.

'Hear that?' Antonia nudged her friend. 'We are beautiful.'

'Here comes that exotic bird—' Barbara pointed.

They watched the cockatoo insinuate itself through the bars of the garden gate and approach Henry with its sideways hop. Henry put his hand down, offering his wrist. 'I think you had better be shut in tonight. Don't nip,' he said, as the bird clawed itself up onto his shoulder. 'Sit tight.'

The bird put its head on one side, raising and lowering its yellow crest.

'Matches the tulips,' murmured Barbara.

'He invited our children here,' whispered Antonia. 'Shall you—'

'Probably – oh certainly, yes. I *wish*—'

'What?'

'Nothing.'

Antonia glanced sharply at Barbara. I wish it too, she thought, drawing in her breath, don't I just. 'I think,' she said, 'that Henry is a prototype himself.'

'Do you?' said Barbara. 'Really? But what about the horses? Was she pulling our legs?'

Antonia giggled. 'It's not possible,' she spluttered.

'Are you two girls going to stay up there all morning

76

tittering, or would you like to come for a swim or a ride before breakfast?' Henry neither raised his voice nor did he look up.

'Oh!' the girls exclaimed. 'Oh!' and sobered, wondering what Henry had overheard.

Henry said, 'Well?'

Looking down at Henry, Antonia said, 'We shall have to telephone our parents and tell them about being engaged. That is, if you don't mind us using your telephone.'

Henry said, 'Please do. And what will they say?' He smiled up at them.

Antonia said, 'My mother will say, "Oh, goodness. I must break it to your father," and he will say, "What about your job?" and "You are awfully young, darling, for such a big decision."'

'And what will yours say?' Henry asked Barbara.

'The same tell your father bit and, "Isn't it rather sudden?" and "Have you really thought it through?"'

'And have you?' Henry caressed the cockatoo, which now clung to his upper arm and peered up at his face with its basilisk eye.

'We have. Long ago,' said Antonia, 'haven't we, Barbara?'

Barbara said, 'Definitely.'

'We only have to get parental consent,' said Antonia cheerfully. 'My father is known as "Stuffy Lowther", but I know how to work on him.'

'They do not want us to rush into marriage and regret it afterwards,' Barbara explained. 'They think "rushing into marriage" is a bad thing.'

Henry said, 'What sensible people.' He transferred the cockatoo from his arm to the wisteria. 'Are you coming or not? If you don't want to swim until the day has warmed up or wait for your future husbands to wake, I could take you for a spin in my Bentley.'

77

'A Bentley!' Barbara was impressed. 'Oh!'

'1926. It was my father's.'

'Thirty years old!' Antonia gasped. 'Wow! Love to.'

Henry said, 'Buck up, then, I haven't got all day.'

Spinning along in the Bentley Henry, raising his voice, asked, 'And what else will your parents say? What will their reaction be? Will they be pleased?'

'Oh, they will be pleased once they are used to the idea. They have been so afraid we might want to marry some penniless person for love and then fall out of it, they will be greatly relieved,' said Antonia.

Henry said, 'I see.'

Barbara said, 'They don't really know us. They don't know that long ago, at least two years, we decided about marriage.'

Henry said, 'And?'

'We decided to be detached,' explained Antonia. 'You might not understand, but we made up our minds not to go overboard, not to go for perfection, to settle for—'

'Security.'

'Well, that too, but what we decided was to choose the kind of husband who would be picked by our parents if they went in for arranged marriages; presentable, right sort of background, enough money, that sort of thing. Do you think that hard-headed and calculating?'

Henry asked, 'Do James and Matthew know about this, your detached attitude?'

'I wouldn't be surprised if James's and Matthew's attitude were the same as ours, with a few minor differences,' said Barbara, 'except that they would never admit it.'

Henry said, 'I dare say you are right there,' rather

grimly. Can all the old battleaxes one meets have started out like this? he wondered. 'Over there,' he said, 'is the lake I swim in. I ride out, have a swim and hack home.'

'Does, I mean, did your wife ride and swim with you?' asked Barbara.

'My wife does not care for horses,' Henry answered evenly. Presently he said, 'Would you two do something for me?'

The girls said, 'Of course, what?'

'If you could pick a few flowers, make an arrangement for the dinner table—'

'That was not what you were going to ask us,' said Antonia astutely.

Henry said, 'No, well, it's this. I bought a dress for my wife. I wondered whether you could pretend it's one of yours, offer to lend it to her for the party.'

'But she never gets out of bed,' said Barbara.

'There are occasions – I rather hoped—'

Antonia said, 'Of course we'll try. We can take one of ours with it, it would look more natural. She is sure to choose yours.'

'If you are prepared to risk a snub, it would be a kindness,' said Henry.

'We'll do the flowers too, of course,' said Barbara. 'It will be wonderful if she comes to the party,' she added encouragingly.

Henry said, 'Yes,' and, 'Thanks. Nearly home.' Turning the car into the drive, he said, 'There are your intendeds wondering where I carried you off to. Shall you delay telephoning your respectable parents until after breakfast?'

Antonia said, 'Before breakfast would be fatal. My father is not human until his digestion has worked and he's been to the lavatory.'

'Mine, who has given up smoking, has to have a

79

surreptitious cigarette. He's all right after that,' said Barbara. 'Ten-fifteen is a good moment.'

'We'd better toss for who telephones first,' said Antonia, waving to Matthew standing on the doorstep with James. Matthew waved back. Barbara, watching Henry's dogs, who had been drooping despondently in his absence, prick up their ears and wag their tails, said, 'How dearly your dogs love you. Look, they are rushing to meet you.'

Henry, slowing the car to a walking pace as the dogs galloped to meet him, said, 'Ah, dogs.'

Comparing Henry's dogs' unstinting affection with his wife's apparent lack of it, Barbara asked pertly, 'Don't you admire us for not rushing as you did into a romantic trap? We shall probably have happy, stable marriages.'

Letting this impertinence pass, Henry said, 'Such hard little heads on teenage shoulders.'

Barbara said, 'We are almost twenty, Henry, not quite the prototypes you thought us.'

Henry laughing, said, 'I agree I got you wrong there.' Bringing the car to a stop, he said, 'I wonder what sort of children you will have.'

8

'Here, give me the secateurs. Crying like that, you can't see what you are doing.' Antonia snatched the secateurs from her friend. The girls were in the walled garden cutting flowers from a border which ran along one wall. Here flowers grew separately from the vegetables, but whereas the vegetables were tended with exactitude, the flowers had to fend for themselves, springing up through disorderly weeds. 'These are marvellous.' Antonia snipped at some nettles and reached towards a clump of Regale lilies. As she cut she laid each stem horizontally in a trug half-full of Mrs Simpkins pinks. As she picked, she sneezed; prone to hay fever, she was affected by their scent. 'These are marvellous,' she repeated. 'I shall make an arrangement backed by artichoke leaves.'

'They'll make it look heavy. And you can't put those on the dinner table, they smell too strong,' said Barbara disagreeably.

'Then I shall put my arrangement on the bar,' said Antonia equably. 'Why must you be so negative? Honestly, Barbara, do stop crying, your face will be a mess. You know your nose swells when you cry.'

Barbara whimpered, 'O-o-o.'

'Nor can I grasp what there is to cry about,' continued Antonia, snipping at the lilies. 'Oh, delicious.'

'My mother—'

'But you said she took it well. And your Pa is

pleased, too. Oh, I say, look at these lilies of the valley.'
Antonia pushed away some invading buttercups.

'They also smell too strong,' said Barbara morosely.

'Oh, there is no pleasing you. They will do beautifully for a centrepiece, we don't need a "cache-mari".'

'What's a cache-mari?' Barbara snuffled.

'A tall arrangement the Edwardians had on dinner tables to conceal their flirtations from their husbands and vice versa; my great-aunt told me.'

'Husbands—'

'Why don't you walk it off, Babsie? Leave the flowers to me,' said Antonia, kindly.

'I—'

'Go on. But come back in time to try Margaret with the dresses. I'm not braving that woman on my own. Here, take my handkerchief.'

Barbara took the handkerchief and left, blowing her nose and mopping her eyes.

Left to herself Antonia muttered, 'Some people!' and crouched down to pick lilies of the valley.

Barbara let herself out of the garden by a door in the wall, crossed a stable yard and climbed a gate into a field of buttercups. As she walked she repeated to herself what her mother had said on the telephone. 'Such a nice young man,' she mimicked her mother. 'Your father and I used to know his family. In a good job, too! Your grandparents will be pleased. A sensible age, not too young. We liked him so much when we met him (she said graciously). I am sure you will be very happy – No, I can't tell your father this minute, he's in the – Of *course* he will be pleased, darling (voice rising optimistically). Such a relief to know you will be safe.'

'Safe,' Barbara shouted. 'Safe!'

A flock of starlings pecking after ants flew up,

startled, their wings rustling, and two horses standing nose to tail under a hawthorn pricked their ears and turned towards her in polite enquiry. Barbara walked up to them and stroked their noses. The comforting smell of horse mingled with the acrid smell of may. She said, 'Oh, silly me,' letting her fingers linger round the horses' nostrils. 'Silly, silly me.' She had stopped crying. 'I bet you never cried over parental approval,' she said, fingering the whorls of hair on the horses' foreheads, pressing her forefinger against the hard skulls.

One of the horses leaned forward and nibbled her shirt, its grey lips making a plopping sound. It tweaked at the shirt with yellow teeth.

Barbara picked at the hair on the bony skull, short and bristly as cliff grass, and remembered how, long ago when she was small, she could not have been more than three, her feet had been bare on the cliff-top and her father said, 'Hold my hand, I won't let you fall. Look at the waves smashing against the rocks; aren't they magnificent?' And, 'Trust me, stupid,' he had said angrily as she stuck in her toes and pulled back from the edge. 'Nothing to scream about. Don't be such a coward,' he had said. 'I have hold of you, you are perfectly safe.' She could still in screaming nightmares feel the stiff grass between her toes as she dragged away from her father and the sheer drop.

'Oh, don't ring off,' her mother had said. 'Here comes your father, he's out of the – It's Barbara, darling, she has news for us. She's engaged to James Martineau, she wants to tell you herself, here's the phone. Tell your father, darling, he'll be so pleased.'

And he had been pleased. 'Congratulations,' he had said. 'Of course you are very young, but I suppose you know your mind or you wouldn't – James Martineau is a sound chap,' her father had said. 'He will look after you. I knew his father, it's a family firm, they say it's likely to expand. And of course there is backing from his mother's family, and someday he will inherit. There's no male heir.'

She had said, 'What?' She was slightly bemused.

Her father had said, 'It's a family trust, hasn't James told you? He will, of course. Of course the uncle is young, something like fifteen years younger than James's mother. He was the result of an afterthought, a last fling,' her father said, 'but it's understood he can't have children.'

'Was it love?' she had asked.

'Was what love?' Her father sounded puzzled in his interrupted flow. 'What d'you mean, love?'

She had said, 'The last fling?'

Sounding grumpy, her father had replied, 'I shouldn't think that came into it, no.'

'I hate my parents,' she told the horse. 'I absolutely loathe them. How *dare* they be so complacent and pleased? How *dare* they assume I shall be safe? I don't want to be safe, there is no spice in safety.'

The horse, taking a shirt button between its teeth, jerked at it.

'Don't do that,' Barbara sobbed, 'you'll choke.'

She pulled away but went on stroking the animal while she thought of her father.

'He's so bloody respectable,' she told the horse. 'He's so boring. If he finds something even faintly amusing he says, "Oh! Ha! That's good enough for *Punch*." I despise him,' she told the horse. 'I have got to get away. Everything he does is right, my mother thinks. She's just as boring as he is. I shall not be like them,' she told the horse. 'My life with James will be quite different. James is in love with me.'

Barbara now contemplated vaulting up, risking a bareback gallop. But a fall would cause bruises which

84

might show at the party. 'No,' she said, 'no, not today,' refusing the risk.

She walked on, leaving the horses, through a belt of beech trees to find herself in the hayfield where, the night before, she had walked with Henry and James and had become engaged to James.

It need not have happened, she thought; it was I who precipitated the decision. It was my choice, I must abide by it now. I was happy last night, she thought; why am I not happy now? She walked quickly, leaving the hayfield and its sweet-smelling haycocks, climbing a gate which led to grassland sloping down to the lake she had seen that morning from Henry's car.

Grazing sheep raised their heads as she passed. There was nobody about.

The water when she reached it looked inviting; it was so still it reflected the yellow flags growing at its edge. She slipped out of her clothes and waded in. The lake washed the buttercup pollen off her shins. She dived. Cool water soothed her malaise, washed the salty detritus from her eyes, rinsed her hair, roared in her ears. In the middle of the lake she turned on her back and floated. As she floated she watched emerald dragonflies zip low above the water and listened to the distant cuckoo's beguiling cry.

It is not like me, she thought, to swim naked. What would my parents think? What would James say? What would it be like if Henry was swimming, too? How would it be between us in this delicious peaty water? The mutinous thoughts which had circled her brain washed loose; when she turned and struck out for the bank she had regained her equanimity.

Henry, taking a short cut across the kitchen garden, espied Antonia. Coming to a halt beside her, he

85

commented on Barbara's absence. 'Leaving you to do all the work?'

Antonia appeared to be stripping the border of blooms; he wondered whether the lilies of the valley would ever recover.

'She is walking off her dudgeon,' said Antonia, squatting by the lily bed, looking up.

'Oh?'

'Floods of tears,' Antonia volunteered disloyally.

'Engagement off?'

'No, no, it's *on*.'

'Then why tears?'

'She was expecting some parental opposition.' Antonia stood up. 'Hoping for it,' she said maliciously.

'She will get it later, perhaps?' Henry suggested.

'Not by marrying James.'

'Ah. Parental approval can be a snare,' Henry agreed. 'And your parents?'

'Oh, I put up with it. I am not romantic.'

Henry laughed. 'So James and Matthew are safe?'

'James and Matthew are safe,' Antonia agreed.

'But you girls are on the wobbly side?' Henry suggested.

Antonia said, 'Well,' drawing out the word, 'well, sort of.' She picked up the trug of lilies, Mrs Simpkins Pinks and lilies of the valley.

She was well aware, Henry thought, of the picture she presented. He sneezed. 'I hope you are not going to heap all that lot on the dinner table,' he said.

'I thought on the bar—' said Antonia.

Henry said, 'Good. I am puzzled by your motives.' He took the trug from her and began walking towards the house. 'Is all this – er – caution necessary?'

'You were not cautious,' said Antonia pertly, 'and look where it's got you. I mean, what were your motives when you married Margaret?'

'None of your business,' Henry answered coldly.

Antonia said, 'Sorry.'

Henry said, 'That's all right,' still chilly.

Antonia wondered how she could retrieve the earlier mood. 'Perhaps,' she said, risking a further snub, 'you got healthy opposition from your family when you married and it spurred you on. That's what Barbara would like. She objects to pushing at an open door.'

'My mother was dead,' said Henry.

'And your father?'

'It was his suggestion,' said Henry sedately.

Antonia thought, Gosh, and tried to assimilate the idea of anyone, far less his father, urging Henry to marry Margaret.

They walked on towards the house while Antonia chased through the passages of her mind for something to say. Then Henry said, 'Here she comes, your cautious playmate. Looks as though she has recovered.'

'I have been swimming in your lake, it is absolutely fabulous,' cried Barbara, coming towards them at a run. 'What are you discussing? You look serious,' she shook her hair, still wet from the lake.

'A puzzle of motives,' said Henry, smiling.

Barbara said, 'Oh?'

'As to why people marry,' said Henry. 'Whether it is to avoid or court boredom.'

'Antonia and I are marrying for love,' Barbara said, '*and* security of course *and* to get away from boring jobs *and* to get away from our parents. All the usual.'

Henry said, 'I see.' These girls were pretty appetizing, not as unintelligent as they made out. 'Some day when you are older I might teach you to take risks,' he said. 'You might enjoy that.'

'We may keep you to that,' said Barbara lightly.

'Are you all right now?' asked Antonia, lowering her voice. She was not sure she was pleased that Barbara had rejoined them.

Barbara answered sharply, 'Of course I am.'

'You have weed in your hair, you smell of mud and you've ruined that shirt. Do you see yourself as Ondine?' Antonia wished that she had had longer alone with Henry.

'Who was Ondine?' asked Barbara, who knew perfectly well. She tossed back her damp hair, ran her fingers through it and glanced sidelong at Henry. 'I must tidy myself,' she said, 'before we go and see your wife. She tells us lots of things about you,' she added.

'That must be interesting.' Henry took a lily from the trug and brushed its orange stamens across Barbara's nose, then did the same to Antonia. 'You must excuse me,' he said, 'I have much to do,' and left them.

'Treating us like children.' Barbara was angry.

'We must learn to grow up. Oh, Babsie,' said Antonia, 'are we doing the right thing? Are we wise?'

'I thought I was the one to have doubts,' said Barbara.

Antonia said, 'Best friends share.'

9

'Where does Henry's money come from? D'you know?'
James and Matthew, having volunteered to collect ice
for the party from the fishmonger and strawberries
from a fruit farm some distance from Cotteshaw, were
driving across country in Matthew's car. Since
Matthew failed to answer immediately James repeated,
'D'you know?', raising his voice.

Matthew, whose parents had brought him up to
believe direct discussion of people's incomes to be
vulgar, replied, 'Inherited, one supposes,' in what he
hoped were inhibiting accents. 'Old money.'

Unaffected by Matthew's tone, James said, 'There
must have been quite a lot. I've seldom seen such well-
kept fences. He's a good farmer, and he has super
stock.'

Matthew said, 'Oh,' and, changing gear at a hill,
'naturally.'

'I am quite interested in farming,' James continued.
'My grandfather farmed in a big way. This was before
one could offset one's farm losses against income tax.
He had an agent, of course.'

Matthew said, 'Of course.' If Antonia were with us
she'd say, 'Ho,' and take him down a peg, he thought.

'Of course the house is shabby as hell,' said James.
'All the money must go on the farm.'

Matthew said, 'I dare say it does, apart from what's
spent on that wife.'

James said, 'Has she got any money?'

Matthew said, 'I wouldn't know.'

James continued, 'I gather that Trask has been here for ever; worked for Henry's father. I don't suppose Henry pays him much and I expect Pilar just gets bed and board. Then that son of hers puts in a bit of work when he's here; I gather he's into interior decorating.'

'You gather quite a lot,' said Matthew.

'I am interested,' said James. 'I like to know how the other half lives.'

'I would hardly call Henry the other half,' said Matthew.

James said, 'Really? Why not?'

'Work it out for yourself,' said Matthew grumpily.

James laughed. 'If your girl, Antonia, were with us, she'd say, Ho to that.'

Matthew smiled. 'Maybe.'

James said, 'I'd like to live in the country but London is where the lolly is, and the work.'

Matthew said, 'The country is OK for holidays.'

'And weekends,' James agreed. 'D'you suppose Henry is lonely? He leads a queer sort of life.'

Believing himself unwilling to gossip, Matthew said, 'I wouldn't know,' and increased the car's speed.

James said, 'I shall bring Barbara here again if she goes on hitting it off with Pilar. And it will help Henry if she gets to know Margaret; we could make a habit of it.'

And it won't cost you anything, thought Matthew, who was himself proposing to come oftener, when invited of course, with Antonia. He said, 'I thought you were into sailing.'

James said, 'So I am, but Barbara isn't keen. I have a boat. I was considering giving it up, but I could post Barbara down here when I have sailing weekends.' He grinned at Matthew 'What are friends for,' he asked cheerfully, 'if not to take advantage of?'

Matthew laughed, admitting James's honesty, then braked hard as a child dashed suddenly across the road. 'You bloody little beast,' he yelled, his voice hoarse with fear. 'I might have killed you. God!' he said. 'Did you see it?' The child raised two fingers and vanished into a cottage. 'Christ,' said Matthew, 'think if I'd hit it.'

James said, 'Well, you didn't. It's all right.'

Matthew said, 'Aah,' letting his breath out. 'Gave me a fright.'

'Does it put you off fatherhood?' James asked as Matthew drove on at a more sedate pace.

'I suppose one could keep them on a lead,' said Matthew. 'No, I'm not put off, just doubly conscious of the risks.'

'We shall start a baby at once,' said James cheerfully.

Matthew said, 'Is that what Barbara wants?'

'I haven't discussed it yet. But I think, don't you, that it's best to get the breeding bit over, establish the ties—?'

'And have fun later,' Matthew slewed round to look at James, 'when you've pegged her down?'

James said, 'Do keep your eye on the road. I don't know about you but I want a family while I'm young. Then, when I've got it, we can travel, have fun, dump the children somewhere if we don't want them with us.'

Matthew said astutely, 'Is that what you would have done with Valerie?'

James said, 'Oh, Valerie. Valerie was different.'

Matthew thought, I shouldn't kick him in the balls, he's not really over Valerie and I can't imagine Valerie settling down to breed little Martineaux.

James stared at the road ahead. Caught unaware, he could still get a catch in the throat. Married to Valerie one would not have bothered to have children; one would not have wanted them taking up Valerie's time and attention. One had been head over heels, obsessed. Valerie's defection had been a bitter blow, the kind of blow which left one cautious, but marriage with Barbara was a whole new ball game; one would have the upper hand.

'I think you and Barbara are wonderfully suited,' said Matthew, sensing James's pain. 'She's a very attractive girl.'

James said, 'Oh yes, she is, absolutely.' With Barbara one would not be risking odious comparisons; would he ever forget the list Valerie had given him of men with better accoutrements, that had been the word she had chosen, than his? Barbara had no previous experience, thank God. 'Of course she is very young and inexperienced,' he said.

'So is Antonia,' said Matthew. 'I think it is to the good.'

'And you are in love with her.'

Matthew said, 'Yes, I am. I fell for her the first time I saw her. We met at her brother's house.'

'Not the brother who was at school with us?'

'That's the one, Richard Lowther. There was another younger brother in another house, but he was dark,' said Matthew.

'I remember,' said James, 'yes. Come to think of it, Antonia is like Richard.'

Matthew said, 'Yes.'

James said, 'Wasn't—' and, remembering Matthew's and Richard's friendship, stopped short. It had nearly got them into trouble. It had been a bit more than friendship; whoever it was who had written that Englishmen liked androgynous girls, and that their taste was formed at their public schools, had it right in Matthew's case. Substituting for what he had been about to say – 'Wasn't Antonia's brother your tart?' – James said,

'Wasn't it about here Henry told us to turn off?'

Matthew said, 'A bit further on, I think. I am keeping an eye—'

James said, 'Antonia is a smashing girl. I think you are very lucky.'

'I think so too,' said Matthew, 'and my parents will be pleased,' and, recollecting various parental hints about it being 'time to look round', he said, 'My father has been saying that he is looking forward to a grandson and using a French expression I can't get the hang of about parking the car.'

'*Il faut ranger ta voiture*,' James supplied. 'Dad uses it too, his first love was French. I've seen photographs, may well have been your father's as well. They were friends. Just think, we might have been brothers.'

'A horrific idea!' exclaimed Matthew, laughing. 'But of course they are right, there comes a time when being a bachelor palls. One needs a hostess, well, I do with foreign contacts to entertain, and someone to – er – well—'

'Fuck,' suggested James. Valerie's vocabulary had been explicit; he had found it sexually exciting.

'I was going to say share one's bed,' said Matthew, 'fall seriously in love with. Of course it's different for you, you are on the rebound from Valerie,' he said with a hint of malice.

'Oh, all that's long past,' said James. 'I am very much in love with Barbara.' Then, feeling that he sounded insufficiently sure, he said, 'Nobody in their senses marries their first love,' and, remembering Antonia's brother Richard in adolescence, gave a yelp of laughter.

Surprised by James's laugh, Matthew said generously, 'One thing I am happy about is that my Antonia and your Barbara are such friends.'

James said, 'It is indeed a bonus.'

Then Matthew said, 'I think this is the turning Henry described; he said turn left at the fork by the blasted oak.'

James said, 'You are right. Poor old Henry, he obviously lacked a wise papa.'

10

Standing in the stone-flagged kitchen, Pilar listened. She tilted her head on its sturdy neck and sniffed like a cat, expanding her nostrils as though the warm air coming in from the yard might bring some message other than the hum of insects and scent of summer. There was the sound of splashing and the clatter of a bucket and Trask's voice – 'Stand still can't 'ee, soon be over' – as he bathed the dogs. The dogs, unwashed, would disgrace the party, she had said, and Trask, obliging, had said, 'Anything for you, Pilar girl,' and patted her rump.

Pilar moved to close the outer door in case a dog should charge in, shake itself and drench the kitchen.

In the house a stair creaked, water gurgled in the pipes, the sound of jackdaws discussing on the stack filtered down the chimney, coke shifted in the Aga, a door whined somewhere in a weak draught.

Resting her weight on her hands, Pilar leaned over the table to scrutinize the list she had written of all that must be done, and alongside it the menu. Henry had praised the menu, had expressed gratitude for her trouble; he had asked whether it was not all too much for her, whether she could not simplify. No, she had said, no, the party must be just so; it must resemble as closely as possible the parties given by his parents. She had not commented, as he stood looking at her, how closely he resembled his father, whom she had revered from the moment he had stopped in his peregrination through the camp in southern France. Towering above her, as Henry did now, he had asked the man who was his guide, 'And these two? Who have they got?' And the man, exhausted by the size of his job and inured to the refugees' pain, had answered, '*Personne*,' closing his mind to her insoluble dilemma. Left much longer squatting on the cold ground, clutching her dying baby to breasts where her milk was failing and hope with it, Pilar would have died; without her young husband there was nothing to live for. But Henry's father had said, '*Je m'en charge*,' and after a time she had found herself at Cotteshaw with a miraculously revived Ebro.

The party must be as close to perfection as she could make it. As far as Pilar was concerned, the party was a celebration in memory of her benefactor. Pilar stared at the menu with unfocused eyes as she remembered Henry's father.

Henry had been away at the war when his father died. He had not been ill long. She had nursed him devotedly, begged him to get better. 'What shall I do, *señor*, without you?' She reproached herself now for her selfishness.

'You must care for Henry. Stay until General Franco dies, then you can go home and spit on his grave.'

She had said, 'What if Henry brings home a wife?'

Henry's father had been silent, then, 'Ah *yes*, I wrote to him. He may get married. There is a letter; d'you see it on the table? Please post it, Pilar.' He had lain quiet for a while; breathing was increasingly hard. Then he had said, on a note of query, 'You will post it?'

She had said, 'Yes, of course.'

'And tell him of my death?'

She had said, 'And that, too,' and then, 'I will pray.'

He had said, 'By all means pray if it helps.' He was a

considerate man, Pilar thought, as she moved to put her list and the menu on the dresser.

Opening the door into the hall, she listened. Margaret, who was not a considerate woman, had not rung her bell for quite a while. As she stood in the silence Pilar remembered the old man had heard her praying. She had known that he was awake and leaned close, in case he wanted to say something. He had said, 'Don't forget to spit,' and died. She had closed his eyes, kissed him for the first and last time and gone out to post the letter before telephoning the doctor.

Now Pilar wished that she had had the sense not to post that letter. I spit on consideration, she thought, as Margaret's bell jangled above the dresser. She started sturdily up the stairs.

Margaret was out of bed watching from her window, standing back so that anyone looking up from the lawn would be unlikely to see her. She wore a pale gold dressing-gown over her nightdress and her apricot hair hung down her back.

Pilar said, 'What do you want?', pausing by the door, her hand on the knob.

'My bed is uncomfortable.' Margaret did not turn round.

'You are able to smooth sheets yourself,' said Pilar, but she came into the room and began smoothing the sheets. 'And puff pillows,' she said, punching and slapping the pillows. 'I am busy.'

'You always say that. Why don't you get those girls to give you a hand?'

'Too young.' Pilar folded back the bedclothes for Margaret's re-entry.

'Ach!' said Margaret. 'Look at that!'

Pilar left the bed and stood by Margaret. 'My husband's "familiars",' said Margaret. On the lawn below the window the dogs circled in mad abandon, running

97

and leaping, pausing to shake themselves, spraying the grass with a mist of droplets. There was a whistle and they careered away as Antonia and Barbara came in sight. 'Which girl is James Martineau's?' asked Margaret.

'The one with brown hair. Let me open the window, it is stifling in here.'

'No, leave it. She is not as pretty as the one who was called Valerie.' Margaret turned away from the window. 'He was in love with that one; how does he feel for this one?'

'Now you are up, shall you have a bath?' Pilar heaved up the sash window, letting in the summer air.

'Is the water hot? Will you scrub my back?' Margaret turned towards the bathroom.

'It is always hot. You must scrub your own back. I am busy.'

'How cruel you are.' Margaret spoke without feeling; she habitually called Pilar cruel. 'You did not answer me about James Martineau's love or not love.'

'I do not know,' said Pilar.

'Of course you don't. How could a peasant like you know about love?'

Used to Margaret, Pilar said, 'I leave you to bath,' but she chuckled as she descended the stairs.

At the foot of the stairs she stopped. Antonia and Barbara were approaching. They appeared to have picked every flower in the garden. Pilar marvelled at their greed. So they would help themselves to life, she thought with sudden fury, and it was not she, Pilar, who knew nothing about love but these innocents. In the darkness of the hall, Pilar remembered the intensity of her love for her young husband and was shaken with hopeless desire for his long dead body.

Antonia and Barbara passed, chattering, into the pantry where she could hear their high young voices consulting as to which vase to use for which flowers.

'This for my high arrangement.' Antonia sounded confident.

'And this, I think, for your great-aunt's cache-mari. What else did she teach you? What other invaluable tips?' asked Barbara.

'One tip I remember, and looking at some of my cousins I wonder sometimes whether she—'

'She what?'

'Whether she acted on it.' Antonia giggled. 'It must be wonderful to have that sort of assurance.'

'Explain,' said Barbara.

'My great-aunt,' said Antonia, 'told me that people who lived on her social echelon had lovers when they were married, and that sometimes their children were not their husband's.'

Barbara said, 'No birth control, of course. Goodness!' She pursed her mouth.

'Apparently,' said Antonia, 'they made sure the eldest was the husband's, but after that it didn't matter so much.'

'Sounds relaxed,' said Barbara. 'Pass me the scissors so that I can snip these stalks.'

In Catalonia, thought Pilar, women would get themselves murdered for such behaviour whereas here in England, if Henry's father had known that she had steamed open the letter before posting it, he would never have forgiven her. On her way back to the kitchen Pilar hoped that in heaven, where he surely resided, Henry's father did not know. Nor would he know, she thought inconsolably, that she here on earth could not forgive herself for posting it.

11

The girls carried their arrangements to the tables in the garden. Ebro spread starched white cloths so that they could set the flowers in place; he exclaimed in praise at their efforts and then began unpacking glasses from a basket and setting them on the bar. Preceded by damp, soap-smelling dogs, Henry came round the side of the house; he was laughing. 'Trask has set his heart on dressing up as a butler,' he said to Ebro.

'Me too. We shall make a pretty pair.' Ebro joined in the merriment. 'We are pandering to Margaret's desire for servants.'

Henry said, 'I don't think it's a good idea, but I can't stop you.'

Ebro said, 'He deserves a reward for bathing the dogs, my mother insisted.' Then he said to Barbara, 'Is not my English impeccable?' He swept her a bow.

Henry said, 'Oh I say! The flowers, lovely. Will they topple over?'

Antonia said, 'Of course not.'

Ebro said, 'Drop some stones in the vase to weight it.'

Barbara said, 'This is my effort, this, on the dining table. I hope you like it? I kept it low so that none of our views of each other are impeded.'

Henry said, 'Wonderful, all these yellow roses, very very pretty,' and made a resolution to impound the secateurs. Then he said, 'Thank you both for all your trouble.' Looking kindly at their upturned faces, he said, 'What about that dress? Shall I show it to you? It comes from Dior. Perhaps you can persuade her, one never knows. I have it in my room.'

Antonia and Barbara said, 'Dior!' and 'Goodness!' Of course they were anxious to see it; they would each bring a dress, then there would be an element of choice. Though naturally Margaret would choose the Dior, it stood to reason.

'Reason is something she stands on its head,' said Henry wryly, 'but it's worth a bash. Meet you at the top of the stairs?'

The girls ran ahead and Henry followed more slowly with his dogs.

As he waited at the head of the stairs, the cockatoo crept under the sash of an open window. When it saw Henry it raised its crest and twisted its neck, glinting at him with one eye. Henry said, 'Aha! I want you. You will be safer shut up.' But as he reached for the bird it dodged out of the window and flew away, squawking. Henry said, 'Damn you.'

'Damn who?' Barbara and Antonia came along the corridor empty-handed; they had decided to see the Dior before deciding on their own dresses. The comparison would be too odious.

'The cockatoo. I missed. I don't want him to bother people at the party, he's been known to nip.'

Antonia said, 'Catch him later. We've not brought our dresses. Where's the Dior? Is it really from Dior?'

'Come. I'll show you.' Henry led the way. 'I live in this wing,' he said. 'The room was my father's. My mother's, too, when she was alive.'

'A separate wing.' Barbara hurried to keep pace. 'Well away from the rest of the house and visitors.' And well away from your wife, she thought.

Henry said, 'Here we are.' He opened a door and stood aside for the girls to pass.

It was a large room, full of sun. Facing the open window was a four-poster, against one wall a kneehole desk; there were armchairs and a sofa; the boards were carpeted with worn Persian rugs, the walls papered in a faded, indistinguishable pattern; there were no pictures, only an inkstain, as though a bottle had been thrown. There was a bookshelf, but no mirrors. The chairs and sofa were covered in a material which, once red, had faded with washing to coral pink. One could see why, thought Barbara, as Henry's dogs climbed each to its habitual place to curl up but remain watchful.

Antonia said, 'Some person threw an ink bottle.'

Henry said, 'Some person did,' but did not explain. Barbara walked to the window to look out and Henry followed her.

Antonia focused on the bed, impressed by its height and width, its beautiful but tattered hangings. From that bed, she thought, Henry can see across the fields to the hills; what an admirable bed. She wished fiercely for a similar bed for herself but Matthew, she was sure, would never put up with it. He would like modern divans. Staring at the bed, Antonia imagined being in it with Henry, who stood with his back to her. Barbara was pointing at something in the garden, standing close to him. Her hair brushed his sleeve; her head barely came up to his shoulder.

In Henry's arms love would be very different to love with Matthew, Antonia thought; she was not sure she cared for Matthew's legs. He had a footballer's muscular thighs. She could see that Henry's legs were not thick, even in those shapeless trousers. They had none of the springy energy she found daunting in Matthew's; they were so long and thin they looked as if they would snap if he played football. So Henry slept in that bed. And who with, she wondered? Not Margaret, that was plain, even if one did not believe half Margaret's hints.

Antonia said, 'What a wonderful bed. I would love to sleep in it.'

Turning from the window, Henry said, 'You would?' It was not an invitation; rather she had the impression that she would sleep there at her peril.

Perhaps after all it would be best to stick to Matthew. She would get used to his thighs; they were not as bulgy as some people's, her brother Richard's, for instance.

She said, 'Just a thought,' and looked away from the bed at the faded wallpaper tempered with dark patches where once had hung mirrors. For heaven's sake, she told herself, I am in love with Matthew.

Henry was saying, 'It's a bit shabby, I'm afraid,' but not as though he cared. 'The dress is in my dressing-room. Pilar thought it should hang; that, left in its box, it might crease.' He watched the girls as their eyes, blue and brown, explored the room.

Barbara said, 'What a lovely room. Is it exactly as it was for your parents?'

Henry said, 'Not exactly,' but made no attempt to tell of any changes he might have made. Barbara thought, I bet his parents didn't throw ink.

Henry said, 'They didn't let the dogs in their bedroom,' and, catching Antonia's eye, laughed.

Antonia said, 'Lying in bed you can see your horses swishing their tails in the shade of a tree.' She pointed to the distant horses.

Barbara said, 'I met them earlier on my way to the lake. Are you – er – are you very fond of them?' Remembering Margaret's snide allusion, she avoided Antonia's eye.

Henry said, 'I bred one of them from a mare called Petronella, who was bred by my father. The other is her foal.'

Barbara said, 'Oh.'

Watching her troubled expression Henry thought that mischief had been sown, then that he was too sensitive; it was ridiculous to be thin-skinned. But when Antonia asked, 'Was your wife's room like this before she had it redecorated?', he was wearily aware that his instinct was right. He answered crisply, 'Quite like,' and watched Antonia flush, turn away and gaze at the view.

He said, 'I see that my wife has been confiding the secret of my bestiality,' and did not try to relieve either girl of her embarrassment in the pause that ensued.

At last the girls spoke together. 'The dress?' Their voices were almost tearful.

Henry said, 'In here,' and opened a door into another room. 'It was my mother's sitting-room. I use it as a dressing-room.' He opened a cupboard and lifted out the dress on its hanger.

Antonia exclaimed, 'How gorgeous!'

While Barbara said simply, 'We could never pretend it was one of ours, not in a thousand years.'

Henry said, 'Try,' and swung the dress to and fro, so that the champagne-coloured chiffon grew lighter and darker as it moved. 'I thought,' he said, watching their faces, 'that perhaps she might be persuaded to get out of bed to wear it.'

Antonia said, 'If she doesn't she's out of her tiny mind.'

Barbara hissed, 'Honestly, Antonia,' between clenched teeth and, reaching for the dress, took it from Henry. Holding it against her body, she said, 'Alas, no looking-glass. May I try your eyes?' and flirted up at Henry.

Antonia, jealous of her friend, said. 'There are plenty in Margaret's room. Come on, let's take it to her.'

'Now? This minute?' Barbara clutched the dress.

'Of course now, this minute,' Antonia said tartly. 'I don't suppose Henry's got all day, have you, Henry?' and looked up to see whether she, too, was reflected in his eyes.

Henry thought that either of these girls would look well in the dress; it would suit Barbara's brown hair and Antonia's fair better than Margaret's marmalade. He said, 'Well, I'll leave you to it,' and held the door open for them.

'This is unbearable,' whispered Antonia as they followed him down the corridor. 'How did he manage to find a full-length dress when they are all shortish this season?'

'It's a wedding dress,' suggested Barbara, also whispering.

'That colour? Couldn't be,' muttered Antonia.

'For a divorcée?' said Barbara. 'I am going to take along my smoky blue; shall you present your pink?'

'Why not?' said Antonia. 'Come on.'

'Good luck, girls,' said Henry. Reaching the stairs, he went down them two at a time followed by his dogs.

'I believe that suggestion about horses is a hoax,' said Antonia when he was out of earshot. 'It would be more likely to be dogs.' She joined Barbara in a refreshing burst of giggles.

Hastening to answer the telephone which was shrilling in the hall, Henry thought that were he a composer he would weave the mix of high-pitched giggles and brazen telephone into five or six anarchic chords. 'Hullo.' He snatched up the receiver. 'Cotteshaw 250.'

'I have a call for Henry Tillotson,' said the operator.

'Speaking.' (The chords would, of course, be treble.)

'Hold on,' said the operator.

Henry held on. Upstairs in his wife's room the two girls would parade in front of Margaret in the Dior dress. Margaret would register each girl's fierce desire to wear the dress at the party, willing her, in spite of themselves, to refuse to come. Perhaps on their way to her room they had tossed a coin to decide who, in event of Margaret's refusal, would wear it? Possibly, since they were such close friends, they had decided to wear it in turn? He remembered how for want of a mirror they had peered into his eyes. 'Such hard little bitches,' he murmured into the receiver.

'Cotteshaw 250, I have a call for you. Are you holding?'

'Yes,' said Henry, 'yes.'

The two dogs flopped exhaustedly at his feet, worn out by the trauma of their bath. The temptation to prevent either Antonia or Barbara getting her hands on the dress would be even stronger than his original hope that Margaret would be unable to resist wearing it. Henry thought, I had not planned to hurt the silly little things, but they are sufficiently ebullient to bear the disappointment. 'Hullo?' he said angrily into the silent instrument. 'Hullo?'

'Henry? We got home sooner than we expected. Are we still welcome at your jamboree?' said a man's voice.

'My God, yes! You certainly *are*,' said Henry.

'Gives me a chance to wear my white dinner jacket,' said the voice. 'Want us to bring anything?'

'Just moral support,' said Henry, feeling his spirits lift. He put down the receiver and went out to meet Matthew and James returning with their carload of ice and strawberries.

12

Stepping forward to help James and Matthew with the ice, Henry realized that he was after all looking forward to the party. 'That was Hector on the phone,' he said cheerfully. 'He's going to wear his white dinner jacket.'

'I thought they were in Italy,' said Matthew, opening the boot of his car. 'I nearly ran over a beastly child. It gave me a terrible fright; your lanes are dangerous. I only have a black dinner jacket. If I'd known—' If I'd known, Matthew thought, I could have hired a white dinner jacket from Moss Bros. It would have pleased Antonia.

Henry, peering in at the blocks of ice, said, 'You seem to have brought the Polar ice cap. In black you can pseudo-mourn for what did not happen.'

'Come again?' said Matthew.

'Henry's convoluted jokes. My dinner jacket is midnight blue; I always think white makes one look like a waiter,' James said disparagingly.

'I can't see Hector being mistaken for a waiter,' said Henry. 'Can't we carry this between us?' He gripped one end of an ice block. 'Come on, James, heave.'

'Did something go wrong in Italy?' asked James, taking reluctant hold of the ice. 'Did Calypso throw a tantrum?'

'She doesn't,' said Henry, and thought, Calypso would never be so mundane. Calypso who, in his teens, he had passionately adored and she, unaware, had married Hector, rich, handsome, old enough to be her father, one of her father's friends, in fact. And she had, goddammit, fallen in love with the man. 'It's Hector,' he said, 'who decides to come back early from wherever they go. He can't bear to be parted from his trees.'

'Typically English,' said James, who scarcely knew the Grants. 'He doesn't like "abroad", retires to the country to plant a wood he won't live to see mature.'

'That's not the point,' said Henry, himself a considerable planter of trees. 'Could you take the fruit through to Pilar?' he said to Matthew. 'We should get this to the scullery,' he said to James. 'Can you manage? Say if it's too heavy and I'll get Ebro or Trask.'

'Of course I can manage,' said James huffily. 'I helped load it. Who else is coming besides the Grants?'

'Peter and Maisie Bullivant and the two Jonathans.'

'That pair of old queens?' Walking backwards, James collided with the hall table.

'Careful,' said Henry. 'They are good neighbours,' he said, resenting James's tone, 'and good company. Calypso likes them and so does Hector. They are my oldest friends.'

James said, 'Oh. Yes. Of course.'

Following with baskets of fruit, Matthew enquired, 'Where are our girls?'

'Upstairs with Margaret, trying on dresses, deciding what to wear tonight. Gossiping, perhaps? A spot of verbal dissection? Who knows?' said Henry. What possessed me, he thought, to clutter up the house with these people? I can't revive my parents' parties, that was another age. 'At least,' he said maliciously, 'the Jonathans won't compete for your girls. Perhaps I should have invited Claire and Evelyn,' he said, the rise of spirit engendered by Hector on the phone beginning to ebb.

James said, 'Who are Claire and Evelyn?', gasping from the weight of the ice, wishing that Henry would not make him walk backwards.

'Henry's local lesbians,' said Matthew, who had briefly met them on a previous visit. 'A scary pair.'

'What a timorous fellow you are,' said Henry. 'First it's a child, now it's two women.'

Resenting their host's acidity, Matthew, following behind Henry, caught James's eye, raised his eyebrows and depressed his lips in a sneer.

While Henry and James set the ice down in the scullery, Matthew carried the fruit through to Pilar in the kitchen. 'Olé!' he said. 'The frutta!'

'Thanks,' said Pilar, who detested having people say 'Olé' in condescending accents. 'Put it on the table.'

'Por favor,' said Matthew, 'what's the grub for the party, senorita?'

'Not senorita, I am married lady,' said Pilar stiffly.

Unrepressed, Matthew said loudly, as to foreigners, 'Of course, of course, my mistake. I was asking what the menu might be for tonight's feast, fiesta to you.'

'Gazpacho, salmon trout, saffron rice with shrimps, asparagus, strawberries and raspberries. Are there not more fruits than these?''

'Yes, yes, lots more—'

'Then—'

'Why don't I fetch them?'

'Exactly.'

'Oh, subito, silly me, subito,' said Matthew, who was apt to confuse Latin languages, and hurried back to his car.

'I've heard it said,' said James, as he followed Henry to collect more ice, 'that Calypso was lovely when she was a girl. Not that she isn't lovely now, but you must have known her, you are about the same age.'

'Just about.' God, I was besotted, thought Henry. 'I

am a few years younger,' he said casually. 'She and Hector married early in the war, I believe.' He had not known that she was married until, in a bar in Cairo, he overheard someone say, 'There's Hector Grant, the fellow who divorced old Daphne – Smith she is now – they never got on and now he has married a popsy half his age called Calypso, said to be a raving beauty. She must have married him for his money; jolly well heeled, is Hector.' I went out and got very, very drunk, thought Henry, and it was the next day, when I had that terrible hangover, that I got father's letter. 'She's an old friend,' he said to James.

James said, 'Broke a lot of hearts, from what one hears.'

Henry said, 'I wouldn't know.' One good thing, he thought, was that Calypso had not known he loved her. If she had known she would scarcely have been affected, since at that time every man she met buckled at the knees. 'It's funny, really,' he said. 'She swears she married for money, but it's an extremely happy marriage.'

'Takes all sorts,' said James. 'I thought about it a lot before deciding on Barbara.'

Henry said, 'One more slab of ice,' remembering Valerie.

'Let me help this time.' Matthew caught up with them. 'You collect the rest of the fruit, James, and I'll take a turn risking a hernia.'

Upstairs in the west wing Barbara and Antonia sat side by side on Margaret's golden sofa; in the bed, Margaret lolled on her pillows. Across the foot of the bed the Dior dress lay like an exhausted ghost.

'Aren't you going to try it on?' asked Barbara.

'I don't think I can be bothered.' Margaret yawned.

'Perhaps you would like one of us to model it for

you?' suggested Antonia. 'Then you could see how lovely it is on.'

'If it fits us, it will fit you,' said Barbara. 'We are all about the same size.' She was unsure that Margaret had believed them when they let her suppose the dress belonged to one or other of them. Margaret did not look the sort of woman who had any beliefs at all.

'I don't think I should find that interesting,' said Margaret. The afternoon sun shone in and exposed a glint in her eye; she said something under her breath which sounded like, 'What a pair of bitches.' Neither Barbara nor Antonia, comparing notes later, could be sure.

'Well?' Antonia stood up. 'Well?' She picked up the dress and, holding it against her, twirled in front of the mirrors. 'I suppose,' she said, twirling, 'that you collected all the mirrors in the house and had them hung in here?'

Margaret said, 'Just about. Put that dress down.'

Antonia returned the dress to the foot of the bed. 'So you *do* sometimes get up and get about?' she said.

'The Jonathans collected them for me.' Margaret watched her.

'Who are the Jonathans?' Barbara asked.

'Two of his fellow sodomites,' said Margaret.

It was peculiar, Barbara thought, the way Margaret referred to Henry as 'he' or 'him', rarely by name. 'We have been arranging the flowers for the party,' she said. 'I hope you will approve.'

'An outmoded method of catching your man,' said Margaret. 'Valerie arranged flowers, although her man was already netted.'

'Who was Valerie?' asked Barbara.

'James Martineau's girl. He was very much in love, still is, no doubt.' Margaret eyed Barbara. 'They had a room down the corridor, made a lot of noise at night, lots of "oh's" and "oops". Quite uninhibited. One wondered how the bed stood up to it.' Margaret laughed, exposing teeth and tongue. 'Hang the dress in the cupboard,' she said to Antonia. 'Leave it with me. Valerie would look good in that colour.'

Seeing her friend's stricken expression Antonia, reaching for the dress, said, 'All right, you think about it. It's a good colour for the older woman, kind to the skin.' She shook the dress then, changing the subject, she said, 'We've not only arranged the flowers but created an Edwardian décor. I had this great-aunt,' she said, moving towards the hanging cupboard. 'She used to tell me how women behaved in her young day – you would probably know this – they had lovers and when they were asked to house parties they made discreet love under their husband's noses, and lots more than that, it seems. Oh, I *say*,' she said, opening the cupboard door, 'you have even had your *cupboards* lined with mirrors. Golly! I see me, me, me lurking in there.' She hung the dress on a rail. 'Don't you weary of seeing you, you, you?' she asked. '*All* the time?'

Margaret said, 'No, I don't,' and ran her tongue over her teeth, exploring her gums.

Antonia said, 'You look like an ape doing that, a golden orang-utan.' She sensed that her friend had not yet recovered from Margaret's disclosure of Valerie, whoever Valerie might be. 'And your cupboard,' she exclaimed, 'is full to bursting with clothes! What a liar you are, telling us you never have anything new except nighties. You must take us for a pair of simpletons.'

'I do,' said Margaret, lolling back on her pillows. 'D'you mind pulling the blind down before you go? The sun gets in my eyes.'

'Oh, pull it yourself,' said Barbara, recovering from her shock. 'Come on, Antonia, I hear voices. James and Matthew must be back.' She jumped up from the sofa and, slipping her arm through her friend's, drew her towards the door. 'We shall see you at the party,' she said, opening the door, 'tonight.'

'Shan't be there,' said Margaret.

Antonia said, 'Ho!' as they went through the door. In the passage she said, 'That woman is a phenomenal liar. Gosh! So Henry now goes in for sodomy as well as horses,' and snorted with laughter.

Barbara said, 'What's sodomy?'

'Oh, Barbara! What they did in Gomorrah.'

Barbara murmured, 'This Valerie, who she said was—'

'Another invention,' Antonia answered stoutly, too stoutly. 'If she had existed,' she went on, 'you would have heard of her.'

'Would I?' Barbara was doubtful about this.

Antonia, equally doubtful, said, 'Of course you would. James is in love with you; when people are in love they tell each other everything, all their past, the lot.'

'The more fools they,' said Barbara with a flash of percipience.

13

Waiting for his guests to arrive, Henry caught sight of his reflection in the french windows. Would it have been wiser to wear his honest old dinner jacket? No, let Hector in his white tuxedo suffer a pang of envy. Let the pipe-stem trousers, mulberry velvet coat worn over a cream silk shirt, pale blue stock and cummerbund, all from Savile Row and Jermyn Street in bygone ages, outshine Hector's sharkskin.

My forefathers, thought Henry wryly, were not in the habit of stinting themselves. I am like them physically, he thought; they wore these clothes at their parties. Then, staring at his faint reflection, he questioned: Am I wise to revive a custom long dead? Would my father have revived it? And my mother? Ah, thought Henry, my mother! We may be built the same, my old pa and I, but it stops there; in our marriages we are poles apart. What would my mother have made of Margaret? She would, thought Henry, turning away from his reflection, have put a smart stop to that flight of Father's fancy. Looking out at the white-clothed tables laid ready for the party, the sparkling glass, shining silver, and Antonia's and Barbara's floral arrangements, he imagined his mother's voice. 'A pretty idea,' she would have said, 'but have you envisaged its consequences?'

His father would have accepted some suggested alternative which would equally serve his purpose. Henry sighed, remembering his mother. Dying, she had told him, 'Take care of your father, darling. Without me he will be a brakeless toboggan.' Furious with her for dying, he had shouted, 'Of course I shall,' and it was years later, when he had come to terms with her loss, that he remembered her adding in a whisper, 'And your emotional brakes leave much to be desired. A bit on the wonky side—'

He had not, in adolescence, cared for this criticism, pushing it aside in a fury of grief. What would she advocate now? Would she suggest a divorce, or would she recognize its impossibility?

Margaret did not commit adultery, nor would she desert him. Counsel, when consulted, had suggested that since adultery and desertion were in the eyes of the law the only cause for divorce, he should sue his wife for the restitution of conjugal rights. 'That might get things moving.'

Appalled by this suggestion, he had exclaimed, 'That's the last thing I want!'

Losing interest, Counsel had said, 'Then I can't help you. If she won't take a lover or desert you, you are stuck waiting for the Grim Reaper.' Then, reviving slightly, 'One hears she's a good looker; surely, if you kept your eyes open, there might be some sexual slip? Bit of hope along those lines? It would be natural, would it not?'

Disgusted, Henry had flared up. 'If anyone commits adultery, as you insist on calling it, it is I who do.'

'Well, well,' said Counsel, positively genial, 'and isn't she interested?' And when Henry answered, 'No,' Counsel said, 'Sad.' And that, apart from his plump fee, had been the end of it and his marriage, such as it was, continued as before.

'What are you thinking, Henry? A penny for your thoughts.' Calypso, coming out through the house, slid her hand through his arm. 'My,' she said, 'you look

115

elegant. That's your dear old pa's get-up, isn't it?'

'His pa's, actually. Father belonged to the Oxford bags era; grandfather's was the pipe-stem. I didn't hear you arrive. Where's Hector?' Henry bent to kiss Calypso's cheek.

'He's parking the car. What were you thinking? You looked rather grim.'

'I was contemplating murdering Margaret,' said Henry, who had reached in his thoughts his usual conclusion. If he had not been in love with Calypso, if he had not heard that she had married Hector, he would not have got so drunk that on receiving his father's letter while still in an alcoholic stupor he had acted instantly, quixotically and fatally. 'I was wondering how to set about it,' he said lightly, glad that Calypso had never known of his passion, a passion long since distilled into friendship. 'But I shan't bother,' he said.

'If you change your mind, let me know how we can help,' said Calypso. 'There would be no shortage of volunteers among your friends.' Then she said, 'Goodness, Henry, this is like old times. I remember your mother at the last party I came to. She wore a stunning dress. She was a lovely person, and so was your father. Look,' she said to Hector, who joined them at this moment, 'look at Henry, he's wearing his grandfather's clothes. Puts you in the shade, doesn't he? Were all Tillotsons your shape, Henry?'

Hector took Henry's hand. 'Tailors were tailors in those days,' he said, smiling. 'Nothing they enjoyed better than dressing a beanpole. Good to see you. I say, look at that.' He stared appreciatively at the dinner table. 'How splendid that all looks! Is Margaret putting in an appearance?' he asked easily. 'Any pretty girls to put Calypso on her mettle?'

'Matthew Stephenson brought Antonia Lowther and

116

Barbara O'Malley came with James Martineau. Both lots, by the way, got themselves engaged last night.'

Calypso said, 'June moon and hot weather, predictable.'

'And as to Margaret,' said Henry, 'her place is laid and she has a dress; the rest is up to her.'

The three friends stood contemplating Margaret. Then Hector asked, 'Who else is coming?'

'The Bullivants.'

'Big feet,' murmured Calypso, 'metaphorically.'

'And the Jonathans,' said Henry.

'The dears,' said Calypso.

'Come along, let me get you a drink,' said Henry.

'I shall flirt with Pilar,' said Hector, as they strolled towards the bar. 'She likes it, I like it and Calypso does not object.'

'You should do your duty and make verbal passes at Margaret,' said Calypso, grinning.

'Too risky,' said Hector, and burst out laughing so hard that his face, tanned by recent Italian sun, went brick red.

Still thinking of his wife as he uncorked champagne, Henry remembered the occasion when he had asked her to divorce him and the malevolence of her refusal. 'And how was Italy?' he asked, pouring the wine.

'Exquisite as ever, but you know Hector; he needs to get back to his trees.' Calypso sipped her wine. 'He thinks they miss him.'

'I am hoping to import some sweet chestnuts from the woods above Carrara,' said Hector. 'I shall get myself snarled up with Customs and Min. of Ag. again.'

'I always supposed you enjoyed such tussles,' said Henry.

'Age blunts my zest, it all takes so long,' said Hector, 'but you must come over soon and see the wood.'

Calypso said, 'Yes, Henry, do; the wood is beginning to look like a wood. You have not been for ages.'

'Not since I brought Margaret,' said Henry.

Hector said, 'Ah. Exactly.'

Calypso suppressed a smile. Hector had been furious out of all proportion when Margaret snapped that beech sapling and uprooted a small yew. (Oh dear! I thought it was a weed!) It would be better, here she agreed with many of Henry's friends, if Henry ceased his efforts to get his wife out of bed. But I must remember my principles and not interfere, she thought. So she smiled at her husband and Henry and sipped her drink.

Watching Calypso, Henry thought, Oh, bugger it, I am taking an awful risk with this party.

Hector, also watching his wife, asked, 'Are all those young people besotted with love?'

'Not so that you'd notice,' said Henry. 'I hadn't really thought, but with the girls it seems more of an—'

'An arrangement?' suggested Calypso. 'I've met their families, pretty drear. Extremely worthy, of course.'

Hector said, 'Now, darling.'

Calypso said, 'But it's true, you must agree.'

Henry said, 'Both girls have been to see Margaret.'

'Did they emerge intact?' asked Calypso.

'Since you saw her last,' said Henry, ignoring Calypso's query, 'she's had her room redecorated.'

'So she tired of the black and white,' said Hector. 'Switched off Cecil Beaton?'

'It is all gold and mirrors now.'

'Must cost you a bomb,' said Hector.

'It's good practice for Ebro, he is taking it up professionally,' said Henry.

'It can't cost as much as taking her to stay at Claridges,' said Calypso, forgetting her earlier resolution.

The friends were silent as they remembered how, a year or two after the war, in an effort to surprise his wife from her habit of bed, Henry had contrived to get her up to London in the hope of distracting her with plays, concerts and exhibitions. Arriving in London, Margaret had holed up in Claridges. It had taken six weeks to extract her, and the promise of a new bed.

Henry said, 'Well,' feeling sheepish.

Calypso said, 'I am not mocking,' and thought, He is afraid of scenes.

Henry said, 'Of course you're not,' rather stiffly.

'I suppose,' said Hector, 'she still plays gin rummy with Trask? And has a masseuse and the lady to do her face and has all her meals brought up on trays and buys clothes she never wears—'

Calypso said, 'Hector, stop it!'

Hector said, 'Lancing a boil.'

Henry said, 'Not the sort of boil that goes away, but thanks for trying.'

'And she isn't mad,' said Calypso. 'I blame your father.'

'My father had nothing to do with it,' said Henry defensively.

Calypso said, 'Yes, he *did*. He pickled you in his principles when you were little. You grew up defence-less. You were *much* too nice! I can't believe he had nothing to do with it.' Then, seeing Henry's expression, she said, 'Sorry, Henry. Hector is about to yell at me to shut up and mind my own business, so I shall, before he does.'

'I was wondering,' said Henry, as he refilled their glasses, 'whether you would like a few young hollies for your wood, Hector?'

'Yes, please,' said Hector. 'Thank you.'

Hector and Calypso thought of the defensive prickles

of holly *vis-à-vis* Margaret and felt a little better about her.

Henry said, 'Good, I'll bring them over in the autumn and help you plant them.'

'Henry,' Pilar called from the house, 'can we bring the food out now?'

Henry excused himself and went indoors. Hector took his wife's arm and they strolled down the garden. He said, 'D'you suppose Margaret is mad?'

Calypso said, 'Sane as they come. Bad. It's not as though she can't get out of bed; she can and does. She simply prefers the horizontal, and solo at that.'

Hector said, 'Henry's father was a crony of my parents before he married—'

'What was he like in those days? I never knew him well.'

'By my father's account he was a sort of Tropic of Cancer character, who souped up Paris in the twenties, but when he met Henry's mother he converted to high principles and changed completely, and with his dying breath wrecked Henry's life.'

'How?'

'He imposed his ideals on his son,' said Hector, not answering his wife's query.

'How d'you know?' Calypso repeated.

Hector, not prepared to admit that he listened to gossip, still did not answer.

'The old man was pretty marvellous when he rescued Pilar,' said Calypso. 'She and Ebro would have died if it had not been for him.'

Hector said, 'True.'

'And Henry goes on being good to her and she repays him. I wish,' said Calypso, 'that *I* had a Pilar to run our house. What a help she would be with Hamish.' (Hamish being Hector and Calypso's school-boy son.)

Hector said, 'Darling, I love you,' laughing.

His wife, who never admitted to personal experience of this emotion, said, 'So you do,' and squeezed his arm.

Hector, speaking half to himself, remarked, 'Henry is flawed, which may be his salvation.'

'In what way?'

'He won't necessarily hold back,' said Hector.

'D'you mean he will murder Margaret?'

'Don't be silly. I mean he won't be over-scrupulous; he will take risks. He will get fun out of life, in spite of Margaret,'

Calypso said, 'I hope you are right. Clever of you to spot it. Should we not go back and meet our fellow guests and brace ourselves against the possibility of Margaret?'

As they sauntered back towards the house she thought that if Henry had been as he was now in her wild and frisky days, she would have nipped him into bed in a trice, and chuckled. And Hector, cognizant of his wife, smiled too.

The long table was now crowded. Three stately salmon lay on grand platters. In death they nestled on beds of glistening watercress. In each fish's mouth Pilar had placed a red rose, but above the roses the great creatures' eyes were blank.

There were sauce boats of mayonnaise, butter-pats sweating in silver dishes, French bread, mountains of asparagus, finger-bowls afloat with flower petals, damask napkins intricately folded, and soup plates expectant of gazpacho.

On the side table, under Antonia's lily arrangements, stood bowls of strawberries and raspberries, jugs of cream and bowls of sugar.

Hector said, 'Yum, yum.'

Antonia and Barbara came out of the house in a

rush, Antonia in palest pink, Barbara in enigmatic, smoky blue. Their hair was freshly washed, their faces unblemished by time. Behind them came Matthew and James, looking pleased with their girls and relatively content with their dinner jackets.

As Henry began introductions, Peter and Maisie Bullivant and the Jonathans arrived in a chattering group. Jonathan called out, 'Here we come mopping and mowing. Are we on time, Henry, or smartly late? Quite a shock to be greeted at the front door by Trask in disguise; for a moment we thought your party was fancy dress, but he reassured us. Mind you, we would have rushed home and dressed in our Pierrot costumes had it been necessary. Dear me, Calypso, how d'you do it? Beautiful as ever. Seeing you one is a teeny bit tempted to do what my old Nanny always said the Good Lord made me for. May I kiss you?'

'Old nannies' hopes are not always fulfilled.' Calypso extended her cheek as Jonathan, brushing back a lock of prematurely white hair, bent to kiss it.

Antonia, who had heard that he was homosexual, was surprised to see that he wore a wedding-ring.

'Darlings, look at that,' he exclaimed, gazing at the dinner table. 'What a feast!'

'All Pilar's work, I bet,' said John. 'Oh, my *dears*, don't those poor fish look dissipated. It will be a shame to eat them, they are so pretty. Is Margaret to play skeleton at the feast, or shall I stand in for her? We are dying to know,' he said, taking Henry's hand between both of his and squeezing it.

'I shall show no pity to the fish,' exclaimed Jonathan, thinking that his lover's mention of Henry's wife was ill-timed if not precisely tactless. 'I am Jonathan the strong,' he said, introducing himself to Barbara. 'He is John the weak. Oh, thank you,' he said, accepting a glass of champagne from Henry. 'Delicious.'

John the weak said, 'What joy, what pleasure,' as he, too, was given a drink. Barbara watched, surprised, as he strained the wine through his luxuriant moustache and thought how disapproving her parents would be to see her in such company. They will shortly have to lump it, she told herself, smiling past them at James. I shall be married and beyond their jurisdiction. 'James and I have just got engaged,' she said, drawing James close by his sleeve. 'He proposed in a hayfield.'

'Romantic if you are not allergic,' said John and souped another gulp of champagne, adding, 'as I am.'

'The poor love is a martyr,' said Jonathan. 'One puff of pollen and it's sneeze all night. Did I hear right, you are engaged?'

Barbara said, 'Yes, and so is Antonia.'

'Your great friend?'

'Yes, greatest.'

'And you do everything together?'

'Well—'

'So nice. You must let us advise you all on beds,' exclaimed Jonathan. 'Many a marriage has foundered on springs. We happen to have done a lot of research and at last we found the – most – gorgeous – bed! You see, if you are of different weights – well, look at your fiancé, a great burly fellow, and you, you can't weigh more than eight stone – with the normally springy mattress the smallest and lightest keeps rolling down-hill as poor darling here used to do and it wasn't always, though sometimes it was, delightful. To cut a long story short, we rootled round the shops and found this marvel, no, not Heal's, I'll write the address for you. It's two friends of ours who have started the business and funny thing, our hostess, I suppose she is our hostess, has one of the early models. Henry of all people discovered them. She is crazy about it, perhaps that's why she—'

'Never gets out of it.' James, not pleased at having such intimate advice thrust on his fiancée, supplied the end of the sentence.

Jonathan said, 'You guessed,' and pushed back his forelock.

Barbara thought, Perhaps James was on inferior springs when he bounced with Valerie, and let off a high-pitched giggle, while Antonia, who was listening, pigeon-holed the snip of information. She had recently been told by her elder brother that Peter Pears and Benjamin Britten shared a bed and refused to believe him.

'What *is* Maisie doing?' said John. 'Do look.'

Maisie Bullivant, clasping her hands together in self-esteem, stood back as they viewed her work. On each fishy eye she had put a nasturtium leaf and tiny blades of grass, making the effect of an eye-patch. 'Maisie, that is altogether too louche,' said Jonathan. 'You will hurt Pilar's feelings. Take it off,' he hissed to John, 'before she sees it.'

While John complied, Peter reproached his wife. 'You always go too far.' But his wife was giving the impression that she never went anywhere.

Calypso murmured to Hector, 'That woman never thinks before she acts,' then more generously, 'but I like that dress she's wearing.' Perceiving Maisie's rueful expression as she realized her *faux pas*, she said, 'That's a super dress, Maisie, where did you get it?'

'So we are on our best behaviour,' said Jonathan to John.

Henry, filling their glasses, murmured, 'Keep it up, boys, keep it up.'

Trask signalled from the house and Henry, going up to him, asked, 'Is Margaret coming down?'

'Doesn't say yes nor no,' said Trask, respectable in a

124

black coat and striped trousers. 'Pilar says give a shout when you're ready for the soup. Her's got her tray,' he gestured upwards, 'in case.'

Henry said, 'You look ridiculous in those clothes.'

Trask replied, 'Look who's talking. What about the soup?'

Henry, glancing at his guests, said, 'They seem fairly happy.'

'At the rate you're pouring the drink they'll be sozzled before they eat,' said Trask.

Henry said, 'Rubbish. All right, tell Pilar we are ready.' Turning back to his guests, he called out, 'Who is for Pilar's gazpacho? Will you arrange yourselves?' He went to help Pilar and Ebro.

Ebro was wearing black trousers and a white shirt. He had slicked back his hair and bound his waist with a red scarf; he appeared on the steps balancing a soup tureen on the upward-turned palm of each hand and stood so poised for the guests' admiration.

The Jonathans said, 'Lovely boy, *lovely*,' and 'My *dear*! What virility,' and were rewarded by a flash of Ebro's enormous teeth.

Pilar was also dressed in black but had stuck a flower behind her ear. As she spooned soup into Hector's plate, he said, 'Calypso and I have been looking forward to this all week. Will you sit with us? Move up, Calypso, and make room.'

Henry stood at the head of the table while his guests arranged themselves. The Bullivants sat together, as did also the Jonathans, but Antonia gestured to Matthew to sit opposite her, next to Maisie. He did so with ill grace, while he watched Ebro take the chair which might have been his. Barbara, dropping quickly into a chair next to Henry, almost excluded James, who was only able to sit near her after asking the Jonathans to 'move down a bit'. With the soup served, Pilar and

Ebro sat among the guests and Trask, shedding his coat ('too tight, too hot'), joined them in his shirt sleeves.

When Henry sat down Barbara murmured, 'I shall try and console you for the absent skeleton,' and brushed his thigh with the hand which held her table napkin. 'Oh, there goes my napkin,' she exclaimed, dropping it between them. As Henry made no attempt to retrieve it for her, she leaned down to pick it up, balancing herself by a tight grip on Henry's thigh. He willy-nilly got a waft of scented shampoo from her freshly-washed hair as she leaned with her head almost in his lap. Edging away towards the empty chair she had referred to, Henry stood up. 'I forgot the candles. Will you help me light them, Ebro?' Barbara, flushing pink, was left to regain her seat by herself.

His guests watched Henry circle the table, tall and mysterious, lighting the candles in the chandeliers to bring velvety darkness at their backs, while beyond the candle-light Ebro moved quietly on the grass to light lanterns hanging from the branches of flowering trees further down the garden.

As Ebro regained his place one of the Jonathans said, 'Instant darkness, how delightful.'

Maisie Bullivant exclaimed, 'Perfect for footsie-footsie. Who am I sitting next to?'

'Your husband,' said her husband.

'And me,' said Matthew, shrinking away from this flirtatious approach. 'Matthew Stephenson.'

Maisie said, 'Oh, oh, Matthew Stephenson.'

'Watch out, she is wearing lethal heels,' said Antonia sitting opposite.

'The seating arrangements are not very formal, are they?' said Maisie. 'It would have been more formal in Henry's mother's day. In her day I would not have been stuck next to Peter, would I?'

'Don't you like your husband, then?' asked Antonia pertly.

Matthew frowned. I shan't let her speak so freely to older women when we are married, he thought.

'Of course I like him,' said Maisie. 'But I like things done right; it's etiquette.'

'What a stickler you are, Maisie. Would you like us all to change around?' asked Jonathan. 'You might get stuck next to me,' he said, laughing.

'Some of us already have changed around.' Maisie looked pointedly at Barbara. Then, feeling uneasy in the presence of these young and pretty girls, she picked up her spoon and addressed her soup, murmuring, 'Pilar's soup, wonderful.' She swallowed the word as she eyed Antonia and wished that Peter, instead of just sitting there, would say something to restore her social courage, which was inclining towards the wobbly.

Then Antonia, smiling at the older woman, said, 'When you need to kick Matthew, please take care. He has delicate ankles.'

'Lucky man,' said Maisie gratefully, 'mine are terrible. Thick. I wish—' I wish, she thought, that I was as young and confident as this girl; she must be thinking me as thick as my ankles. She sighed and ate her soup and wondered what to say next.

Antonia took stock of Maisie. There was something in the woman which reminded her of her mother; she tried to pin-point it. Too much eye shadow? Someone should tell her. Did her husband squash her in private, as her father squashed her mother? No, it was her age, the age when features no longer fitted, noses grew larger and chins doubled. I shan't allow it to happen to me, she thought; I shall keep my looks as Calypso Grant has kept hers. She smiled across the table at Maisie.

Maisie said, 'When we were introduced I did not quite catch your name.' The girl was lovely, there was no need to be scared of her.

'Antonia,' said Antonia. 'Antonia Lowther, and that's Matthew Stephenson next to you. We are engaged to be married.'

'Oh!' cried Maisie, delighted. 'Oh, how nice. Antonia Lowther, of course. Your father is that MP one is always reading about, the very red one, almost a communist. How interesting.'

'No!' said Matthew sharply. 'No. Antonia's father is in *steel*.' He stressed the word.

'A relation, perhaps?' Unconsciously Maisie belittled Antonia's parent. 'An uncle or something?'

'No relation,' said Matthew firmly, 'none at all. He's Lowther's Steel.'

Maisie looked discouraged.

Antonia said, 'Not even a "something", I'm afraid.' There was no need for Matthew to snap at the poor woman. 'I've heard,' she said, 'that that Lowther makes witty jokes in Parliament. My father's not in the same league. Matthew is anti-red,' she said, grinning at Maisie and avoiding her fiancé's eye.

Failing to catch Antonia's eye, Matthew realized an implied reproof. She was looking very pretty in the candle-light, more mature than her years; he would forgive her.

Calypso, who had been listening to this exchange, glanced at Hector but made no effort to break a silence which began to spread around the table. Henry had regained his place and was eating his soup. Barbara sat on one side of him; the chair on his left was empty, backed by the dark yews. James, ignored by Barbara, tried to catch her eye; she should, he thought, pay attention to him. He cleared his throat but, unwilling to look a fool, stayed silent and listened to Peter Bullivant who, having finished his soup, was almost shouting past his wife to Henry at the head of the table.

'I hear,' Peter said, 'that your wife's had her quarters redecorated; it can't be long since she had it all done.'

Henry said, 'No.'

'What is it this time? Somebody told me she's gone in for gold.'

Henry said, 'Yes.'

'Must cost you,' said Peter. 'I mean, you don't get paint and paper and re-upholster furniture for nothing, do you?'

Henry said, 'No.'

'And labour,' said Peter. 'That costs, these days.'

Henry said, 'Yes.'

'It's vulgar to talk about money, Peter,' Maisie whispered.

'Not etiquette, I suppose,' snapped Peter, 'not done, bad form.'

'Well, it is,' said Maisie out loud.

'What?' said Peter.

'Bad form,' said Maisie.

'So are red MPs,' said her husband. 'Don't teach your grandmother—'

Henry laughed.

'I love the way you two squabble in public,' said Jonathan. 'It's refreshing.'

'Where was I,' asked Peter, 'when old stupid here interrupted?' He sounded quite affectionate.

'Cost of labour,' John prompted.

'Oh yes,' said Peter, 'that. Yes. I suppose, when you spend so much on Margaret, you let the rest of the house go hang. Let's face it, it's jolly shabby.'

'Yes,' said Henry.

'But your land,' said Peter, 'you keep that in good heart, nobody could fault you there. Your farm is terrific.'

Henry said, 'Thanks.'

'And this party,' Peter carried on, 'it's splendid. You don't stint your guests. Jolly good food, and the drinks—'

'He's been costing them,' said Maisie.

'I haven't,' said Peter.

'You always do,' said Maisie. 'When we get home you know exactly what the wine has cost. He might be a wine merchant,' Maisie informed the table at large, 'so clever.'

They could almost see Peter resist calling her stupid.

She smiled hugely round the table at her fellow guests, proud of her husband. 'It's all right if you do it in private,' she said.

The Jonathans, Calypso and Hector burst out laughing and presently awkwardness evaporated and conversation became general while Ebro and Trask collected the soup plates, replacing them with fresh ones for the salmon, which soon ceased to look pretty and dissipated as they were transferred from their beds of watercress to diverse digestive tracts.

From time to time Henry circled the table, replenishing his guests' glasses, catching, as he went, snatches of talk. Hector and Trask were deep in forestry, Ebro discussing pop music with Antonia. The Jonathans were instructing Maisie on the novels of Camus which was, he guessed, an affectionate tease, it being common knowledge that Maisie never read a book if she could avoid it. Peter was trying to engage Barbara's attention without success and Antonia, only sparing half her attention for Ebro, was watching Henry move in and out of the shadows, his presence betrayed by the glint of a candle on the bottle he carried. He refilled her glass and moved on.

Why, thought Antonia, watching Henry, did he never raise his voice? She compared him with

130

Matthew, who was talking embarrassingly loudly to Calypso while ignoring Maisie sitting next to him. How was it Henry looked so elegant in his *outré* clothes? They made Matthew's excellent dinner jacket look dull. How was it Barbara had managed to sit next to Henry? Why should Barbara sit next to Henry and not she? Antonia pushed back her chair with her neat little bottom and, taking her plate of salmon with her, moved into the empty chair beside Henry.

When Henry resumed his seat he said, 'That's nice,' but Barbara, on his other side, failed to respond.

Maisie, observing the move, and sorry to see Antonia move away, wondered whether this sort of general post was the new mode among the smart set in London, and whether to try it at her next dinner party. But I am not silly enough to suggest it to Peter, she thought. I lack the nerve.

14

Calypso was the first to see Margaret; she nudged Hector, who was turned away from her talking with Trask. It had grown quite dark as they ate their salmon; the candles on the table accentuated the severity of the yew hedge's dark backdrop. In the flower borders tulips raised their pale faces and Antonia's lily arrangement on the bar seemed to hover in the gloom.

Amused by the girls' manoeuvres, Calypso had been watching the head of the table; now she stared at the point where she had seen a movement, a lightness which shifted from Henry to Antonia to Barbara. Perhaps she had been mistaken? Was what she saw a shift in the shadows caused by a flickering candle? The candles flickered again when Peter's breath gusted in laughter as Maisie began teasing Jonathan and John, reminding them of the days when they had both clung to the same name.

'You made yourselves ridiculous,' she said, 'both called Jonathan. That's what they did,' she said to the table at large. 'Used the same name! It was almost possible when we were all young, but ludicrous when they began living together—'

'A beginning which has no end—' Peter's laugh tinged on the cruel. 'So far,' he said.

The shape in the shadows shrank back. 'We were equally entitled to the name,' cried the younger man. 'We were both baptized Jonathan.'

'It made them look silly,' persisted Maisie. 'It made the neighbourhood laugh.'

'We don't care about the neighbourhood,' cried the younger man, 'never did.'

'Obviously not.' Peter backed his wife.

Why are they being so petty? What's this all about? Antonia wondered, and liked Maisie less than before.

'Henry's father was our sponsor, our godparent. He chose the name,' protested the older man. 'Who were we to question his choice? Our mothers didn't.'

'He wouldn't have suggested the same name if he'd known what you would turn into—'

'Steady on, Maisie,' said Peter.

Henry said, 'Jonathan was a favourite name of my father's. It's all ancient history, Maisie. There was some sort of entertainment value in telephone calls: can I speak to Jonathan? Which Jonathan? Oh, that Jonathan, and so on, but it did pall. It was graceful of the younger to give way and abbreviate to John.'

'Are you suggesting I am not graceful?' said Maisie, bristling. 'That I am insensitive?'

'Since you ask,' said Jonathan, answering for Henry, 'yes! You take a touchy subject and worry it like a terrier. You have no tact; you are almost as insensitive as Margaret, our absent, our quasi-hostess. Where is she, by the way? Weren't we promised—'

'Oh!' Maisie's cry was full of indignation and hurt. 'Oh, you old—'

I have not given them the right proportion of alcohol, thought Henry. Perhaps I should top them up? If I defend the Jonathans, who are able to defend themselves, I shall offend poor Maisie, who can't. He stifled a longing to laugh.

'Hector,' said Calypso in a low voice.

'Yes, darling?' Hector did not immediately turn to her, allowing Trask to finish a long and convoluted arboreal sentence. 'They should not tease the boys,' he said.

Calypso slipped her hand in his. 'Look who's here,' she said quietly.

Hector said, 'Look? Where? Who?'

'I thought at first it was a trick of the light, but it's Margaret. She's behind Henry, look.'

Hector said, 'Ah!' and closed his fingers over his wife's. 'I see her,' he said. 'What d'you suppose she is up to?' he said, speaking with his mouth close to her ear. 'Now she's gone. No, she's there, behind Henry. There. Gone again. D'you think he's aware?'

'He's too far away for me to see the hairs rising on his neck. Mine would.' Calypso glanced over her shoulder.

Peter had taken over from Maisie and was in full cry teasing the Jonathans, listened to with a mixture of surprise and distaste by Matthew and Antonia.

'Peter Bullivant's an offensive bastard,' said Hector quietly. 'Never heard the word tact.'

'There she goes again,' whispered Calypso.

Hector, who assessed his wife's nerve as normally steely, recognized a tremor of fear and tightened his grip on her hand.

'Henry may not have noticed,' he whispered. 'He's got to deal with Peter,' he said as Henry pushed back his chair and stood up.

'Now then,' Henry said, 'would you two girls collect these sordid plates while I circulate the wine and Pilar and Ebro bring the pudding?' If I top up my foolish guests, he thought, they will swing from the offensive to the sweet – with luck. He advanced on Maisie and Peter armed with a fresh bottle of wine.

Antonia and Barbara jumped up and began collecting plates, and as they moved along the table Hector and Calypso saw Margaret shrink back into the shadows. They strained their eyes, but could not see her. Hector said, 'Did we imagine her?'

'I didn't imagine that.' Calypso chuckled as Antonia deliberately let a load of dirty plates slide into Peter's lap. 'Well done, girl!'

'Oops,' said Antonia, mopping with Peter's napkin. 'So sorry. I've got grease all over your pretty trousers.'

'You did that on purpose, you are making it worse.' Maisie snatched the napkin.

'Oh no!' said Antonia. 'Oh dear, I'm sorry.'

'She should sound sorry,' said Hector.

'I think Henry has noticed,' Calypso said. 'His shoulders have gone all stiff. But he's not letting on.'

'M-m-m,' said Hector. 'And what happens now?' He sat alert, holding his wife's hand.

It was then that the cockatoo, furtively climbing up by the table-cloth, attained its goal and let out an ear-splitting screech. The diners jumped and there was laughter. The bird, as though acknowledging applause, raised and lowered its crest and began picking its way among the spoons.

'He is fond of fruit,' said Henry. 'Here come the strawberries,' he said as Pilar and Ebro placed the fruit on the table. 'Careful, Maisie, he is not so funny drunk.'

But Maisie, unheeding, offered the bird her glass. 'I don't suppose he's got psittacosis,' she said, watching the bird sip. 'I'd like to see him pissed.' She was annoyed with herself for hurting the Jonathans and annoyed with them for being hurt. I always think people should watch their own backs, she thought.

Henry put a hand down to catch the bird but it hopped sideways to the middle of the table, where it stood raising and lowering its crest, ignoring the people who offered fruit, saying, 'Pretty Polly,' in dulcet accents.

Trask said, 'Best leave her be.'

Maisie, feeling at fault, said, 'Oh, I thought it was a cock, I didn't know it was a she. How d'you tell the difference?'

'By looking under its feathers,' said Trask, 'as with skirts.'

With Henry moving round the table, and Barbara and Antonia parlour-maiding the plates, there were now three empty chairs at the head of the table. It was a shock to everyone when Margaret materialized seated in the middle chair. 'Well,' she said, 'well,' sitting with her hands folded. She smiled at the assembled guests. 'Sorry to be so late,' she said. 'Any salmon left for me?'

With her red-gold hair piled high on her head, Margaret looked beautiful. The candles gave a peachy glow to her skin, enlarged her eye sockets, softened her mouth and flattered the cleavage between breasts pouting under the Dior chiffon.

Henry's guests stared, speechless and gormless. Calypso shook with laughter and Hector chuckled out loud. The cockatoo was forgotten.

Trask said, 'You had your salmon on your tray hours ago.'

Still smiling, Margaret said, 'Dear Trask, so I did, but I'd like more.'

'None left,' said Henry cheerfully. 'But you are in time for the pudding, coffee and brandy. Why don't you move up beside her, Jonathan and John? Take your glasses and take this bottle with you.'

'Does he not dare go near her?' murmured Calypso.

'I wouldn't in his shoes,' said Hector. 'She's ousted the virgins rather effectively.'

'I was enjoying the spectacle they made,' said Calypso, watching the diners rearrange themselves.

'Dear Jonathan,' said Margaret as her cavaliers took their seats, 'and dear John.'

'You were snooping!' said John.

'Listening,' said Margaret, 'wondering whether I would be welcome.' She looked down the table at Henry, who had found a seat next to Calypso previously occupied by Ebro.

'Quite a turn-up for the book,' he remarked as he sat down.

'She is a beautiful woman,' said Calypso. 'It's not only the candle-light.'

'And she is making herself agreeable to the boys,' said Hector, surprised.

'And she has silenced Peter and Maisie,' said Calypso.

'She can be agreeable,' said Henry. 'It's been known.'

At the head of the table Margaret was smiling as Jonathan on her right heaped her plate with fruit while John on her left scattered sugar and poured cream.

'The two girls,' said Hector, laughing, 'are looking pretty, too, sitting back with their men. We enjoyed watching them casting themselves at your head.'

'Net practice,' said Henry. 'The slow bowl.'

'It's had the desired effect,' said Calypso. 'Both James and Matthew look smug and possessive.'

Henry said, 'Ah, possessive,' and appraised Antonia and her friend.

'Hector is possessive,' said Calypso. 'I recognize possessiveness when I see it.'

'She likes it,' said Hector. 'Have you ever been possessive, Henry?'

'Yes.' Henry frowned. 'But it was half-hearted, a mistake. I desisted. It was in the nature of a bad taste joke, an act,' he said, wincing at an unpleasant recollection.

Sensing his hurt and recognizing a private pain,

Calypso said, 'We trip ourselves up when we are bored.'

Gratefully, Henry said, 'That's it, yes. I was bored, I wanted something to happen. It backfired,' and enlightened them no further.

Catching his wife's eye, and switching the subject back to their fellow guests, Hector said, 'One wonders whether those two fellows will be sufficiently heavyweight for their girls, whether they will come up to scratch.'

'Women don't always want perfect husbands,' said Calypso. 'The imperfect allow more scope. I say,' she said, 'I think we had better listen to this—'

Others were listening: Maisie open-mouthed, Peter frowning, Antonia and Barbara leaning towards Margaret. A question had been asked by James. Why had Margaret married Henry? He was to excuse himself later, explaining that his hostess had asserted that she had always despised Henry, that he was mean, insensitive and a moral coward. How the subject of Margaret's union with Henry had arisen nobody afterwards was clear. They all, however, heard Margaret say, 'I was sorry for him.'

In the ensuing silence Margaret assessed her audience.

Antonia said, 'Go on.'

Barbara gaped but said nothing.

Matthew said, 'I think—'

Antonia said, 'Shush.'

James was mute.

Margaret said, 'I had been married to a brute. He not only beat me, he subjected me to psychological violence. He spent my money, he flaunted his women, he drank. And worse, he took drugs.'

James sucked in his breath and released it. 'Phew!'

Jonathan murmured, 'You poor, poor thing.' His

lover was heard to say, 'Matrimonial martyrdom.'

Margaret took a spoonful of strawberries. 'Not enough sugar,' she said, and John tenderly helped her to more. 'I was a good wife.' Margaret took a mouthful of fruit. 'That's better. I considered him too much. I was subservient.' She spooned in the fruit. 'I tried my best. I bore it, but my love shrivelled. He did things to me which I could not even whisper to my confessor – the indignities!'

'Never knew she was a Catholic,' muttered Hector, who was of that persuasion.

'Finally,' said Margaret, laying down her spoon and letting her voice rise, 'I had had enough. I divorced him.'

'Quite right,' said Jonathan. 'More fruit?'

Margaret, ignoring him, said, 'I am a romantic.'

John said, 'Of course you are, dear. And then?'

'Well then, when Henry laid siege with little notes, with pretty presents, with expensive flowers, with – with – well, as I have admitted before, with such persistence it amounted to pestering, I gave in. And look,' said Margaret, her voice suddenly harsh, 'at what I got.'

The candles were guttering by now, their light wavery, but Margaret's audience were able to see the look of bane she gave her husband.

Peter jeered. 'A mean, insensitive moral coward, a monster.' Drunk and enjoying himself.

Pilar rose and asked, 'Coffee, Henry?'

Henry said, 'Yes, please, Pilar. And fresh candles, if we have them.' Then he said to Calypso and Hector, 'Come round the garden with me, we've heard the best of it.' He was laughing.

As she got to her feet Calypso said, 'I don't think you should be laughing, Henry. It isn't funny. Hector isn't laughing.'

Henry said, 'But Hector is married to you,' and stopped laughing. 'Hector,' he said as they walked away from the dining table, 'would never have got himself into a ridiculous situation.'

'Oh, I don't know,' said Hector. 'My first marriage was a flop.'

'But not ridiculous,' said Henry. 'You were unhappy. I am ridiculous. There's a nuance which is hard to miss.'

'I don't think your wife makes you ridiculous,' said Hector.

'It isn't my wife,' said Henry shortly, 'it is the person responsible for the whole bloody situation.'

15

Barbara whispered to James, 'Must go to the lavatory, can't wait. Listen carefully and tell me later.'

James said, 'Oh, all right, but don't be long,' keeping a fascinated eye on Margaret.

Barbara slid from her chair and faded into the dark; James did not notice that she headed not for the house, but down the path after Henry and the Grants.

Strolling between the two men, Calypso said, 'You should do something, Henry, put a stop.'

'What do you suggest?' Henry asked snappily.

Calypso said, 'You know I'm not given to prying. Hector knows more about your marriage than I do. He was in Cairo when you married—'

'I know very little,' Hector interposed. 'I never—'

'He never lets on, he's discreet, he's told me nothing,' said Calypso. 'But you can't let your wife talk as she does. I do wish, Henry, that you would tell us something of what really happened. Then we might be able to help.'

'I don't see how you could,' said Henry shortly.

'We could at least stop that rot about her first husband. It's so preposterous it can't possibly be true.'

'How did you guess?' Henry began to laugh again.

'It's no laughing matter,' said Calypso. 'And now Hector's laughing,' she said. 'What's so funny?'

'The first husband,' said Henry. 'A mouse of a man, wasn't he, Hector?'

'Nice little chap,' said Hector. 'Still alive, I believe,

141

rather older than she is, works in the States.'

'Oh, come on, Henry—' Calypso's clear voice carried back to Barbara. 'Tell.'

Thinking she would hear better if she closed in a little – Henry's voice, deep and rumbling, was difficult to hear – Barbara quickened her pace as Henry said, 'Oh, all right. There's no point in shutting up, I suppose. Let's go and sit over there and I will tell you the sordid tale. I take no pride in it.'

As he spoke Barbara tripped over one of the dogs which, following at Henry's heels, had paused to sit and scratch. The dog yelped and Barbara, stumbling forward, nearly fell.

Hector said, 'We have an eavesdropper.'

Barbara exclaimed, 'Oh gosh, have I hurt him? What's this one called?' as the dog jumped up and tried to lick her face. I wish I could die, she thought.

'Their names are Humble and Cringe,' said Henry nastily.

'Last time somebody asked, you said they were called Spot and Rover,' said Hector, thinking, Bloody stupid girl.

Henry, regarding Barbara, said, 'My dogs answer to Hi or any loud cry.'

Calypso said, 'You know what they say about listeners; we might have been discussing you, Barbara. That's your name, isn't it?'

Barbara, choking, said, 'I am too insignificant, I suppose,' loathing the older woman.

Henry said, 'Now, now, no need to be unkind; she's blushing and wishing herself dead. Come along,' he said, taking hold of Barbara's wrist, 'we are going to sit on that seat over there while I strip the skeleton from my cupboard.'

'You are hurting my wrist,' said Barbara.

'Splendid, glad to hear it,' said Henry.

142

'Who is being unkind now?' murmured Hector.

'Won't your fiancé miss you?' Calypso was chilly.

'I am on my way to the lavatory,' said Barbara desperately.

'Then cross your legs and shut up,' said Henry. 'Here we will sit and watch the moon while I rattle my skeleton.' He sat on the bench, pulling Barbara roughly down beside him.

Hector grunted protestingly and muttered words to the effect that Henry was being unkind to young girls. He made room for his wife between himself and Henry.

'I enjoy being unkind to young girls,' said Henry. 'I enjoy young girls.'

'You told me he was flawed,' said Calypso, speaking to her husband.

'She might as well stay,' said Henry more moderately. 'It doesn't really matter,' he said. 'We know that anything she might have heard would get garbled. She may as well begin her garbling from a truthful source. Learning the art of gossip at her age is as complex as learning the facts of life. Do you know the facts of life?' he asked Barbara, tightening his grip on her wrist.

'Of course I do.' Barbara was close to tears.

'Enough, Henry,' said Calypso.

'I would like to know,' said Henry, 'since you *are* here, exactly what my wife had been telling you and your equally nubile friend.' He ignored Calypso.

'She told us,' said Barbara, speaking between her teeth, 'that you are a sodomite and can only do it with horses.'

Henry let go of her wrist. 'I am sorry if I hurt you,' he said. 'I feel a bit winded,' he said, turning to Hector. 'The accusation isn't new, but the esoteric combination is.'

'Perhaps we could get back to the bones,' said Calypso. 'The contents of the cupboard.'

'At least your wife gives you full marks for versatility,' said Hector, lightening the atmosphere with a laugh. 'Your truth will have to be a lot stranger than fiction to surprise us after that revelation.' He chuckled again and murmured to himself, 'Horses!'

'Shut up, Hector.' Calypso, too, tried not to laugh. 'Now you've *got* to tell us,' she said, curbing her mirth. 'You were about to begin when Barbara here fell over Humble and Cringe.'

'Their real names are Hector and Lysander,' said Henry, 'but when Hector comes to dinner—'

'You prevaricate. What was the start of your dilemma?'

'Love,' said Henry morosely.

'Love?' Calypso's voice rose in astonishment.

Barbara muttered, 'I must go, I—'

'No, you don't.' Henry recaptured her wrist. 'There was this girl I used to watch,' he said. 'She became an obsession. She was older than me, very lovely, always surrounded by adoring men. It began when I was thirteen or fourteen. Each time I saw her she was lovelier than before, more out of reach. I don't think she noticed I was there, but I fantasized and dreamed and convinced myself that when I grew up and was free of acne I would marry her. At times I was sure she would be waiting. Lots of people have this juvenile experience.'

'Is she still around?' asked Hector.

'Oh yes.'

'Middle-aged by now?'

Henry said, 'That is the case.'

Calypso said, 'Stop interrupting. Go on, Henry.'

'Where was I?'

'You were imagining she would be in her perpetual prime. What happened?'

'The war happened.'

144

'And?'

'I was caught up in it. You can't want my martial record. I found myself in Cairo.'

'Stick to the love part. You must have been grown up, or nearly so; did you still have this obsession? Did you suppose she would still be there after you had finished with the war?'

'Believe it or not, I did.'

Calypso said, 'Oh. Wouldn't your mother have helped? I'm sure if Hamish ever got himself into a fix like that, I would get him out of it.'

'My mother died in the thirties and after her death my father was caught up in the war in Spain, extracting Pilar and Ebro. He wasn't actually ever of much practical use to me and not much of a letter-writer—'

'He wrote letters to *The Times*,' Calypso interrupted. 'Very trenchant they were.'

'But not to me,' said Henry. 'He had a theory that one should only write letters if one had something of vital importance to say. One must not clog the mail. That being so, if I did get a letter from him I paid special attention.'

Somewhere in the garden, a blackbird, disturbed by a marauding cat, set up a loud screech and chatter. Henry's dogs sat up, ears pricked. In the silence which followed Calypso sighed and said, 'So you got a letter?'

'Two. One from the Jonathans, who wrote quite often. Sandwiched in their gossip was the news that my "amour", as I thought of her, had got married. Before I read my father's letter I went out and got drunk. I was drunk for several days. I happened to be on leave. When I read my father's letter I was in a state of moribund alcoholic gloom.'

Hector clicked his tongue. 'I know the feeling.'

Calypso said, 'And what did your father say?'

145

Letting go of Barbara's wrist, Henry exclaimed, 'It is so ridiculous, so inexcusable, so utterly crass. I—'

Calypso said, 'Come on, Henry.'

Henry said, 'Oh, dear God.' Then he said, 'My father wrote to tell me he was dying. He thought I should know. Not long, he said. Pilar was being wonderful and the Jonathans kindness itself, but there was one thing, this urgent idea he had of helping – You knew him, Calypso.' Henry turned to her.

'Oh God,' said Calypso, 'I did. Philanthropic and idealistic, an absolute menace. My parents, who were boringly sensible, thought he was insane. What was the idea? I suppose he passed the baton on to you?'

Henry said, 'That was what it amounted to. He wrote that he was concerned for innocents caught up in the war, particularly for unfortunates who were dubbed enemy aliens in error. He had heard of an English-woman who had married a German and, although now divorced, found herself in danger of being interned in Egypt; would I look her up? She was a friend of a friend of the Jonathans. A worthy cause, is what he called her.' Henry paused, staring out across the moonlit garden.

Beside him Barbara held her breath and thought, He has forgotten I am here. And Calypso, feeling for Hector's hand for comfort, thought, This is spine-chilling.

'My father wrote,' Henry went on, 'that it behoved everybody to do what they could in however small a way and quoted the kindness of an old neighbour who, recently widowed, had at his suggestion married a German Jewish lady. It was neither here, he wrote, nor there, as mischievously suggested by the Jonathans, that the poor man needed a cook/housekeeper. The Jonathans knew of an English poet who had offered to marry the daughter of a German writer. They themselves seemed unable to volunteer, but here, and he gave it, was the address. Before he had known he was dying he had intended proposing himself by cable, but in the circumstances it would be of little use, so would I—'

'And it was Margaret,' said Hector.

Calypso said, 'How could you have been so *stupid*?'

Henry said, 'I managed.'

Hector said, 'And I suppose you thought what the hell, I've lost my girl and I shall get killed anyway.'

Henry said, 'That sort of thing.'

Calypso said, 'The girl you were in love with should never have led you on.'

'She didn't. She hadn't an inkling of my feelings.'

Thinking of Henry's father, Calypso murmured, 'What a pity he didn't die before he wrote that letter.'

Excusing his parent, Henry said, 'He had never done good by proxy before.'

Hector said, 'Margaret's ex was German, an archaeologist. He'd lived and worked in Egypt all his life. His application for Egyptian nationality came through after he divorced Margaret, so she was left German while he was in the clear. People thought it frightfully funny. I wonder what his sexual deviations were.'

'Nil,' said Henry.

'People liked him, though; he was dull but decent.'

'No need for Margaret to expand on that,' said Calypso, 'I should have thought.'

'But she does,' said Hector. 'And your aged pa is responsible for the mess you are in.'

'I should have thought Jonathan and John were the ones to blame,' said Barbara.

'So you are still there,' said Henry. 'I'd forgotten you.'

147

16

'I think I had better go back, I am a neglectful host,' said Henry. 'See what's cooking.' He rose to his feet. 'Don't you two move if you are happy,' he said to Hector and Calypso. Humble and Cringe rose as one dog, and Barbara rose too. Henry absently took her hand.

Watching them go, Hector said, 'I am bothered about that girl. Henry can be pretty bloody.'

Calypso said, 'It is more likely she will hurt him than he her.'

Hector said, 'Oh? That is possible,' and, putting his arm round his wife's shoulder, drew her close. He wondered whether she had guessed the identity of Henry's infatuation.

She said, 'How well did you know him in Cairo, in the war?'

'He was only around when on leave from the desert. I didn't see much of him, but I knew Margaret's husband. I was interested in antiquities. Then of course I became a prisoner of war and out of touch. I only got to know Henry properly when we came to live down here. But you must have known him as a girl? You were neighbours.'

'All I remember is a gangly, spotty youth one sometimes got stuck next to at parties. I was on another tack, aiming high, craving to escape from home and find myself a rich husband.' Calypso leaned against Hector, brushing her head against his chin.

Hector said, 'Me.'

'You.'

'Us,' she said, looking out across the moonlit garden, considering herself fortunate and blesed in her *trouvaille*. 'I would not like you perfect,' she said.

Hector said, 'That's a comfort.'

Strolling back towards the party, Henry said, 'You are now free to go to the lavatory, Barbara.'

Barbara said, 'That was an excuse. I'm sorry.'

Henry said, 'I am sorry if I hurt you. You had better get back to James.' When Barbara said nothing, he said, 'I take it you are in love with him.'

Barbara said, 'I suppose so,' without ardour and waited for Henry to question her lack of enthusiasm but he did not, so she stopped and Henry stopped too, and Humble and Cringe sat down. Barbara said, 'What does a man like you do about sex?'

'What makes you think I do anything?' He was amused by her temerity.

Barbara said, 'One can't possibly believe your wife.'

Henry said, 'That's good news.'

'And you seem quite normal,' she pressed on.

He asked, 'Are you propositioning me?'

Barbara said, 'Of course not! I am interested. Your situation seems so strange and you say you were once in love, so—'

'So you imagine I have ordinary urges?'

'Yes.'

'Aren't you being rather impertinent?'

'Curious.'

Laughing, Henry said, 'There are such things as call-girls.'

'Tarts?' Barbara was taken aback. 'I hadn't thought—'

'Then you don't do much thinking,' said Henry patiently. 'Listen, child, before they married my father and his friends rogered village girls. I grew up to see

149

my mother looking askance at the local adolescents, hoping not to see a likeness. The two Jonathans, for instance, are results of my father's pre-marital era, though not his, I hasten to say. My mother never took to them and resented my love for them; they reminded her of my father's habits before she met him. I incline to what solace London may offer. Satisfied?'

Barbara said, 'Was Valerie a call-girl?'

'Valerie? What Valerie?'

'The Valerie James brought to stay here.'

'Oh, that Valerie. No, not a call-girl.'

'Oh.'

'How, by the way, did you hear of her?'

'Your wife.'

'It's amazing,' said Henry, exasperated, 'what a fount of mischief that woman can be. The little trot James had with Valerie was of no importance. Anyway,' Henry said, remembering James lovelorn and sulky, 'it's all over long since. I don't suppose he ever gives her a thought. James is patently in love with you. Now, if you don't mind, I must get back to the others.'

'But I just wanted to ask—' Barbara persisted.

What Barbara wanted to ask Henry was never to know and Barbara forgot, retaining only a blurred impression of their questions and answers since they were overriden by the screams, shouts and yells coming from the dinner party. Henry broke into a run.

The dinner table was a shambles. Maisie was screaming, Trask swearing and Pilar yelling, 'Aie! Aie!' at the top of her voice. Some of the candles had been snuffed, some had fallen and spitted their grease as Margaret danced on the table among the debris of the meal. As she danced she crushed the lilies of the valley underfoot. She had ripped the Dior dress, tearing the bodice, so that she was naked to the waist. Flame from a candle had scorched up her skirt; the smell of singeing mingled with the lilies. But worse than the smell of burning Dior was the stink of scorched feathers as she whirled the cockatoo round her head, then dipped it low to catch in the candles. Maisie was screaming on a high, hysterical, undulating note and Peter was being sick into the tulips.

Trask, Ebro, James and Matthew made futile grabs at Margaret but, evading them, she stamped and danced, whirling the cockatoo.

Then Antonia leapt upon the table. Margaret crowed, 'I dare you to come closer.' As Antonia hesitated she tore off the bird's head and flung it in Antonia's face, shouting, 'Hah! Come on! Come on!' and began ripping the bird's wings.

Henry, bursting past Ebro, hurled himself on to the table and, catching Margaret round the knees, brought her down among the glass and china. As she went down she tore at his face with her bloody hands. The table collapsed under their weight and Antonia, terrified, cried, 'Help! I am falling!' And Margaret, struggling with Henry, bit him in the neck.

Matthew said, 'Oh *dear!*' and helped Antonia to her feet. Maisie and Pilar stopped screaming, Barbara ran into James's arms, buried her face against his dinner jacket and sobbed, but nobody spoke until Henry said, 'Give us a hand, somebody,' and extricated himself and his wife from the broken table, setting her carefully on her feet as Hector and Calypso arrived at a run to see what was happening.

They heard Henry say, 'You must not get cold, Margaret.' He was quiet and solicitous after the shrill pandemonium. They saw him take off his jacket and wrap it round her nakedness. 'Are you all right?' he asked. 'Are you hurt? No? That's good.' The bite on his neck was bleeding but he was gentle with Margaret, setting her upright, holding her steady.

Margaret said, 'Well yes, I am a bit chilly. Perhaps I will go back to bed. It would be nice if Pilar or somebody would bring me a glass of hot milk.'

Henry said, 'One of us will.'

As they walked towards the house Margaret said, 'That *was* a good party. I *did* enjoy it. We must do it again. Good night, everybody,' she called over her shoulder, 'so glad you could come. Come again some time, but not you who is being sick all over the tulips. You do have peculiar friends, Henry.'

Hector was to comment later on the macabre behaviour of the dogs. Humble retrieved what was left of the cockatoo, while Cringe, unable to locate the head which Matthew, mindful of his fiancée's sensitivity, had covered with a plate, contented himself with a mouthful of feathers to be carried in his master's wake.

Calypso overhead Matthew say *sotto voce*, 'I expect after that you would like me to take you straight back to London.'

And Antonia's robust reply: 'Don't be so wet.'

'Those girls have no manners.' Margaret leaned against Henry. 'Not the sort of behaviour I learned at home. All that screaming.'

Henry held his jacket round his wife's shoulders; he did not ask where 'home' had been. The Jonathans, who had tried to delve into Margaret's mysterious antecedents, claimed that she had confided that she was born in Leeds, but at other times she had said Alexandria or the Lebanon.

'My feet are hurting,' Margaret whimpered. 'If you were going to buy me a dress you might at least have gone the whole hog and bought me shoes to match.'

I do not even know what size she takes, thought Henry. 'Kick them off,' he said, 'the grass is soft.'

'I can't walk barefoot,' Margaret snapped. 'You did buy the dress?' she accused.

'Yes,' he said, 'I did.'

'I thought as much. What do you take me for?' Henry did not answer. Margaret giggled. 'Oh, how those two girls desired it!'

'Did you tread on glass?'

'I may have done.'

He led her to the house. Pilar was already in the hall. 'Could you bring Margaret some hot milk?' he asked her.

Pilar nodded.

'With honey?' he suggested.

'No sweetener,' snapped Margaret, 'idiot.'

Henry led his wife up the stairs. Pilar, watching, made a wringing motion with closed fists.

At Margaret's door Henry said, 'Wait,' to the dogs, who sank down on reproachful haunches. He led Margaret into her room and closed the door.

Margaret stood in the middle of the room while Henry drew the curtains and pulled back the bed-clothes for her. She was a beautiful creature, he thought objectively, and wondered whether any man had ever wanted to have her, whether she could arouse desire. 'Let me help you,' he said as she fingered the tattered dress. 'Better take it off.'

'Any other colour would have been better. You have no taste,' she said.

'Come on.' Gently he drew the torn dress over her head, letting it drop and blend with the carpet, the walls, the bedspread, the nightdress he handed her and her hair. Her pubic hair was rust colour; he had not seen it before and was shocked to find it ugly.

'I am sick to death of this colour,' she said.

'Are your feet all right? Let me see if they are cut.'

'Of course they are not cut! That old bag Calypso's

153

hair is the colour of hay,' she said, 'pretty musty hay. She should tint it, liven it up.'

Had she livened her bush? 'If your feet are all right, you should get into bed,' said Henry quietly. 'Here is your milk,' he said as Pilar knocked at the door.

'Don't let her in,' exclaimed Margaret. 'I don't want her in here.' She got into bed. 'As tomorrow I shall not want you.'

Henry brought her the milk.

'Too hot,' said Margaret. 'Put it down. I shall consult with your sisters what colour to have next.' She looked at her golden room with narrowed eyes.

'Sisters?'

'The Jonathans, the quasi-men, the silly old sodomites, your spiritual sisters. Can't you sit down?' she said irritably. 'I shall keep all the mirrors.'

Henry sat with his back to the window, his jacket across his knees. In the wood owls hooted and he thought of Trask, the old man's love of birds and kindness to him as a child. Weary, he yawned.

Margaret was talking.

'I have my own money,' she was saying belligerently, 'I can pay for it myself if you start being mean.'

'I would rather you did not use your money. I do not know what money you have, nor do I want to know,' said Henry. It would be an obscenity to use her money on the house, he thought; I would rather pay myself for whatever grisly colour she chooses.

'Your sisters know! Those old queens pry! They call themselves my friends, but I know they betray me. But they do not treat me as you do. You treat me like an animal,' she said viciously.

Henry said, 'Yes,' and fingered his neck where she had bitten him. His fingers came away sticky. She is a wounded animal, he thought and yes, he was treating her as such, far more kindly than he would a woman.

He was always gentle with animals, more tender than he had been tonight to poor silly Barbara.

'You do not treat me as you should a woman.' Margaret reached for the glass of milk.

Henry stiffened. Would she throw it at him? Spilt milk smelt disgusting.

'You don't begin to know how to treat a woman.' Margaret drank the milk. 'You and those Jonathans are alike, your sexual parts atrophied from lack of use. All that gristle dangling about, useless and untidy.'

Henry laughed.

'And you had the nerve to ask me to marry you!' Margaret almost shouted.

Wearily Henry said, 'Margaret, you needed a British passport. My father had heard of your plight; he wrote, suggesting I should marry you to save you being interned. It's ancient history.'

'The stupid old man! And who put him up to it? Tell me that!'

'He thought it a helpful idea,' said Henry temperately. 'He was given to acts of kindness.'

'It was not kindness! It was mischief. Your friends, your sisters put him up to it,' Margaret crowed.

Henry flinched. Was she speaking the truth? Oh, the Jonathans—

'You cannot divorce me,' Margaret was saying. 'You will never get rid of me. I will see to it that you never have children.' She drained the milk.

Henry stood up and took the empty glass from her. 'Will you sleep now?' he asked. He tried to imagine Antonia, Barbara, Calypso or even poor Maisie Bullivant voicing such spleen. 'Try and sleep,' he said. 'Good night.'

Margaret said, 'I am glad I bit you.'

17

There was a shamefaced tidying up. As is usual at times of social disaster, those present felt guilty and responsible. Antonia and Barbara collected the residue of the meal, a lot of which had spilled on the grass. Matthew and James tried to right the trestle tables. In so doing they got in Trask's and Ebro's way, causing unconcealed animosity. Pilar had followed Henry and Margaret into the house. Several chairs had suffered in the fracas, and broken glass endangered fingers.

Maisie, shocked into silence, dusted Peter down and they slunk away in a drone of apologetic and sibilant goodbyes. As the sound of their car faded, Jonathan said to John, 'It will be some time before Henry asks them to the house again. They egged that harpy on.'

John replied tartly, 'I should imagine that stricture would apply to us all. Not, of course, to you and Hector,' he said to Calypso. 'You weren't here.'

Antonia, who had kept quiet since Henry removed his wife, exclaimed, 'Oh, my God! Oh Christ, look!' She had come upon the cockatoo's head, hidden by a plate, crushed into a butter dish.

'Leave it, leave it,' exclaimed Matthew. 'Let me deal—'

Ignoring Matthew, Antonia turned to Calypso. 'We had forgotten he was there. Margaret was behaving normally; she was being quite amusing, or so the men seemed to think. He waddled up the table towards her. She held out a strawberry, he laid back his crest and she grabbed. Then she climbed on the table. You helped her,' she said to Matthew. 'She began to shout and dance, and Peter cheered her on! She ripped the dress with one hand and the bird – she shook it. Did you see?' she asked Calypso, almost shrieking.

Calypso said, 'Thankfully not,' her voice steady.

Antonia cried loudly, 'My face! She threw its head in my face, she—'

Matthew said, 'Now then, darling, it's all over, don't get hysterical.'

Antonia hissed, 'I am not hysterical; there is a difference between shock and hysteria. Oh!' she cried, crashing the pile of plates she had collected on to the table. 'What a pompous ass you are! You laughed. You thought it funny when she – You thought, this is some sort of old world binge. A relic of the *Folies Bergère*. An excess of spirit. In a minute you would have been drinking out of her sweaty shoe. God!' she said, raising her hand to strike. 'I can't think how I could ever have got engaged to you.'

Hector, who had been standing a little apart, now spoke. 'Bedtime, girls. Off you go.'

Surprised, Antonia lowered her hand. Barbara said, 'Come on, I'm whacked. Good night, everybody,' and, putting her arm round her friend, led her away.

Halfway to the house Antonia turned and shouted, 'How can Henry be so magnanimous?'

Calypso murmured tiredly, 'How indeed?'

James said to Matthew, 'Hadn't we better see that they are all right?' and the two men followed their girls at a discreet distance.

Hector said, 'I don't know about anybody else, but I could do with a swallow of Henry's brandy from the drinks table in the sitting-room.'

Jonathan said virtuously, 'We can't leave this mess.'

Hector said, 'Yes, we can. Trask and Ebro are dying

to get shot of us. You are, aren't you?' he asked Trask.

Trask said drily, 'Since you ask, yes.'

John said, 'In that case, I think we two will be on our way.'

'Shouldn't one of us see how Henry is?' enquired Calypso.

Henry appeared, answering for himself, 'I am quite all right.'

'Your throat? Your face?' Jonathan lingered.

'Plastered, as you see, by Pilar; scratches duly dabbed with Dettol. Are you two off?'

'Yes,' they said, 'yes. Good night.' They said, 'It was a most, a most unusual party, dear boy, thank you for asking us.'

'Have Maisie and Peter gone?'

'Evaporated,' said Jonathan, 'as we must also.'

John said, 'We are sorry there was, so sorry there—'

'Was a storm in a teaspoon,' Henry finished his sentence for him. 'I will walk you to your car.'

Hector said, 'Brandy. Come on,' and led Calypso into the house.

She said, 'He looks rather dishy, all plastered and haggard. I am not surprised the virgins wooed him.'

Hector said, 'The virgin who jumped on the table was on the point of busting her engagement.'

'Might be a good thing. She won't, though she rightly called him wet.'

'Dampish, I agree.' Hector poured a little brandy into a glass. 'For you?' he offered.

'No, thank you, I'll drive home.'

Hector poured more brandy into the glass and gulped. 'Ah, that's better.'

Joining them, Henry asked, 'Have *la jeunesse* gone to bed?'

Calypso said, 'So one supposes.'

Henry said, 'I would suggest sitting on the terrace, but it's immediately under my wife's window.'

Calypso said, 'It's very nice here,' and settled on the sofa.

Hector said, 'Couldn't you divorce her?'

Henry asked, 'For killing a cockatoo?' As neither Hector nor Calypso answered, he said, 'And who would look after her if I did?' He took the brandy Henry handed him. 'Tonight was my fault,' he said. 'She is OK left in bed. I get impatient. She *does* get up. *When* she wants to. *If* she wants to. I should have left well alone.'

'Well?' Calypso raised an eyebrow.

Henry said, 'Well enough. Better than tonight, let's say. I should never have bribed her with that dress.'

'She looked lovely in it,' said Calypso.

'I did not foresee the consequences. She was intoxicated by the girls' desire.' Henry gulped his brandy. 'No,' he said, 'I can't divorce her, I've been into all that,' and yawned.

'Come on, Hector, we must go home.' Calypso got off the sofa. 'We must let Henry get some sleep, he's exhausted.'

'A bath,' said Henry, 'then it will be time for haymaking. This is a busy time of year.'

Driving through the scented lanes with the car windows down and Hector half-asleep beside her, Calypso heard him say, 'That girl called him magnanimous.'

She said, 'So he is.'

'But not necessarily to young girls,' her husband murmured.

'You disappeared,' said James, overtaking the girls. 'I was worried stiff,' he told Barbara. He held her arm above the elbow, bringing her to a halt.

'I was with Henry,' said Barbara defensively, as Antonia walked on with Matthew.

'With Henry? Why?'

'Why not?' Barbara faced her lover. 'He is our host. We are staying in his house. It is customary to be polite to one's host, is it not?'

'Don't be like that.'

'Like what?'

'Snappy. You are engaged to me. I can't have you chasing Henry.'

'I am *not* snappy.' Barbara took stock of her intended. 'I was not chasing him,' she lied. 'If you must know,' she said crossly, 'I wanted to ask him about Valerie.'

'Valerie? Who is Valerie?' James's heart thumped in shock.

'Valerie with whom, so Margaret told us, you bounced in bed until the springs made such a racket you kept her awake. That Valerie.'

'Oh, *that* Valerie.' James attempted a laugh. 'She was just a friend. So has Margaret been making mischief? And what,' he asked rather cleverly, as he thought, 'did Henry tell you?'

'He said she was not a call-girl.'

'Well, there you are,' said James, relieved.

'And he said you weren't in love with her, but I took it that was just men sticking together. Weren't you in love with her?'

James lied courageously. 'Valerie was just an ordinary friend. She married some chap in insurance. I love *you*, darling, no one else. I should have thought I had made that pretty obvious. You can't have believed Margaret; she is one of those people who can't bear to see people happy. She's a nutcase.'

'I did believe her.'

'Oh, darling.' James put his arms round her. 'You

must not allow random malice to come between us. Margaret is mad.'

'She is not mad.'

'Malicious, then.' James stroked Barbara's hair.

'She ruined the party. It was a lovely party. She ruined that dress; it was *such* a beautiful dress.' Encompassed by James's arms, Barbara mourned the Dior dress. 'What an awful waste.'

'Some day I'll buy you a dress like that.'

'How soon?' She raised her face to be kissed.

'When we are married. A Dior maternity dress.'

'A *what*?' She pulled away from him.

James corrected himself. 'I'll buy you a Dior dress to celebrate our first baby.'

'Have I got to have a baby?' Barbara was dubious.

'Isn't that what marriage is for?'

'Suppose I don't want babies?' Barbara was discovering the pleasures of being difficult. 'Do we then bounce and break springs without the approval of Church and State?'

'Joking,' said James. 'I was joking.' There was much to be said for bouncing without strings, but Valerie had left him high and dry, bereft. 'Would you like me to come into your bed tonight,' he whispered, 'just for a cuddle?'

'Antonia is next door, she'd hear. And you wouldn't really want me to sleep with you before we are married.'

'People do,' James muttered, breathing into her hair.

'Not this person,' said Barbara virtuously. 'I am not Valerie.'

'Damn Valerie!' James exploded.

'So you *were* in love with her?' Barbara niggled.

'I was *not*,' James snapped, 'not one bit. If you insist on picking a quarrel,' he exclaimed, 'and ruining our engagement, that's OK by me.' I would be free, he

161

thought wildly; I could recapture Valerie, be her lover again. She knows she looks best naked; *she* doesn't bore on about Dior dresses.

Barbara began to cry. 'You are horrible. I thought you loved me. I am so tired.'

'I do love you, I do. Listen, sweetie, we are saying things neither of us mean. You must rest, have a hot bath, a good long soak, and a long sleep.' He kissed her wet cheeks. 'There, don't cry, tomorrow will be lovely.'

Barbara said, 'Oh, James,' and let him lead her to the house. 'You are right, I'd better hurry. If Antonia gets there first she takes for ever and all the hot water.' She kissed James fondly and raced up the stairs.

Antonia, too, had a dubious time with her intended. Matthew keenly resented being called wet. He was not to know that in years to come, when he had become a Member of Parliament, the term 'wet' would be considered by many to be one of approval. 'I am not wet,' he had said the moment he got Antonia alone. 'I will not stand for abuse.'

'I was upset,' Antonia riposted, 'and so would you have been if you had had a dead bird thrown in your face.'

'Only a bit of it.'

'A *bloody* bit,' Antonia raised her voice, 'and still warm.'

'Don't swear,' said Matthew. 'I can't stand women who swear.'

'You put up with a lot of swearing from Richard,' said Antonia, delving into the past, when Matthew had been her brother's friend.

'Richard was a boy.'

'He still is, though I sometimes wonder how much of one. Why are we talking of Richard?' she asked.

'You brought him up apropos swearing. You went off at a tangent.' Matthew remembered that Richard, much less lovely now than in his teens, had had the same evasive trait. 'You were telling me how shocked you had been by Margaret. I was more startled by the sight of her breasts.'

'Wobbling.' Antonia giggled. 'I *wish* she had not torn that dress, it was so beautiful. I longed to have it.'

'Must have cost Henry a pretty penny,' said Matthew. 'Commodities he is short of. The more fool he.'

'Is he badly off, then?' Antonia was surprised.

'Of course. Haven't you noticed how shabby the house is? The curtains in my room are rotting, I daren't draw them at night.'

'But Margaret's room?'

'Keeps her happy. Ebro's in the business. Gets a discount, I expect.'

'But the party. So lavish! All that drink.'

'I expect when he's used up his father's cellar, it will remain dry.'

'Poor Henry.'

'Of course he keeps his land in good heart, that's what he lives on. If you work as hard as Henry does, you make a living.'

'Why are we discussing Henry? And Henry's means, as I suppose you would call them. You want to be a man of means, don't you? I can smell it,' said Antonia.

'Nothing wrong with money,' said Matthew. 'It's only wrong when you haven't got it.'

'We've got miles from the point,' Antonia exclaimed. 'I thought we were standing here so that you could comfort me for the disgusting shock I suffered.'

'I thought you had got over it,' said Matthew, who, having himself recovered from the horrid scene, imagined Antonia would have done likewise.

'What *is* it going to be like married to you?' Once again Antonia felt like hitting her fiancé. And yet, she thought, I shall marry him.

Refusing to be drawn, one of the things which Antonia would later find supremely irritating, Matthew said, 'I think you are tired. God knows I am.'

'Good night, then,' Antonia snapped and left him without a kiss, racing to her room where, seeing her face in the glass still streaked with the cockatoo's blood, she felt quite sick, tore off her clothes and rushed to the bathroom, only to find the door locked. 'Barbara, let me in,' she shouted, thumping the door.

Barbara called out, 'Find another bathroom. I *must* soak in peace.'

Antonia leaned low to the keyhole and hissed through it, 'Bugger you, I hate you,' as though they were still at school, best friends having a tiff.

Muttering with rage, Antonia snatched the bedspread off the bed and wrapped it around herself. Setting off to find another bathroom, she padded barefoot to the head of the stairs. The house had gone quiet; there were no lights. Here, where the banisters sloped slippery to the hall, the cockatoo had launched himself. Antonia gulped. There would be a bathroom near Matthew and James, but for the moment she wanted no truck with Matthew. Margaret had a bathroom; she savoured the thought of running a bath, using preternatural force and drowning Margaret in its golden depths. She put her hand to her face, felt the cockatoo's blood still tacky on her cheek and retched. Her need for a bath was imperative.

Backtracking, she tried doors which opened into an airing cupboard, an empty room, a door leading to an attic stair, her own door and finally, very angrily, she tried Barbara's, but Barbara, anticipating this attack, had leapt from her bath, locked the door and returned to soak. Short of setting up a great hullaballoo and rousing the house, there would be no dislodging her.

Venturing further, Antonia explored until at last she was rewarded by the sound of a running tap; she opened a door and there, to her joy, was a bath in the middle of the room, a wash-basin on one wall and a lavatory. Beyond it a window stood open to the dawn and the sound of robins, thrushes, tits, wrens and finches revving up for another day.

As she hurried towards the basin there was a stirring by the bath as Humble and Cringe half-rose in welcome. In the bath Henry lay in steaming water, an open book blocking his view of the intruder. He said, 'Not now, Trask, please.'

Antonia said, 'It's me,' and froze.

'What do you want?' Henry lowered the book.

'I was looking for a bathroom. Barbara has bagged ours. She's so selfish. I've got to wash. My face is smeared with blood. I feel unclean. I can't bear it, I simply cannot.' Antonia's voice rose by several decibels. She was almost hysterical with disgust.

'Wash it in the basin.' Henry made no attempt to move.

'May I?'

'Of course.' Henry laid his book on a chair beside the bath and sank back in the water.

Antonia said, 'Oh! Right, I will. Thanks.' She ran the taps in the basin and, using both hands, splashed her face repeatedly.

Henry said, 'Now you will feel better. Use my towel.'

Drying her face, Antonia said, 'I am sorry to butt in on you.'

Henry said, 'That's all right.'

Antonia said, 'I felt if I went and used Matthew's

bathroom he would – er – he would start up all over again. We've had a row.'

Henry said, 'Yes.'

Antonia said, 'You have a lot of bathrooms for such an old-fashioned house.'

Henry said, 'My father had a thing about bathrooms. I suspect it was a guilt-induced desire to cleanse his sins. It's a usual form of mania; my mother approved of the plumbing so, although she kept him in check otherwise, she connived at the bathrooms. She used to say, there is no greater frustration than getting locked out of a bathroom.'

Antonia said, 'How I agree. I could have murdered Barbara just now and she's my best friend. She soaks for absolute hours.'

Henry said, 'So do I.'

Antonia said, 'With blood caking my face, feathers jarring against my teeth, I thought I'd go mad.'

Henry said, 'I am sick of that subject. Sit down.'

Antonia gaped at his lack of feeling, but sat obediently on the chair. She had not seen a man in a bath before and was at a loss as to how to behave. She said, 'Why didn't you bash your wife for killing it?'

Henry said, 'I try not to do what she wants me to do. To have hit her would have made her evening.'

Antonia said, 'How convoluted,' and tried not to look at Henry's penis swaying up like a periscope in the warm water. Modestly she drew the bedspread tighter round her shoulders.

Henry said, 'Shan't be long now, but as you are here, will you turn on the hot tap?'

Antonia complied.

Henry whooshed the water round, then, holding his nose, ducked under until he was completely submerged. When he did this Humble and Cringe stood up and looked anxiously into the bath. As Henry came

166

up, Antonia said, 'They were afraid you would drown.'

Henry said, 'Pass me my towel,' and, getting out of
the bath, said, 'It's all yours.' He pulled the plug,
wrapped the towel round his waist and left the room,
followed by the dogs.

When the water had gurgled away Antonia replaced
the plug and turned on the taps, bending over the bath
to stir hot water in with cold; she felt her head swim.
She realized that she was intoxicated, had been so for
some time, and that in that state she had insulted her
lover publicly.

18

Matthew and James met in the kitchen. The door and windows were open to the yard; they heard Pilar's voice and the clucking of hens.

James said, 'D'you suppose we are to find our own breakfast?' He sniffed doubtfully towards the stove. 'Aha! Coffee,' he said, relieved, 'and hot milk.' He lifted the coffee pot. 'For you?' he offered.

'Black,' said Matthew. 'No sugar.'

'Like that. I see,' said James. '*I* didn't overdo it. I'm pretty perky. I wonder where our girls are? Still asleep, no doubt.' He answered his own question. 'The girls, I said, my Barbara and your Antonia.'

Matthew grunted and, picking up a cup, held it while James poured coffee.

Had it been imagination or had the girls behaved a bit oddly with Henry last night? There goes my fertile imagination, James told himself; I must not let it rip. Henry was host; they were obliged to play up to him. 'Your hands are shaking,' he said to Matthew.

Matthew said, 'Belt up,' and sat at the table holding his cup with both hands. 'God, I needed that,' he said. 'Shouldn't have had that night-cap.'

'You should drink a glass of water and swallow two aspirin last thing after a party,' advised James. 'I do.'

Matthew made no reply.

'Good morning. Lovely day.' Pilar bustled in from the yard. 'Fresh,' she said, holding up a colander full of eggs. 'Still warm from the hen. Who would like omelette or eggs and bacon, our own pig?'

Flinching, Matthew said, 'No thanks.'

James said, 'Super! Eggs and bacon, splendid.' He sat at the table.

Matthew said, 'Dry toast,' adding, 'please.'

Pilar pursed her lips and replenished Matthew's cup, murmuring, 'Aspirin,' as she placed a tactful bottle to hand. 'Take two now, two later,' she said gently.

With his back to the light Matthew muttered, 'Thanks.'

Pilar urged: 'Go on, swallow.'

'What I need is Fernet Branca,' said Matthew, but catching Pilar's eye popped the pills in his mouth.

Pilar said, 'Well done,' and set to work on James's breakfast.

At the first hint of bacon fat Matthew took his cup and moved to the open door.

'In a moment, dry toast,' Pilar called after him.

Watching Pilar turn the bacon in the pan and break in eggs, James thought, Valerie taught me the aspirin trick. Full of handy tips, that girl. One would not want Barbara to be so experienced. One would wish to be the one to inform Barbara; a wife should learn from her husband. He cast his mind back, trying to remember how Valerie had got on with Henry.

Pilar said, 'Lovely day for a swim or a ride.' She flipped the bacon rashers over. 'Or a long walk,' she suggested, 'if you cannot ride?'

'Of course I can ride,' said James huffily. This is like riding, Valerie had said, and the other way up, she had said, Ride me, ride me. Oh Lord, how would it be with Barbara? 'Oh, thanks,' he said as Pilar dished up the bacon and eggs. 'Delicious.'

Matthew turned his back and accustomed his eyes to the sunlight.

'Hullo, hullo, hullo.' Antonia came rushing into the kitchen, followed by Barbara. 'Good morning, everybody. What a gorgeous day! Oh, lovely smell of coffee. Any for us?'

Barbara bent to kiss James's cheek which bulged with bacon. 'Morning, greedy.'

Antonia sidled up to Matthew, putting her arm around his neck. 'Oh, Matthew, darling, I was terrible to you last night. Will you forgive me? Say you will. I haven't slept a wink, tossing all night in an agony of self-reproach and remorse.'

'You look very well on it.' Matthew drew away.

'Darling, please, darling.' Antonia swayed closer.

'You were overwrought,' said Matthew, responding to her soft pressure.

'I was,' Antonia admitted. 'I was indeed.'

James, with his mouth full of egg, said, 'Jolly plucky, the way you leapt on the table and tackled that—'

'That's enough,' Pilar broke in. 'Today is today and beautiful.'

'Quite right, Pilar. I would like to spend all day alone with you,' Antonia whispered in Matthew's ear and nuzzled his neck. 'Darling.'

Matthew felt a rush of pleasurable emotion. His eyes filled and he heard himself exclaim, 'I believe I could manage some breakfast after all, Pilar. Perhaps a little crisp bacon with tomato?'

Pilar repeated, 'Tomato, crisp bacon with dry toast.'

With her fiancé's arm round her waist, Antonia thought, Phew! That's over, and with her father in mind renewed her resolution regarding alcohol and cross words.

Barbara had not spoken during this exchange, but put bread in the toaster, helped herself to coffee and ranged butter and marmalade by her plate. She now announced: 'The first thing I must do this morning is

170

visit Margaret. She must be feeling dreadful, poor woman, after last night.' She enjoyed the surprised silence she caused, a silence broken only by the clatter of toast leaping in the toaster.

James said, 'What magnanimity! Gosh!'

'No gosh about it. Common manners.' Barbara spread butter and marmalade while James stared at her, thinking, Valerie would never in a thousand years have thought of this. Valerie—

'And speaking of manners,' said Barbara, biting her toast, 'you haven't even said good morning, James, sitting there stuffing bacon and eggs.' She laughed, aware that on the snakes and ladders of courtship she had moved up one.

'I suppose you wouldn't like to take a picnic to the lake and swim,' suggested James, 'after visiting Margaret? Just us. Walking hand in hand?' He watched her reaction. 'Spend the day?' he said. 'Together?'

'Love to, but first we must go up there.' Barbara pointed in the direction of the ceiling.

James said, 'Very well,' and, leaning across the table, kissed her. 'Good morning, Barbara.' Barbara looked pleased. She had walked with Henry holding her hand last night and it had been strangely agreeable, yet earlier, sitting with Hector and Calypso, he had been as cruel as his wife made out; James would not be cruel. Inept, yes, but not cruel. Nor would he indulge in call-girls.

Matthew said, 'If it's OK by you, Pilar, Antonia and I will picnic. Or we could get lunch in the pub if you'd like that?' Antonia nodded. 'We can sit on one side of the lake while you sit on the other,' he said to James. 'But what about Henry? Shouldn't we—'

''E is working on the hay with Trask. 'E said, you amuse yourselves.' Pilar grilled bacon for Matthew's toast.

171

'And Ebro?' Matthew asked. If James had not absorbed Barbara's hint about manners, he would show that he was not lacking. 'How is Ebro?'

''E cleared up last night's mess and went back to London. 'E has work.' Pilar, amused, let her eyes travel from Matthew to James. 'I was thinking,' she said, 'with this good start you all have as happy marriage as Hector and Calypso. Your breakfast.' She put Matthew's plate in front of him.

'But Calypso only married Hector because he's rich,' Antonia and Barbara chorused. 'She was not in love with Hector, Pilar.'

'That's what she says.' Pilar showed her horsey teeth. 'Is joke.'

'He loves her, that's possible, she did after all give him a son. But she? Oh *no*, Pilar, it was for money, definitely.'

'Is good marriage,' said Pilar tartly. 'See if you can do as well.'

'She is foreign, of course,' said James as he climbed the stairs with Barbara. 'Foreigners have peculiar standards.'

Barbara said, 'Hum. Yes, I dare say.'

Left with Matthew, Antonia said, 'All the same, there is something about the Grants that is enviable. Apart from their money, I mean.'

Irritated, for his stomach was still unsettled, Matthew said, 'One might as well envy that pair of queens who were here last night.'

Antonia grinned. 'They seemed happy, though.' Tamping down a smidgin of doubt, faint residue of last night's rage, she said, 'Come on, eat up, Matthew. Let's get cracking and have a wonderful day.'

'Shall we get it over, then?' James caught Barbara's eye as they stood, hesitating, at the top of the stairs.

Barbara, taking a deep breath, said, 'Yes,' and nerving herself tapped on Margaret's door, then without pausing for an answer walked in. She would show James that she was strong, not to be trifled with, that she was not in the same league as Valerie, if indeed Valerie existed. She would show James that she was no nincompoop who believed tall stories invented by a dangerous lunatic who danced on tables, strangled cockatoos and ripped up Dior dresses.

'We have come to see how you are,' she said, advancing into the room, 'after the party. Not too tired, we hope?' she said, trying to keep her voice sympathetic and non-belligerent.

My word, thought James, she's plucky, she has a splendid nerve. Bully for her, that's my girl.

'Oh, do come in,' said Margaret. 'How nice to see you,' she said sweetly. 'Wasn't it a splendid party? I did enjoy it. Isn't Henry wonderful to plan a surprise like that? He is so good to me, so kind.' She lay against her pillows and smiled at her visitors. 'It's lovely to see you, do sit down, my dears. How are the other two?'

'Gone out,' said James and sat quickly on a small gold chair to enjoy the spectacle of Barbara coping with this volte-face.

Barbara, fearing for the small chair, positioned herself on the sofa and drew a deep breath.

'They are so in love, those two,' said Margaret. 'As you must be.' She smiled at Barbara and then at James. 'It is good of you to come and see me, I *am* pleased.' Margaret watched them. She looked rather younger than last night and more beautiful. Her hair lay loose on her shoulders, her eyes sparkled like silver in her pale face, her mouth this morning wore no lipstick. 'It's a joy to watch young people in love,' she said. 'Rewarding.' She savoured the word and repeated it. 'Rewarding.'

James crossed his legs and cleared his throat. Barbara said, 'We—'

'I have been thinking,' Margaret said, 'in the night. I am not a good sleeper, you know. How nice it would be if you all came more often. It would be wonderful for me, and company for Henry. He gets lonely. Not that he complains, oh no, but with me always in bed, and he works so hard on his wretched farm, he needs people of his own sort, not just Spanish servants and poor old Trask—'

James cleared his throat. 'Didn't Trask work for Henry's father?'

'If you call it work, yes. Some people say, or shall I say, it has been said? There's a subtle difference. I believe that Trask is really Henry's uncle. You know how those old country families get mixed up with their tenants. Tenanting is the word, I think.'

'I think that's rubbish,' said Barbara from the sofa. 'They aren't in the least alike.'

Margaret said, 'No, of course they are not. Silly me. I just love a bit of embroidery. What a nice literal girl you are. I got a rise, though, didn't I?' And she winked at James.

James uncrossed his legs.

'What it amounts to,' said Margaret, 'is that Trask should be pensioned off, but Henry won't hear of it, he's too soft. The man's got his old age pension, but no, Henry won't. He can't afford a proper man, he spends so much on me, the house is shamefully shabby, and last night was pathetic or should I say bathetic; he wore his grandfather's clothes because he can't or won't afford new ones. Then he gives that party! So generous. So kind! His generosity is boundless. How can I repay him?'

Barbara opened her mouth.

James said, 'I—'

174

'I do try to economize,' said Margaret. 'I only have my face done once a month, and that's for Henry's sake. I tell him he should let part of the house or take paying guests, but he won't hear of that. He insists he will only have his friends. I tell him other people make their friends pay, but he won't listen. Good Lord,' Margaret went on, 'if all his friends who bring their girls for weekends paid their whack – and it's not always the same girls – are you uncomfortable, James?' she asked, for James had risen.

'Afraid my weight would break the chair,' said James urbanely. 'My mother used to scream at me if I sat on unsubstantial but precious chairs. I was about to move to the sofa and put my arm round the girl I bring down for weekends.' And he suited the action to the word, encircling Barbara with his arm. 'Actually,' he said, 'we mustn't tire you; we only popped in for a minute. We are going to picnic by the lake and swim, if it's warm enough.'

'Then I mustn't keep you. Have a good time.' Margaret seemed to lose interest.

'I couldn't get a word in edgeways,' said Barbara as they walked downstairs.

'One would think,' said James, as they set off across the fields to the lake, 'that nothing out of the ordinary took place last night.'

'I do mourn that dress,' said Barbara.

'I promise I will buy you one. You are a brave and splendid girl.' James stopped, put his arms round her and kissed her warmly.

Barbara said, 'That's nice, do it again.'

'I feel,' said James, 'what the French call *ému*. What's the word in English?'

'Doesn't matter,' said Barbara, kissing him. They walked on hand in hand.

James said, 'Actually, it's rather a good idea.'

Barbara said, 'What is? Buying me a dress?'

'No. What she suggested. Coming here as paying guests, we could sort of share. It would be cheaper than a cottage and Pilar keeps it running, anyway.'

Barbara said, 'James!'

James said, 'If we did pay, just a bit, not all that much, we could come whenever we wanted, not wait to be invited.'

'James, she's a crazy woman.'

'It isn't a crazy suggestion. I shall think it over. We could come here often and bring the children.'

Barbara said, 'What children?'

'Ours, silly. I shall talk to Matthew. Henry may have discussed it all with Margaret.'

'They are not on those terms,' said Barbara.

'You never know what goes on between married people,' James said sententiously.

Barbara grinned and said, 'What a funny mind you have.'

'What d'you mean by that?' James eyed her sharply.

'You'll find out when we are married.' She laughed.

'And if you don't like sailing, you could come here while I sail.' James spoke half to himself.

'Or go shopping *chez* Dior,' said Barbara. 'Super!'

James made no reply but took her hand.

'There's the lake,' said Barbara, 'over there, look.'

James said, 'I wonder what it's like to swim in?'

Barbara said, 'Let's find out,' remembering and keeping to herself her magical swim of the day before.

'There are the others,' said James. 'Let's go the other side; they will want to be on their own. I dare say Antonia wants to make it up to Matthew, she behaved rather badly last night.'

'What makes you think that?'

Not liking her tone, James said, 'She called him—'

'Wet,' said Barbara, 'and he was.'

'Barbara.' James was stirred by masculine loyalty. 'Matthew is not the sort to be wet—'

Scenting trouble, Barbara said, 'Why don't we strip? I can see that the others have.' And I wonder how I compare with Valerie, she thought, as she took off her clothes.

But James was not comparing her with Valerie. 'You are lovely,' he said, 'absolutely smashing,' and tried to catch her before she dived. I am a lucky fellow, he thought, nipping out of his trousers.

Catching up with Barbara in mid-lake, James trod water. 'Let me kiss you,' he said, and when they had kissed, 'I shall ask Matthew what he thinks.'

'About what?' She shook the water from her ears.

'Sharing Henry's house.'

'Not a good idea.'

'Yes it is.'

'Antonia won't think so,' Barbara jeered.

'I bet you are wrong there and Henry—'

'Do we share Henry as well as his house? I'm getting cold, I'm going in.' She swam for the bank.

James shouted, 'Don't be like that,' and followed her. 'It would help Henry,' he said as he climbed the bank.

Barbara said, 'I don't see how, and I am like that.'

James said, 'I don't want to argue.' It suddenly seemed of vital importance to get his own way. He had rarely got his own way with Valerie.

'Ask Matthew then and see what Antonia says.' Barbara dried herself and stepped into her knickers. 'Hand me my sweater,' she said, 'I am cold.'

'Matthew will see the sense of it, leap at the idea. And Antonia—'

'Antonia will say, You must be joking,' scoffed Barbara. 'That you are out of your tiny mind.' Suddenly an argument which had started half-joking

177

became serious. It had not occurred to James that men in couples engaged or married did not run the show, but here was Barbara overruling him.

'Let's go and ask them,' said James, who had put on his shoes. 'Race you round the lake.'

Barbara, with one shoe on and one shoe off, watched him run; he ran well, she thought. He looked rather splendid. She pulled on her shoe and ambled good-naturedly in his wake. 'I should have hurried,' she said later to Antonia, 'put on a spurt.'

'It would have made no odds,' her friend replied.

Arriving, Barbara found that James had set his idea in train and Matthew was listening. One of the things Barbara had yet to discover about James was that in matters of business he could be both brief and imaginative. Matthew, sitting by the lake on a hot summer day, was enthusiastic.

'It could work a treat,' he said. 'Save everybody a lot of trouble.'

'How d'you work that out?' asked Antonia.

'And money,' said Matthew, ignoring her. 'Syndicates are the thing these days.'

James said, 'Absolutely.'

'Nice to be near friends,' said Matthew.

'What friends?' asked Antonia.

'The Grants—'

'You hardly know them,' said Antonia.

'Don't quibble, darling.' Matthew stretched out and took her hand.

'What about Margaret?' Barbara had not yet spoken.

'You saw her yourself this morning,' said James.

'And how was she?' asked Antonia.

'As kind and normal as any country house hostess I've ever come across. Barbara will bear me out on that. Very concerned for Henry. She thinks he over-works; she thinks he's lonely. Actually, in a way, it was

178

she who started the idea. I suspect she worries about the place getting run down and leaps at the idea of putting a bit of life into it.'

'That's not what she said,' said Barbara.

'It's what she meant,' said James.

Barbara, thinking of Margaret and the insinuations she had made when she and Antonia had visited her first, opened her mouth to speak but closed it; it was not for her to resurrect Valerie or spread rumours of Henry's sexual mores.

'You must admit,' James was saying, 'that she couldn't have been nicer this morning.'

'But what about last night?' said Antonia.

'Some sort of *crise*,' said James. 'A joke which turned sour, something like that.'

Antonia and Barbara exchanged glances.

'No harm in putting the idea to Henry,' said Matthew, yawning. 'Are you going to swim again? There's a lot to be said for a private lake. I'm going in. Race you across, James.'

Barbara stood with her friend watching the young men swim naked, racing like seals.

Antonia said, 'They shrink in cold water.'

Barbara said, 'What?' and as Antonia did not reply she said reproachfully, 'You did not put up much of a fight.'

'Because I'm not altogether against it,' said Antonia and began to laugh. 'Oh my, my!' she said, laughing. 'I foresee repercussions.'

Part Three

1958

19

'Don't let her take all the best veg this weekend, you know what she's like.' Jonathan eased his back and leaned on his hoe.

'Don't hoe any deeper than that,' said John. 'Remember the carrot-fly.'

'She's avaricious,' agreed his older friend. 'My poor back,' he said, 'is giving me gyp. What time are they coming?'

'They usually arrive about six to suit infant Susan's bedtime, as you well know,' sighed John.

'Ah,' said the older man, 'that baby! If we don't watch out, she will have those carrots. It isn't only your back; mine is in sympathetic agony,' he said, stretching. The friends laid their hoes aside and relaxed on a seat under a fig tree.

It was four years since the summer dinner party; there had been changes at Cotteshaw. For eighteen months now the Jonathans had rented the walled garden from Henry, adding its produce to that of their own cottage and retailing it from a stall at the local market, along with their hams, sausages, bacon, eggs, chickens and herbs.

'If we don't watch out she will have those carrots,' repeated John crossly. 'I spotted her eyeing them last week. It's a sin to mash baby carrots, let's fob her off with spinach. It's supposed to be good for infants.'

'An exploded myth,' said the older man. 'But she won't know,' he added cheerfully.

The 'she' the Jonathans referred to was Antonia Stephenson, who nowadays came regularly with Matthew and their baby for weekends to occupy a pair of bedrooms they had redecorated with Ebro's help, and make free with the drawing room and other downstairs rooms, as did James and Barbara who came less regularly, but whose foothold at Cotteshaw was equally strong.

'She told Pilar that she wants another child,' said John, puffing out a moustache longer and more luxuriant than it had been at the party; it almost concealed his lower lip.

'Oh God,' said Jonathan. 'As if the world was not overpopulated. I bet it's Matthew, not Antonia, who wants it. Antonia's not particularly maternal.'

'Matthew wants a son; poor little Susie is the wrong sex,' said the younger man. 'Does Antonia know Henry is away, one wonders?'

'The absence of Henry is balanced by Pilar,' said Jonathan. 'Their au pair has the weekend off and Pilar is potty about babies and takes the little mite off her parents' hands.'

'Lucky mite.' The two men surveyed their rows of spring vegetables: trim, neat, succulent, geometric; their *oeuvre*.

'We shall get a fine crop of figs,' said the younger man, looking up into the tree. 'Babies don't like figs.'

'Nor do they like artichokes,' said his friend.

'Tell you what, why don't we pull these carrots now? Then, what the eye doesn't see, the heart won't miss.'

'Good idea,' said Jonathan, getting to his feet. 'She has to learn. Last year she and Matthew scooped the lot. We'll tell her they had carrot-fly and we lost the crop; she knows nothing about gardening.'

'Is Barbara coming?' asked John, as they set to to pull the carrots. 'And James?'

'I heard Pilar say James is sailing this weekend, so she may come alone.'

'That's no way to match up with Antonia,' said John thoughtfully.

'Does she want to?' asked Jonathan.

'They have always run in tandem, it would be funny if she didn't. I was a bit surprised she let Antonia produce first,' said John. 'Not that I enjoy watching the process. Although the end result is OK if one goes by tiny Susie.'

'Barbara's effort will also be dumped on Pilar. Those girls take advantage,' said Jonathan.

'Pilar doesn't mind; they are a change from Margaret.'

'At least Margaret remains barren,' snorted Jonathan. 'And fair do's, they pay rent, which helps Henry keep the house going; no use hankering after old times.'

'These new times, though – sometimes you'd think the whole place belonged to that lot,' grumbled John.

'Well, at least they won't get these carrots,' said his lover amiably. 'And if Barbara starts off with a boy, Antonia's nose will be twisted.'

'We'd better give a bunch to Pilar for Margaret,' said Jonathan as they ambled towards their car. 'She refused to eat them last season, so she may like them this. What do you think?'

'She threw the vegetable dish at Hector and Lysander, according to Pilar; they gobbled them up off the carpet,' said John. 'All right, it's worth a try, but make it a small bunch, darling.'

'Is Henry delivering the new potatoes?' questioned Jonathan. 'If he is, it's very good of him.'

'A consignment for Barbara and James – James doesn't want his new car sullied by sacks of pots. Matthew and Antonia are not so precious,' said John.

'Matthew and Antonia have not got a new car, my dear.'

'And why,' said John, 'is it so good of Henry to ferry a bag of potatoes for us, if I may make so bold as to ask?'

'It wastes time which might be better occupied,' answered the older man. 'He doesn't often get away from the farm.'

'And how, one wonders, does Henry occupy his time? I believe you would like him to be trolling round the sleazy joints of Soho.'

Jonathan laughed. 'I would like to think he was lunching with a pretty woman and doing what comes naturally afterwards. But you know, and I know, he visits his bank and his solicitor, has his hair cut, buys Margaret an expensive present he can't afford, browses among the new books at Hatchards and, if he feels peckish, has a sandwich in a pub.'

'Right,' said the younger man. 'And the odds are that Margaret chucks the expensive present out of the window.'

'Let's face it, my dear,' said the older man, as he climbed into the driving seat. 'Henry leads a pretty boring life.'

'And who is responsible for that?' niggled the younger man, expecting no answer and receiving none.

Henry drove west towards Chelsea to deliver James and Barbara's sack of new potatoes. He had visited his bank and his solicitor, and had his hair cut at Penhaligon's. From Fortnum & Mason he had bought Margaret a present, the cost of which had made him linger less than usual in Hatchards.

James and Barbara's small, steep house was in that part of Chelsea equidistant from the Brompton and

King's Roads; it faced north but had a garden at the back which was sunny. Here, in their first flush of marriage, James had planted a wisteria and Barbara a vine.

Henry's brakes squealed as he drew up. He humped the potatoes down the area steps and rang the bell. Anybody passing could help themselves to the potatoes, he thought, as nobody answered. Perhaps the cleaning lady was operating the Hoover; he would try the front door. Idly he pressed the bell with his thumb. The door flew open. Barbara stood in the half-dark of a narrow hall. She said, 'Oh!' and, backing away, tried to shut the door.

Henry put his foot in the jamb. 'I brought the spuds you wanted from the Jonathans.'

Barbara said hoarsely, 'Oh, thanks, Henry. Could you move your foot?'

Henry said, 'No,' and pushed the door.

Barbara pushed back.

Henry said, 'What's the matter, Barbara?' and pushed harder.

Barbara said, 'I was washing my hair.'

Pushing the door open, Henry said, 'So I see,' and walked in, closing the door behind him.

Barbara had a towel wrapped round her head, but under it her face was white with greyish blotches and her nose and eyes were puffed and swollen.

Henry said, 'Have you been crying?'

Barbara answered crossly, 'I got shampoo in my eyes.'

Henry looked past her into the hall. 'Would you like to come out to lunch?'

Barbara yelped, 'No,' and tears coursed freshly down her cheeks.

Henry said, 'What's the matter, Barbara? What's wrong?'

Barbara shook her head and tried to wipe her tears with a corner of the towel. 'Nothing.'

Henry said, 'Where is James?'

Barbara said, 'Sailing,' spinning the word into a wail.

'Who with?'

Barbara let out a loud hiccuping cry.

Henry put both arms round her and held her close; she leaned against his chest and howled. The towel round her head fell off. Henry held her with one hand and gently stroked her damp hair with the other. He said, 'You've had a row.'

Barbara nodded against his shirt.

Henry said, 'Delicious shampoo.' Then he said, 'You'll give yourself a headache.'

She said, 'I've got one.'

He still stroked her hair, teasing it away from her face. He said, 'Let's go and sit down somewhere,' and led her upstairs to her drawing room. The sun was shining in quite nicely through the window at the back and the wisteria and vine framed it as Barbara and James had hoped it would. Henry made Barbara sit on the sofa and sat beside her with his arm round her and his legs stretched out. He said, 'This row?'

Barbara said, 'Valerie,' her voice choking up into a whoop.

Henry's eyebrows went up, but he said nothing. Barbara pushed back her hair with a shaky hand and said, 'I've ruined your tie.'

Henry squinted at his tie, which was indeed smeared with tears and snot. He said, 'No matter, it will clean.'

From another garden came the sound of children's voices, squeaks of enjoyment and laughter. Henry said gently, 'This row?'

Barbara snuffled, took a deep breath and said, 'He's gone down to his boat on the Solent; he likes sailing.'

Aware of James's penchant for small boats, Henry said, 'Yes?'

'It's the baby,' Barbara began. 'The baby he wants to have. He wants it so much that I've become infected; *I* want it too. I never particularly – well, not much I don't think, well, not until Antonia – Then, when Antonia did, of course I thought I would too. I threw my Dutch cap out of the window and *nothing happened.*' Barbara's voice, husky with crying, trailed to a halt.

Henry remained quiet, holding her with her head against his shoulder. She said, 'Have you got a handkerchief? This towel is soaking and making my nose sore.' Henry fished a handkerchief from his cuff and gave it to her. I could do with some new shoes, he thought, looking down at his feet. I got this pair in the war, they are years old but lasted well. He crossed his feet at the ankles. Barbara dropped the towel on the floor and blew her nose in the handkerchief. 'We had a *terrible* row,' she said. 'He's been niggling at me for not getting pregnant.' She balled the handkerchief in her fist. 'Making biblical allusions to barren women. It's stupid because he never reads the Bible, hasn't since school, I should think. Anyway, he keeps saying it's my fault, that I'm not fertile, that I can't, that I'm not trying, that I don't care. And all the time I *know* it's him.' Barbara sobbed again, gasping for breath.

There was a blackbird singing in a neighbouring garden, the chatter of sparrows. In the street a taxi drew up. Its door slammed, it drove away.

Barbara said, 'You see, it's James. He doesn't know I know he went to see a specialist – he'd made *me* go ages ago; it was horribly embarrassing. He doesn't know I looked through his letters and read the result of the tests he had, he doesn't know I know there's a ninety per cent chance he may never father a child, he doesn't know I know his sperm isn't active or up to

189

much. He doesn't think I'm the sort of girl who reads her husband's letters – so when, this morning, he said he was going sailing and why didn't I come for once, sea-sickness wasn't morning sickness, it popped out. We'd been arguing about moving house; he'd said, "We will need a bigger house when we have a family." I said, "What family? We are not very likely to have a family with your pollen count so low." I'd forgotten the proper medical term, of course. Oh, Henry, he *exploded.*'

Henry murmured, 'Pride.'

'Of course,' Barbara shouted, 'his pride. Henry, he yelled at me. I've never seen him so worked up; he positively screamed. He went on and on and then quite suddenly he stopped, stared at me, then went to the telephone and I heard him ring up Valerie and ask her to go sailing with him. Henry, do you suppose he's been seeing her all this time?'

'And did she say she would?'

'I wouldn't know. I'd left the room, slammed the door, shut myself in the loo. Of course she said yes.'

Henry murmured, 'Mm.'

'The dreadful thing is, Henry, that I never really believed she existed. I half thought, I hoped she was one of Margaret's inventions. You know what Margaret's like.'

Henry said, 'Boring girl. She married a millionaire.'

'So she *does* exist! What is she like?'

'Dull.'

'But in *bed*?'

'I wouldn't know.'

'Oh.'

'Look, Barbara.' Henry sat up straight. 'I'm starving, it's long after my lunch-time. Put some black specs on and come and eat.'

'Henry!'

'Buck up. Come on, your hair is dry.'

'I can't come like this.'

'Yes you can, don't argue. You don't have to impress me.'

Henry took her to a quiet and dark restaurant, which seemed even darker viewed through her black glasses. A waiter led them to a remote table. As Barbara sat down, she said, 'James will never forgive me for reading his letters.'

Henry, studying the wine list, said, 'He is probably relieved that you did.'

Barbara said, 'Oh?', disbelieving.

Henry ordered wine and asked the waiter to bring it quickly. It was delicious, sliding down her throat, sore with weeping, as innocuously as barley water. Barbara drained her glass while Henry ordered lunch; the waiter refilled it, and brought smoked trout.

Barbara said, 'I am too upset to eat.'

Henry said, 'Don't be a fool. Eat some bread and butter with it,' and she obeyed.

When tiny lamb cutlets with green peas, French beans and minuscule new potatoes appeared she failed to protest, but ate them with mint and redcurrant jellies while admiring the conjunction of colours.

The waiter changed their plates and brought them succulent artichokes from Brittany. Barbara drank more wine.

Henry said, 'What garbage did Margaret concoct about Valerie?'

Barbara scraped an artichoke leaf across her lower teeth. 'She said they bounced in bed and the springs made so much noise it kept her awake.'

Henry said, 'Well, I never!' and laughed.

Barbara said, 'It is not at all funny.'

Henry said, 'I find it so, and anyway James had not met you in those days.'

191

'But it happened, and he yearns for her.' Barbara's voice rose.

Henry said, 'Don't start up again, you will embarrass me.'

Barbara said, 'I shouldn't think, after being married to Margaret all these years, that anyone could embarrass you.'

Henry said, 'I see you feel better. Let me refill your glass.'

Barbara allowed this. They were on to their second bottle and finishing their artichokes. She regretfully ate the last bit of heart and, dabbling her fingers in the finger-bowl, tweaked at a borage flower floating in the water.

Henry said, 'Could you manage crême brulée or mountain strawberries?'

Barbara was game. Henry ordered, and coffee for both of them. He said, 'If you were to see Valerie, you would stop fussing.'

Barbara said, 'I don't *want* to see her. What's she like?'

Henry said, 'Blond, tall, rather long torso, big bottom but beginning to sag in front, a voice that grates.'

Barbara said, 'Grates?'

'On the nerves,' Henry said. 'And I seem to remember she didn't smell too good.'

'Smell?'

'Wrong kind of scent, too strong. One wondered what it covered up.'

'Oh!'

Henry asked, 'More coffee?'

Barbara said, 'I think I'd better,' rather primly.

Henry ordered more coffee and asked for the bill.

Barbara said, 'James is kind, James is sweet, I love him.'

Henry said, 'Of course you do,' and calculated the tip.

192

Barbara went on, 'I want to make him happier and be more wonderful than Valerie ever did. I want to hold him close in my arms but so far I disappoint him.'

'You weren't in love with him when you married him.' Henry was matter-of-fact.

Barbara cried, 'But I am now,' her voice rising.

Henry said, 'I'll walk you home,' and led her out into the street.

Barbara said, 'Gosh. The sun! Mine eyes dazzle,' and rocked on her high heels. Henry took her arm.

20

On the doorstep Henry asked, 'Got your key?' Taking it from her, he let them into the house. The hall was cool and dark, the street noises muffled. Barbara kicked off her shoes, took off her dark glasses and, laying them on the hall table, stood adjusting her eyes to the change.

Henry said, 'Upstairs. It's time for a siesta,' and gave her a push. In her bedroom he helped her undress.

In bed Barbara said, 'I've never done it like this,' and, 'I say, I like that!' and, 'I wonder whether James—' and, 'I bet Valerie doesn't—' and, 'I never knew you could—' and dissolved into helpless giggles.

Henry got out of bed and drew the curtains.

Barbara said, 'I'm sorry I laughed.'

Henry said, 'Half the fun of bed is laughter,' and settled back in the bed with his arm round her shoulders.

Barbara said, 'I had not realized about the laughter. Thanks.'

Henry stretched his legs down the bed until his toes stuck out at the bottom.

'Margaret,' Barbara said, 'told Antonia and me that you were homosexual.'

'And?' Henry yawned.

'Horses.' Barbara snuffled with merriment.

Henry said, 'Go to sleep,' and turned on his side.

Barbara said, 'Call-girls! You told me call-girls, long ago. Is this what you—'

Henry said, 'Oh, Barbara, grow up.'

When Barbara woke, Henry was gone. She sat up, pushing her hair from her face. She felt extremely well. She got out of bed and began picking her clothes off the floor. As she put her dress on a hanger and moved towards the cupboard to hang it, the telephone rang; it was Antonia.

'Are you coming down this weekend? We thought you'd be here and you're not.'

'I had a sort of migraine.'

'You don't have migraine.'

'Well, I *did*. It's better.'

'Are you coming? It's so lovely. Henry is away. The boyfriends say he went to London and took some of their potatoes.'

'He left some in our area. I was out.'

'Are you coming? Do come, it's dull without you. We are going to swim.'

Barbara said, 'I'll see, I might come tomorrow. James is sailing.'

'Then you must come, don't be lonely.'

Barbara said, 'I'll see—' and replaced the receiver.

She felt relaxed and lethargic. She tidied the bed, changing the sheets, slapping the pillows, humming a tune. She opened the window wide, pulling back the curtains. The blackbird was singing again in the neighbour's garden. Someone had their radio on; it was Mozart, no, Bizet. She ran the bath.

Lying in the bath, she heard James's key click in the front door. He shouted anxiously up the stairs, 'Darling?'

Barbara called back, 'I'm in the bath,' and listened as he slammed the front door shut and raced up the stairs. She sponged her face, pressing the warm sponge to her nose.

James came in and stood looking down at her.

Barbara looked up at him. James said, 'Darling, I love you so. Oh God, why don't you say: And how was Valerie?' His face was white.

Barbara smiled.

James said, 'I've had a rotten day. The tide was all wrong and no wind. Valerie wasn't with me; you knew that, I suppose? I made it up, I pretended I was talking to her. I sailed alone and got stuck on a mud bank, I've been thinking of you all day. I'm so ashamed. So sorry. Oh, darling!'

Barbara said, 'Help me out of the bath,' and held up her hands.

'Are you hurt? Are you all right? What happened?'

Barbara said, 'I'm fine, never better.'

James wrapped her towel round her and held her. He said, 'I was monstrous. I love you so much, I can't think why I – Oh, Barbara!' He was near tears.

Barbara said, 'Hush my love, hush. I love you too,' and put her arms round his neck. 'I'll make you all wet,' she said.

'As if it mattered,' James exclaimed. And then, 'Do you think it's too early to go to bed? I do so want to hold you and – oh, I've been thinking of you all day—'

Barbara said, 'Not a bit too early, get undressed.' Her voice was still throaty from the morning's tears. 'Hurry up,' she said as she pulled back the sheet and, picking an almost black hair from the pillow, got into bed. 'I'm still damp,' she said. 'Antonia telephoned, wanted me to go down to Cotteshaw—'

James said, 'Oh God, I might have come in and found you gone. What an awful thought. I should have been totally suicidal, thought you'd left me.'

'I haven't left you.'

'No, thanks be. And let's stay here, have the weekend – Unless you want to go down, then of course we—'

She said, 'No, no. All I want is to be more wonderful and loving and fun in bed than Valerie.'

James said. 'I can't *think* what I saw in Valerie. She chucked me, you know. I never told you, did I? But she was already going off, I mean her looks, like soft fruit. And she went right off *me* and she had such a sharp tongue. Oh, darling, let's forget about Valerie.'

Barbara said, 'Willingly.'

James said, 'Then later on we will go and have a super tremendous dinner. I'll think of a restaurant. Did you have any lunch?'

Barbara said, 'I had a sort of snack,' and kissed him.

As she drifted off to sleep Barbara remembered Henry's socks. Handknitted and longer than the socks James wore, Henry's socks reached to just below the knee. They were cable-stitched in brilliant scarlet silk and the braces which supported his trousers were scarlet, too. I must get some for James, she thought; blue would be nice.

While Barbara slept, James felt an immense tenderness and an absurd, it must be absurd, gratitude to Valerie for bringing this about. He realized that he had fallen in love with his wife and was filled with inordinate desire and lust. Valerie was nothing. Barbara was no longer second best.

21

Four years after the June dinner party Antonia still had to nerve herself to visit Margaret on her own. 'She gives me the creeps,' she would say to Barbara, 'but I quite enjoy it if you are with me.' Since their marriage Matthew left social duties he wished to avoid to his wife. 'Antonia does these things so well,' he would mutter, edging away from embarrassment or boredom. 'Women are naturally good at them.'

So she nerved herself. 'I have brought you some flowers.' Antonia swept into Margaret's room. 'To cheer you up,' she added, closing the door with a swish.

Margaret said, 'Put them where I can't see them.'

'What a terror you are,' said Antonia with false bravado; she set the vase on the dressing table where the mirror would reflect it in triplicate. 'These are the first sweet peas,' she said, 'not many, but lovely.' She sat in one of the golden chairs and tried to grin cheerfully at Henry's wife. She wished, as she grinned, that she were able to develop some rapport with the woman by pitting obstinate and optimistic cheer against Margaret's negative destruction.

Margaret said, 'The way you behave one would think you lot owned this house.'

'We pay rent. Help with repairs, take turns with the cooking; Matthew has painted the front door.'

'The front door.'

'Yes.'

'You fill the house with squawking babies.'

'Only one baby.'

'You won't stop at one.' Margaret shuddered.

'No,' said Antonia bravely, 'we won't. Matthew wants a son.'

Margaret said, 'Gertch!'

Antonia laughed.

'Where's the other girl?'

'Couldn't come this weekend. James is sailing.'

'She does not like sailing. I used to sail on the Nile with my lover.'

If one was to believe her, Margaret had had a posse of lovers. 'Which one was that?' Antonia leaned forward to tweak a sweet pea into a better position. She and Barbara doubted whether Margaret was capable of love, yet she must have inspired it, otherwise Henry—

Margaret sneered. 'Lady of the manor.'

'What?'

'This act you and your friend put on, picking my flowers, helping yourselves to fruits of my earth. Little so-called ladies.'

'Fruits of the Jonathans' hard work and Henry's earth.'

'Dumping that disgusting infant on my servant.'

'Pilar is *not* a servant and Susie is *not* disgusting.' (Oh, why do I rise to these jibes?) 'You are jealous,' said Antonia, 'poor barren woman, of our youth and fertility. You crouch in bed wallowing in your agora-phobia. You are agoraphobic,' she said, marvelling at her nastiness. 'Agora means—'

'I know what it means,' said Margaret. 'Do you? I bet you don't. Agora is Greek for market-place. In Greece with my lover we ate sucking pig and drank retsina in the market-place.'

'The same lover or another lover?'

199

'I am not afraid of any market.' Margaret ignored Antonia's question.

Feeling cheap, Antonia persisted, 'Then why do you never go out?'

'I prefer to stay in.'

'But aren't you terribly bored?'

'As to boredom,' said Margaret, 'look who's talking.'

'Me?' Antonia was startled. 'Me?'

'If it hasn't dawned on you yet – as they say in the cinema, FORTHCOMING ATTRACTION COMING SOON: marital tedium, boredom, ennui, one big yawn,' said Margaret.

Antonia turned the vase of sweet peas slightly to the right and, switching the subject a little, she said, 'Henry has gone to London. I wonder what he will bring you? He always brings you a present,' she said. Margaret watched with her silvery eyes. 'Why do you throw his presents in his teeth? It seems—' She hesitated to use the word perverse in case Margaret should use it against her.

'He once threw something at me,' said Margaret.

Disbelieving, Antonia said, 'Oh?'

'I had a knife,' said Margaret. 'He threw a bottle of ink.'

'Had he given you the knife? Had you given him the ink? Was this what's known as an exchange of presents?'

'He missed,' said Margaret. 'He had been trying to rape me.'

Antonia gaped; she remembered the stain on Henry's bedroom wall.

Margaret repeated, 'He was trying to rape me.'

Antonia rose to go. 'You used to tell us that Henry was homosexual and went in for bestiality; now you suggest rape and that he is brutal. He can't be all that versatile,' said Antonia, moving towards the door.

'Henry can be very kind. He is kind to us and wonderfully kind to Susie.'

'In your shoes I should be watchful in that quarter.' Margaret smiled at Antonia, calculating and malicious.

'What on earth do you mean?' Antonia's hand was on the door knob.

'Paedophile derives from the Greek as does agora.' Margaret chuckled as Antonia sped from the room.

In the rooms she and Matthew shared with their child, Antonia bathed her face and rinsed her mouth to expunge Margaret's insinuations. Pressing her face into a towel she muttered, 'Poor Henry, oh poor Henry.' In the bathroom she heard Pilar exclaim as Susie splashed and chuckled in the warm water. She opened the door and looked in. 'Mama!' said Pilar. 'Look, Susie. Mama!' The baby gurgled and slopped her flannel about in the water.

'All right?' asked Antonia, 'Happy, darling? I'll be up later with daddy. Thank you so much, Pilar, thank you.'

Pilar called out, ''Appy, yes!'

'I'm going down to cook the supper,' Antonia told Pilar, 'see you later.' And, bubbling with good intentions, she ran down to the kitchen. 'I must be nice to Henry,' she said aloud as she wrapped an apron round her waist. And extra nice to Matthew, she thought as she tied the tape tight. And, how does she know how I feel about Matthew? She never sees us together. 'Trask,' she said as Trask came in from the garden, 'does Margaret ever get out of bed these days?'

'She took premature to her eternal rest when Henry brought her home as a bride.'

'I know that,' said Antonia, 'and I remember the dinner party, but does she—'

'Walks,' said Trask.

'Walks?'

'And watches and listens. You wouldn't see her. Ain't much she misses.'

'You mean she spies on us?'

'Could call it that.'

'But when?'

'Any time as spirit moves her.'

'How creepy.' Antonia flinched, 'Why?'

'Likes to get under people's skin,' said Trask.

'You don't seem to mind.'

'When your skin's as thick as mine it ain't worrying.'

'My skin is not very thick.'

'T'will thicken in time,' said Trask reassuringly. 'Where's Matthew?'

'He went for a walk rather than visit Margaret.'

Trask smiled and Antonia wished she had not said this about Matthew, not in that tone of voice. I love Matthew, she told herself; I really should not let Margaret upset me. 'Does Margaret like anybody?' she asked Trask.

'We gets on so-so and she likes the two boys.'

'Boys?'

'Jonathan and John. She talks to them.'

Antonia was still uneasy. 'Would she, would she – I mean, she is so horrid about Susie, would she – er—'

'No,' said Trask. 'That's all talk.'

'You sure?' (Was it safe to leave Susie asleep, as she would be tonight while they ate supper? Was it safe?) 'Are you sure?' she repeated.

Trask laughed. 'Your Susie ain't no parrot.'

'I am not reassured,' said Antonia. 'I wish Barbara was here. Oh Lord, I must get cracking and cook the supper, pull myself together.'

I am making myself ridiculous in Trask's eyes, she thought. Margaret scared me; I should be used to her fantasies. She is an unfortunate, she gets her kicks in

202

strange ways, that's all. I wish Trask hadn't told me she walks and spies.

'Sharp tongues don't cut babies,' said Trask with intent to reassure.

Antonia said, 'Oh, Trask.' She laughed, 'You wouldn't know what paedophilic means, would you?' she said.

'No. No more than them dogs.' Trask gestured out of the window to where Henry's dogs crouched, noses on paws, patient, expectant, listening for the sound of Henry's car. 'He will be home shortly,' said Trask. 'They know that and I know that and when Henry's been to London he comes home hungry.'

When Henry arrived he kissed Antonia's cheek and chirupped to the dogs. Antonia said, 'You are nicely in time for supper. What did you buy Margaret?' She watched Henry stack parcels on the dresser. 'Books,' he said, 'for me and shoes for me.'

'And Margaret?' Henry put a small packet on top of the books, reaching across the dogs, who leaned against him whimpering with pleasure, lashing their tails. 'Not caviar, I hope. Remember when you did bring caviar, she threw it and her room was braided with globules of sturgeon; it took even Humble and Cringe an age to waffle it up.'

Henry said, 'Hector and Lysander, please. They may not care for what I brought this time.'

'What? Oh, not scent!' Antonia threw up her hands in protest.

'Yes.'

'Even the best scent smells dreadful, spilled and stale.' Antonia looked longingly at the parcel.

'Get Matthew to buy you a bottle.'

'He will demur. He demurs a lot these days; he has the expenses of paternity. Besides, he is saving up for a son.'

Henry asked, 'Where is Pilar?'

'Putting Susie to bed. I said I would cook supper.'

'Matthew?'

'Gone for a walk.'

'He might have taken the dogs.' Henry stroked Lysander's throat.

'They wouldn't go, they were expecting you home,' said Antonia loyally. Matthew had refused, shut the dogs in with her.

Henry said, 'So what's for supper?'

'Wonderful spring veg from the Jonathans, and delicious tender lamb cutlets, and for pudding strawberries and cream.'

Laughing, Henry asked, 'No smoked trout?'

'We can't get smoked trout round here.'

'Crême brulée?'

'I don't know how to make it. Are you teasing me? If you wanted smoked trout, you should have thought of it in Fortnum's. Are you criticizing my efforts?'

'Are there green and ruby jellies to eat with the cutlets?'

'Of course there are,' said Antonia huffily. 'I may not be as expert as Pilar, but I try, and if you want exotica you should go to a restaurant.'

Henry said, 'Of course. A restaurant,' amused.

Antonia eyed him as he sat in the window, his dogs adoring at his feet. 'I'll go and fetch some claret from the cellar,' he said, still laughing.

Antonia flushed. 'Actually, Matthew's done that, because of the temperature, and he, we thought you wouldn't mind – um, as we share – sort of share – so much – he—'

Henry said, 'I am in favour of sharing.'

'I wish you'd share the joke,' Antonia said rather crossly, for Henry was smiling still.

Henry said, 'Some day, perhaps. You look fine,' he said, changing the subject. 'Brown.'

204

'We swam, lay in the sun. Susie paddled.'

Henry said, 'Good,' stifling a yawn. 'Good.'

'I telephoned Barbara,' said Antonia. 'She's on her own. James is sailing. Bloody selfish. I said, Come down, be with us, don't be lonely. She said she had a migraine.'

Henry said, 'A migraine?'

'She doesn't have migraines,' said Antonia. 'I guessed, of course, but keep it quiet; she will want to tell us herself. What she's got is morning sickness.' Antonia lowered her voice.

Henry said, 'Oh.'

'I haven't told Matthew or anybody. I can't think what took her so long to get started. She's pregnant.'

Henry pursed his mouth in a whistle.

Antonia said, 'Could you move your legs? I want to lay the table.'

Henry moved his legs. Antonia was looking very pretty, he thought. Maternity had improved her; she had lost the last bit of puppy fat. Having a child had honed her features.

'Are you going to change your clothes?' Antonia asked. (Barbara will be furious with me for letting on, she thought.) 'I only ask,' she said, 'because if Margaret throws that scent over you, no cleaner will get it out.'

Henry said, 'Thanks for your concern. There have been presents she did not throw.'

Antonia said, 'Name one.'

'A box of comfits which got lost in the post.'

Something was amusing Henry. Antonia hated to be laughed at. 'And the decapitated cockatoo,' she said. Then, 'I'm sorry. I shouldn't – I'm sorry. But your suit, it's such a good one. Forget my lack of tact, consider your suit. I was brought up,' she joked, 'to believe no gentleman would be seen dead in a brown suit in London, and look at you! Oh, do stop laughing, Henry!'

Entering the kitchen at that moment, Matthew said, 'Has my wife uttered a witticism? Might one share the joke?'

'She is making fun of my suit.'

'Looks all right to me,' said Matthew. 'Can't see anything laughable. Actually, it's a jolly unusual piece of gent's suiting,' and he leaned past Antonia to finger Henry's sleeve.

'In a moment,' said Antonia, 'you will be asking what it cost.'

Matthew said, 'And suppose I do?'

'More than your boring pin-stripes.'

Henry said, 'It's some material my father chose and never had made up. I inherited it. One of my happier inheritances.'

Matthew said, 'I like these little flecks of colour. Look, darling, red and blue and green, just here and there. What a dandy you are, Henry. No one else would get away with it. Look at your socks. And that tie! You would never let me wear a tie like that, would you, darling?'

'You dress extra dull,' said Antonia.

'Dear me, snappy snappy.' Matthew blinked.

She *had* been snappy, she remembered years later when, wandering through an exhibition, she came upon an Augustus John of a man of gypsy appearance with very dark hair and a red scarf round his neck and was reminded of Henry and of how she had compared his appearance with that of her husband. It had been Matthew, she remembered with remorse, who had noticed the flecks of colour, Matthew who had said, 'I wish I had the nerve to wear red socks.' But at the time Matthew had asked, 'And what is my wife giving us for dinner?' She, in a surly way hoping to embarrass him, had answered, 'Lamb cutlets, as you well know. You asked so that you could fetch up the wine.' Matthew,

206

maddeningly sweet-tempered, had said, 'Whatever she has cooked, it will be delicious. I speak as a fond husband.' She, turning back to the stove, had prayed that Matthew's host-like attitude in Henry's house did not get up Henry's nose as painfully as it did hers. She remembered that evening well.

Matthew had said, 'I must go up and say good night to my daughter,' and while he was out of the room she had been silent. Henry had kept silent, too, sitting in the window stroking Hector's and Lysander's ears.

They were joined at the meal by Trask and Pilar. Ebro was absent or not noticeably present; she could not remember as she walked round the gallery on a harsh winter's day. But she remembered Matthew saying, 'I was thinking this afternoon on my solitary walk of how it is time for me to have a son.' He had popped more peas in his mouth and another piece of cutlet pasted with jelly, and none of them round the table had spoken. She had watched him swallow and gulp some wine and heard him say, 'Yes, Antonia and I will be having a son before long, so I have been thinking—'

She had said, 'You have been thinking—'

And Matthew had answered, 'Well, yes, in the first place—'

And she, bristling, 'And in the second?'

And he, 'Darling, don't keep interrupting. I need to tell Henry.'

Henry, refilling their glasses, had said, 'Congratulations. When is he due?'

Matthew said, 'Oh well, as to that, I am a spot premature planning ahead; I haven't actually set the mechanics in motion. But what I am building up to, Henry, is this: when we have a son, we shall need more room. How would it be if I got Ebro to decorate another room for him? The one next to Susie's beyond the bathroom would do very well. I will pay for the work, of course.'

Henry had looked at Matthew; indeed, they had all looked at Matthew. It occurred to Antonia all these years later that perhaps Matthew had been drinking; too late to find out now. While they looked the door opened, Antonia remembered, and Margaret came in. Was it the dogs who alerted them, or a draught? Margaret had gone straight to the dresser and picked up the parcel of scent. She undid the parcel, prised the stopper from the bottle and doused the dogs with it.

22

'There is someone at the door,' said Calypso.

'At this hour?' Hector pulled his spectacles down his nose. 'I was about to stop reading and cuddle up to you, prior to sleeping or whatever. It's very late.'

'There goes the bell and knock, knock, knock,' said Calypso.

Hector said, 'I wish I was deaf.' The knocking persisted. 'We should let the dogs sleep in the house.' He groaned. The bell renewed its appeal.

'It is you who insist they sleep in the stables.' Calypso closed her book, marking her place with a finger. 'It must be an escaped lunatic. Are you going or are you not?'

Hector grumbled, 'I was warm and comfortable and loving, but I suppose there may have been an accident.' He got out of bed and felt for his slippers. 'Or perhaps the house is on fire and some kind person has noticed.' He wrapped himself in his dressing-gown. 'I should have thought we were too far from the road.'

Calypso said, 'Don't catch cold,' opening her book.

'It's bloody midsummer.' Hector departed, muttering, 'I'm coming, I am coming.' His slippered feet slopped downstairs and across the hall and the front door opened. Calypso listened. There was a murmur of voices, the sound of shuffling, the door closing, then silence. She thought: It's burglars. Hector's been hit over the head. 'I'm coming, darling, I'm coming,' she shouted. 'Oh darling, do take care,' and not pausing to put on dressing-gown or slippers she leapt from bed and catapulted downstairs. 'If you've touched a hair of his head I will kill you,' she shouted.

In the hall Hector stood looking at Antonia, crouched in a foetal position on the sofa with Susie clutched in her arms. Susie stared up at Hector, her mouth agape.

Calypso said, 'I thought you'd been mugged. Are you all right?'

Hector said, 'Not mugged. She doesn't seem able to talk; she's incoherent.' Aware of their scrutiny, Antonia huddled lower on the sofa, her hair shrouding her face.

'Spent all her energy getting here,' Calypso suggested. The girl looked a mess, she thought; she held out her hand. 'Come along,' she said, 'plenty of beds made up.' She took Antonia's hand. 'Bring your baby to bed.'

'A drink?' Hector suggested. 'Brandy? Whisky?'

Calypso, shaking her head, mouthed, 'Hot bottle.'

Antonia wailed, '*Bilge*. Couldn't stand any more *bilge*.'

Calypso said, 'Try tottering up the stairs,' and gave Antonia's hand a tug. Antonia lurched to her feet, holding the baby.

Looking out of the door, Hector said, 'She's left the lights of her car on, the engine running and, dammit, it's on the lawn!'

Reaching the stairs, Antonia clutched the banisters. 'I must apo – I must apolo – I must not impose – I must—'

Calypso said, 'Tomorrow,' and gave a guiding push. 'Keep it till tomorrow.'

Hector went out to Antonia's car. Returning presently, he saw his wife emerge from one of the spare rooms and shut its door. She leaned over the banisters.

'Coming up?' she asked. 'Reminds me of old times.'

Hector ignored this. 'Bloody girl,' he said. 'She left it with no brakes on, all the lights on and plum in the herbaceous border. What d'you suppose it's all in aid of? We hardly know the girl.'

'She'll tell us tomorrow,' said Calypso, getting into bed. 'At least she didn't hit a tree. Or she may not tell.'

'Lucky she wasn't stopped by the police,' said Hector. 'That baby might have been killed.' Calypso held the covers back as he climbed in beside her. 'This is where we'd got to when that infernal racket started.' He took Calypso in his arms.

She said, 'I thought you'd been mugged. Your feet are cold. Come close.'

Holding her, Hector said, 'It's a very quiet baby.'

Calypso said, 'It's a very *drunk* baby.'

'Drunk?'

'On mother's breath,' Calypso said.

Hector said, 'Oh, darling, I wish you wouldn't make me laugh just when I was getting an erection.'

In the spare room Antonia kept the light on and prayed for the room to stop spinning. What was she to say to the Grants in the morning? How to explain her intrusive arrival?

'It will be the last straw,' she said to her baby, 'if you pee in this wonderful bed.' I must not sleep, she told herself. I won't undress; I'll get up presently and creep away, write a long letter of grovelling and profuse apology. None of this would have happened if Barbara had been there; we've always shared everything, sharing makes things bearable. In her arms Susie snorted in her sleep. Her ears thrummed as though she was coming round from an anaesthetic and the room continued spinning.

*   *   *

211

'What would you like for breakfast?' Calypso enquired when Antonia came into the kitchen. 'Coffee? Orange juice? Toast and marmalade? We are tucking into bacon and eggs.'

She looked disgustingly well and young for her age, Antonia thought. She's almost my mother's age, must be. 'Oh – I – er—' she said.

Hector folded his newspaper and rose to pull out a chair for her. 'Why don't you put the child on the floor?' he suggested. 'Hamish used to be happy on the floor at that age. Does she like dogs? It is a girl, isn't it?' He peered closely at Susie.

Antonia said, 'Yes,' and sat. 'Yes.'

'Then put her down.' Hector indicated a pair of Labradors lolling by the Aga. 'There's a mug of milk to keep her quiet, and Calypso found some rusks.'

'They may be a bit stale,' said Calypso.

Antonia said, 'I—'

'First of all, coffee for you,' said Calypso. 'Strong. Here you are. Then I'll coddle the baby an egg, that's what they like.'

Dubiously Antonia lowered Susie among the dogs, then accepted the coffee. Useless to tell Calypso that Susie hated eggs and would spit them out. But the coffee was delicious. She gulped it greedily and watched Calypso put a mug of milk in Susie's hands. 'Keep it steady,' she said. 'Now for that egg,' and turned towards the stove.

Grasping the mug with both hands Susie drank, goggling over the rim at Calypso's back. When she had downed the milk Hector took the mug from her and handed her a rusk, which she thrust first in her mouth and then at a Labrador, who took it with a furtive glance at its master.

Hector refilled Antonia's cup.

Antonia searched her mind for a mode of speech

which would explain and attempt to excuse arriving drunk on the Grants' doorstep in the midnight hours, when she hardly knew them. At least I was not sick, she thought, and Susie didn't pee in the bed.

Calypso broke a lightly-boiled egg into a cup, added salt, stirred, and handed it to Susie. 'Eat that.' Susie ate. Antonia whispered, 'She hates eggs,' amazed.

Calypso said, 'Children are like that. Now, toast and marmalade? Make Antonia some toast, darling.' Hector reached across the table and put bread in the toaster. 'It only pops up for Hector,' she said. 'Have you noticed how mechanical objects hate women?'

Antonia said, 'I – er—'

'I hope you don't mind,' said Hector, 'but I moved your car. It's in the yard.'

Antonia said, 'Oh, God. I must explain – I – Oh, I am so sorry, I—'

Calypso said, 'She gets on with dogs, doesn't she?' as she watched the child hold the eggy cup for the second Labrador to lick. 'I expect she is friends with Henry's Humble and Cringe. Eat your toast while it's hot,' she said. 'Nothing worse than soggy toast.'

Hector put the toast by Antonia's plate. 'Henry is a tactful fellow,' he said.

Antonia gripped a piece of toast. 'I should – I must, I really should – I can't think what I—'

'We know their real names are Hector and Lysander. It's excessive sensitivity on Henry's part, don't you think?' Hector bent down to retrieve the cup from the Labrador.

Gripping the toast so hard it broke in her fingers, Antonia said, 'I must explain, I must apologize.'

'I promise you it isn't necessary,' Calypso said. 'Honestly not. Would you like to stay for a bit?'

Antonia flushed, 'Oh, no. No. I must get back – he – I

mean, they don't know where I am, but I *want* to apologize.'

'Have a bath before you go,' said Calypso, stemming the apology.

'I slept in my clothes.' Antonia began to weep. 'Oh, God.'

Calypso said, 'More coffee. I will lend you some clothes.'

Antonia sobbed. 'Perhaps when I have it straight in my mind I can come and explain?'

But she never did.

Watching Antonia drive away, Calypso said, 'At least she wasn't sick.'

'For someone who dislikes babies,' said Hector, laughing, 'you behaved admirably.'

Calypso said, 'Tolerance comes with age. I thought you were splendid,' and she took Hector's hand. Hector held her hand then tucked it warmly into his pocket and held it there. 'She did say one illuminating thing,' Calypso said. 'While we were upstairs choosing clothes, she said she could not endure the spectacle of Henry being kind to Margaret.'

Hector said, 'Now that *is* interesting.'

'Here comes the runaway,' said the younger Jonathan, looking out of the window as they sat eating a late breakfast. 'Shall you spring to the telephone and allay Matthew's fears?'

'Let's give her a minute,' said his lover. 'I don't mind Matthew worrying.' He went out to help Antonia out of her car. 'Let me hold Susie,' he said. Taking the child from her and bending to kiss her cheek, he asked, 'Have you breakfasted? We are in middle of ours; come and join us.'

'I have, but I couldn't eat. I drank some coffee. Susie ate all right, she ate an egg.'

'An egg? She hates – What a little puss. Come along in.' He led her towards the cottage. 'Never mind the geese,' he shouted as a gaggle of geese came heavy-footed and honking round the house, 'such good watch-dogs. Don't be afraid of them. Piss off,' he hissed. 'You look uncommon smart this morning,' he said, standing aside so that Antonia could go into the house. 'Isn't she elegant?' he said to his lover. 'Super outfit, darling.'

'It's Calypso's,' said Antonia, 'borrowed.'

'So that's where you've been! We heard you'd eloped; the troops are out looking for you, you know. Well, not the troops, your husband, to be precise. It would never occur to him to look for you there. We promised him we would telephone if we got wind of you.'

'No,' said Antonia, 'please.'

'Not yet,' said the younger man, kissing her also. 'Come in, sweet girl, and share our meagre fare, and tell all.' He laughed and his moustache blew out like the feelers of a friendly crustacean. 'Matthew was looking pretty po-faced,' he chuckled. 'Concerned for his car. You, too, of course, and Susie. Now, what would you like to eat? There's muesli and fruit. We are risking coronaries with bacon and eggs.'

Antonia sat at their table. 'Fruit, please, or muesli. Oh, why didn't I come to you?'

'Matthew was here at six a.m., that's why we are breakfasting late; we overslept.'

Antonia cried, 'I made a complete ass of myself at the Grants. I drove into their flower-beds. I was inebriated.' She drew out the word. 'Dear boys, it's good to be here.' She smiled at the Jonathans, who beamed back, and Susie in the older man's arms chuckled. 'Was Matthew sober?'

'You couldn't call it sober,' they said.

'If Barbara had been there, nothing would have happened,' Antonia said. 'I say, can I change my mind and have bacon and eggs? I'm starving.'

'Of course you can, but didn't the Grants offer?'

'They did, they were incredibly kind, but I was choking with embarrassment, dying to escape. They were hideously tactful.'

'You can loosen your stays here,' said the older man. 'Bacon and eggs it is. Try and tell us as you eat. Begin at the beginning, do.'

'The Grants didn't ask any questions, they behaved as though it was all the most natural thing in the world,' said Antonia.

'That's Calypso all over. She disassociates herself from other people's lapses.'

'She was kind. A bit brisk.'

'We are kind but not brisk, we are devoured by curiosity. Come on, darling, tell us what happened. We promise to pass it on so garbled no one will ever think it was you.'

Laughing, Antonia said, 'All right. It began yesterday afternoon. I missed Barbara. Matthew and I had been swimming; it was such a lovely day. Henry was in London so we were on our own. It's not the same without Barbara, much less fun. Anyway, I rang her up to ask her to join us. I knew James was sailing but I couldn't see why she couldn't come without him; she could have caught a train or something. She sounded odd, queer, said she had a frightful migraine. I couldn't persuade her. She said she was waiting for James and that she had to write a letter or something. God knows who to. Of course I guessed at once, she's pregnant.'

'Pregnant!' said the lovers. 'Well, well! Population explosion.'

216

With her mouth full, Antonia asked, 'May I have some mustard?'

Passing the mustard they said, 'Go on. That can't have – Did you have cross words with Matthew?'

'Not exactly.'

'Not exactly,' said the older man. 'What then?'

'Well, I didn't tell Matthew what I thought. I went up to visit Margaret. I don't mind visiting Margaret when Barbara is with me, but on my own I am falsely jolly and I mind her jibes. This time she suggested we make use of Henry and don't pay our way, that sort of thing. I, retaliating, suggested she has agoraphobia – I'd read an article about it in a magazine.'

'Bit risky.' The older man sucked in his breath.

'That led to other things,' said Antonia. 'Oh dear, d'you mind if I skip that bit? It was true, you see.' Antonia's eyes filled with tears.

'No, no, don't tell us,' cried the younger man. 'Not that we aren't dying to know, but not if it hurts.'

'Of course it hurts,' said his lover. 'Margaret's talent is finding the weak spot and inserting the stiletto. But do go on, love.'

Antonia said, 'Thanks,' and sniffed. 'Henry came back from London while I was cooking supper,' she said. 'You know how different the London Henry is from the country Henry? I teased him a bit; he always brings Margaret a present, I teased him about it. God knows why he takes the trouble.'

'It's to stop himself hitting her, that's our theory.'

'Really? How daft of him.' Antonia stared at the two men. 'You are percipient.'

'What did he bring this time?'

'Gorgeous scent, Guerlain.'

'And?'

'So we had supper. Matthew, who'd gone out to avoid visiting Margaret, was back by this time.

217

Actually he had been back quite a while, because he'd fetched wine from the cellar, and that made me twitchy because it's Henry's cellar and it was Henry's wine and Henry wasn't back when he did it. It's not that Henry minds, but Matthew does sometimes take things for granted.' Antonia, having finished her eggs and bacon, put her knife and fork down. 'That was delicious.'

'What else?' asked the younger man.

'Well, I take things for granted, too, I know that!' said Antonia. 'Pilar doing practically everything for Susie, all the things I dislike or am bored by, it was just that at supper, Matthew – oh dear, I can't tell you that either.'

'Not to worry,' they said. 'None of our business.'

Antonia said, 'So we ate our supper, we discussed the beauty of Henry's London suit, we drank quite a lot. Oh, dear boys, it's so easy to get carried away by you two sympathetic dears and get bitchy and disloyal.'

'We love it,' said the moustached lover. 'Please get carried away.'

'Honestly,' said Antonia, laughing, 'I can't. Anyway, in the middle of all this in came Margaret.'

'Oho!'

'And?'

'She went straight to the dresser where Henry had put the scent. She tore the parcel open, she ripped off the stopper—'

'And poured it over Henry?'

'No! The dogs.'

'Whew!'

'It was whew,' said Antonia. 'The dogs went mad. They rushed whimpering round the kitchen, then disappeared into the yard and Margaret sneered, "He expects me to anoint his feet and dry them with my hair".'

'And then?'

'Henry laughed and offered her a glass of wine. I told you we'd been boozing a bit more than usual. All Henry said was, "Oh, Margaret, the poor creatures, they will now find some really terrible stink and roll in it." Somehow his being so nice to her made me want to throw up,' said Antonia. 'I used to believe he was heartless and a lot of other things she told us, but there he was wheedling her to sit down with us and telling her she looked beautiful.'

'And was she looking beautiful?'

'Of course,' cried Antonia. 'Then Matthew began sucking up to her. He put his arm round her and said, "What's upset you, woman?" (So awful, that use of woman.) And guess what? She kissed him and he kissed her back. What possessed Henry to marry that bitch?' cried Antonia.

'There was some suggestion of persuasion, we believe. It was a long time ago.' The lovers avoided each other's eyes.

Antonia said, 'Huh!'

'And? Then?'

'I – er – I went and telephoned Barbara again. Things seemed to be getting out of hand. If she had been there, it would have been different, felt different. She might have found it comical, it was comical, but on my own I couldn't take it.'

'And what did Barbara say?'

'I felt I could kill her. I was drunk, of course, I freely admit it.'

'And cross with Matthew.'

'Cross! *Murderous*!' Antonia wailed. 'Don't laugh, you two.'

'We are not laughing,' they said as they dissolved into helpless giggles. 'It's a tragic story,' they cried. 'Terrible. What next?'

'I thought, to hell with it, to hell with them all. I went upstairs, I collected Susie, wrapped her in a blanket, put her in the car and drove off into the night, and came to rest in the Grants' herbaceous border.'

'But what had Barbara *said*?' cried Jonathan 'What?'

'Barbara said she couldn't talk now, she and James were catching the midnight train from Victoria for Paris.'

23

'Here comes Henry, I wonder what he wants.' Maisie Bullivant watched a car approach up their drive.

'It isn't Henry,' said her husband, glancing up from his newspaper.

'It's Henry's old Bentley, stupid.'

'Matthew Stephenson's driving.'

'But he has his own car,' said Maisie. 'I told you it was time to get your eyes tested.'

'Test or no test, that's Matthew.' Peter put his paper aside and rose to his feet. 'Bye, bye, Sabbath peace,' he groaned.

'I wish people wouldn't drop in before I've done my face,' said Maisie as Peter went to meet Matthew.

'Hullo, Matthew, what can we do for you?' Peter had reached the hall.

Matthew came in. 'You don't happen to have seen Antonia? Good morning, Maisie,' he said, looking round the room.

'I was just going to do my face,' said Maisie. 'What's happened, have you lost her? You look terrible,' she said, 'really terrible.'

'Not lost, mislaid,' said Matthew. 'I hoped she'd be here.'

'She's not,' said Peter. 'Do sit down.' Matthew was already slumped in an armchair. 'Where has she gone?'

'If I knew where she'd gone, I wouldn't be here,

would I?' Matthew raised his voice. 'God! How stupid can you get?'

Peter Bullivant swallowed. 'Have you tried the Jonathans?'

'Of course I've tried the Jonathans,' Matthew shouted.

I must keep my cool, Peter thought. 'Not there?' he said.

'Would I be here if she'd been there?'

'No need to be aggressive, Matthew,' said Maisie, wounded.

Matthew said, 'Sorry, I'm half out of my mind. She took the child with her.'

'Took little Susie?'

'Yes.'

'Why ever should she do that?'

'She's its mother,' said Peter.

Matthew said, 'I wish I had not come here,' and rose to go.

'No, no, don't go, we want to help,' exclaimed Maisie. 'Please tell us what happened; we sound stupid because we don't know. Even stupider than usual,' she added humbly. 'Would you like some coffee?' she asked. 'Or a drink?'

'I'll get him a drink,' said Peter. 'He's had a shock of some sort.'

Matthew watched Peter leave the room and listened to the clink of glass against decanter in the next room.

Maisie thought, He's too upset to notice I haven't done my face. 'Have you tried Mrs Watson at the Post Office?' she asked helpfully. 'She never misses anything.'

Matthew said, 'I've tried Mrs Watson at the Post Office, I've tried the whole bloody neighbourhood, now I've come to you.'

'Last resort,' said Maisie sadly.

Peter handed Matthew a stiffish whisky. Matthew gulped the whisky, then said, 'Sorry to be so rude, I am terribly anxious.'

Maisie said, 'Of course you are. Could you try and—'

'I *love* my wife,' said Matthew violently and took another swallow. 'I *love* her.'

'Did she take the car?' asked Peter. 'You driving Henry's old thing suggests—'

'Of course she took the car.'

'Gone to mother?'

'You don't know her mother.' Matthew snorted.

'Ah. No. We don't know her mother or for that matter her father,' said Peter. 'So you don't think she'd go to them? The Lowthers?'

'No.'

'What about Barbara?' Maisie brightened. 'She and Barbara are so close. That would be London, of course.'

'Tried her first, there was no one there.' Matthew put his glass down. 'Oh God,' he said. 'Oh God, oh God, oh God!'

'She wouldn't do anything silly?' suggested Maisie.

'Like suicide? No,' said Matthew. 'No.'

'Of course not, not with little Susie.'

'I don't see why little Susie should avert it,' said Peter. 'One reads—'

Matthew said, 'I'm drunk,' and began to cry. 'You topped me up,' he accused.

'Oh dear,' Maisie said. 'Oh, Peter, how could you?'

Peter did not reply.

After a bit Matthew said, 'Henry has *no* sense of morality.'

Peter said, 'We are not with you. How does Henry come into this?'

Spacing his words, Matthew said, 'Henry went to London yesterday, right? Henry goes to London from

223

time to time and he comes back bringing Margaret a present, which Margaret either chucks at his head or at someone else. You with me?'

'Yes,' they said, 'just about. It's common knowledge.'

'Margaret's a beautiful woman; she joined us at dinner.'

'So she got out of bed?' Maisie was astounded.

'Must have done if she joined them at dinner.' Peter was withering. 'Go on, Matthew.'

'I was sorry for Margaret,' Matthew said. 'She does not have much of a life.'

'It's of her own choosing,' said Peter.

Maisie said, 'I chose you and I don't have—'

'Shut up, Maisie. Carry on, Matthew,' said Peter.

'Henry gave her wine. We'd been drinking a rather good claret,' said Matthew. 'I sat beside her and tried to jolly her up. She drank her wine, she may even have had something to eat, I can't remember. Antonia had cooked a smashing meal, Henry had taken the dogs out, I forgot to say Margaret had smothered them in some expensive scent he'd brought her. Terrible waste of money. The more fool he.'

'Oh,' said Maisie, 'how awful. Poor dogs.'

'Go on,' said Peter.

'There's not much more,' said Matthew. 'When she asked me to help her up to her room – we'd been getting on rather well – of course I did. So we went up, taking a bottle with us, may have been two bottles, that's what she seemed to want and I've always understood that it's dangerous to their peace of mind to interrupt the flow when someone's baring their chest. I'm mixing metaphors but I dare say you get the gist? Anyway, reaching her room, Margaret got into bed and I sat on the edge and held her hand – I think I held her hand, it felt as though I did. We talked as people do. I told her how I love Antonia and about the

224

son we are planning to have. Well, I suppose it's chiefly me that plans him, and she was so understanding, she really was! She thinks it's selfish of Antonia to hold back, as of course it is, and that although she personally had been spared or deprived, I think she said deprived, of the traumas of parenthood because of Henry being what he is, she'd always understood that any "real man" wants a son. Well,' said Matthew, sighing, 'we had this confidential and highly-interesting chat.'

Peter said, 'I've always wondered why she married Henry.'

'I can tell you that,' said Matthew. 'It was pity.'

'Her pity for him or his pity for her?' Peter's eyebrows rose.

'Henry's pity for her,' said Maisie. 'It's obvious.'

'That's quite a percipient remark,' said Matthew, 'for a stupid woman. Any more whisky?'

'You've had enough,' said Maisie, huffed.

Peter took Matthew's glass and went to refill it. When he came back he said, 'Go on.'

Matthew drank. 'Terrible story,' he said. 'I mean, for someone who loves their wife as I love Antonia, it's a terrible story. Oh dear, oh dear.'

'And I love Maisie, come to that. Do go on,' said Peter.

'Not much more,' said Matthew. 'When she tumbled to the pity bit, she made up her mind to make the poor sod's life a misery. Now, I'm not saying she's right, but that's what it's all about, the staying in bed, wringing cockatoos' necks – shall we ever forget that? And chucking away his presents, she is out for misery for Henry.'

'But it doesn't work,' exclaimed Maisie. 'Henry is *not* miserable.'

'You've done it again!' exclaimed Matthew. 'Spot

on, Maisie. You really are quite bright.'

Peter laughed. 'So what does she get out of her marriage?'

'Security, of course.' Matthew gulped the last of his whisky.

'Well, yes,' said Peter. 'But do they ever – I mean—'

'I did ask,' said Matthew. 'We'd grown pretty intimate. She was so confiding, amusing in her way, you know how it is, yes, I asked.'

'And?'

'She said yes, then no, once, just to see if he could, she suggested he try. Those were her words, that he try. They rang rather true. She said come and sleep with me or words to that effect. Prove you are a man? Something like that, perhaps? Henry refused and she, taking umbrage, went for him with a knife and he threw an inkpot at her and missed.'

'And you believe that?' asked Maisie.

'Sounded true,' said Matthew.

'He wouldn't miss,' said Peter, 'never. Henry's got a marvellous eye. She filled you up with a bundle of poppycock, old boy.'

Seeing that Matthew looked annoyed, Maisie said, 'And what did she tell you after that?'

'I'm afraid I can't tell you.'

'Was it something too awful?'

'I fell asleep,' said Matthew.

'In her bed?' Maisie asked, wide-eyed.

'On it, actually.'

'Pissed,' said Peter, regretting his waste of whisky. 'And Antonia?'

'Vanished.'

'Telephone,' exclaimed Maisie as the telephone began shrilling in the next room. She went to answer it. 'Hullo?' she said, reaching for the receiver. 'Maisie Bullivant here.'

'And Antonia Stephenson here. Have you got my husband, by any chance?'

'Yes,' said Maisie, 'he's terribly upset.'

'Still drunk,' said Antonia. 'I'm coming to fetch him. Don't let him drive.'

'She sounds rather cross,' said Maisie, returning to the listening men.

Half an hour later, watching a tight-lipped Antonia drive her husband away, Peter said, 'What do you suppose Matthew means by saying that Henry has no sense of morality? I don't get it.'

Maisie said, 'He hasn't any more than his father had. Like father, like son.'

'I don't see the comparison,' said Peter. 'Henry's father was an old do-gooder.'

'Not in his youth,' replied Maisie. 'You can't have heard the village on the subject.'

'Gossip,' said Peter. 'Henry farms his land very well and keeps an eagle eye on things.'

Maisie snorted. 'Didn't keep much of an eye last night, did he? Letting Matthew spend the night with his wife.'

'Don't exaggerate, Maisie.'

'No need to,' said Maisie. 'Would Antonia have bolted into the night, taking little Susie, if Matthew had come to bed in the normal way? Even I, stupid as I am, can grasp that he woke up in Margaret's bed.'

'On Margaret's bed, he did say *on*, outside the bedclothes.'

'All right, outside, a detail which would be lost on poor Antonia. What I'm asking is, what was Henry up to, allowing such behaviour?'

'I expect he had gone to bed,' said Peter. 'But you can ask him when he comes to fetch his old crock.'

'If that's a dare,' said Maisie, 'I'm not taking you up on it.'

24

The dogs, pressing against him, woke Henry with their shivering. He lay, shoulders propped against a bale, in the middle of a hayfield. The sun was not yet up to counter the full moon riding high; looking up, he could see stars. A sheep coughed in the next field and Lysander whimpered, flattening his chin on to Henry's chest. He was cold except where the dogs pressed against his ribs; he sat up, caressed them. 'Good dogs, keep still. Listen.'

A wren sang a few loud notes, fell silent, was joined by a robin chortling its aria in full. In the wood beyond the field a pheasant cackled in alarm as a vixen trotted home across the stubble. A jay shrieked. Hector and Lysander followed the vixen with their eyes, straining their necks, noses twitching. Henry said, 'No,' and they subsided on to quivering haunches.

He was lying in muffling mist. Spiders were weaving their traps in the stubble; he listened to the pre-dawn silence and then, as the chorus of birds got under way, he got to his feet, dusted himself down and resumed the walk he had begun the night before when he shed his town clothes, put on corduroys, sweaters and an old jacket and took the dogs across the fields to the lake to rid them of the stink of Guerlain and himself of thoughts of his wife, his lodgers, his life.

'Run, dogs, run,' he had cried to the dogs as they came splashing out of the dark lake and he had run with them as they circled crazily in the moonlight, crashed through the reeds, startling waterfowl, then rolled and twisted on the grass to dry before following him as he circled his land through the wood and over the hills until, tired, he had stopped in the hayfield and fallen asleep.

Now he walked towards the reddening sky; it was going to be a hot day. As he walked, the mist evaporated and one by one grasshoppers set up their dry chirrup. He forgot his irritation with Matthew. Pilar and Trask would have manoeuvred Margaret back to bed; it had been better to get out of the way. There was nothing he could have done. Anger with Margaret was futile; rather, he thought with wry amusement, he was these days inclined to be grateful to her. For so long he had wished himself free of her; now in some perverse way she represented freedom.

Thinking of this, he stood looking down a narrow valley at the foot of which lay a wood still in shadow. There as a boy he had hidden and dreamed of Calypso, gnawed by love, yearning with all the force of adolescence for the impossible, weeping with frustration, refusing to abandon hope.

Who would have imagined as she broke my brittle heart that she and Hector would become my dear friends? They love each other; it has lasted, Henry thought admiringly. That woman had sense.

Looking down the valley, he hesitated; should he go down? There was work to be done, hay to bring in, another field to cut. He turned back and his thoughts turned dispassionately to Barbara and Antonia, who had shown less sense than Calypso. Their families were no worse, no more boring than Calypso's had been, and both lots had the advantage of money, whereas Calypso's had been poor. Those girls could have waited, thought Henry; surely they could have done better for themselves? What a potential mess they are making, he thought. 'Not that I,' he said out loud to his dogs, 'am not quite happy to aid and abet.'

Henry felt at peace this lovely summer morning; he loved his land, enjoyed working it. The house and garden survived, thanks to the Jonathans and his lodger friends. He must not let things irritate him. Life might be a whole lot worse; freedom was precious.

Across the fields there came the sound of a tractor. Trask, coming into view, drove up to stop beside him, quelled the engine.

'You slept out,' he shouted, as though the engine were still running. 'You'll be getting rheumatics.' His long upper lip worked reproachfully. 'Or perhaps you was walking back from the village?'

Henry said, 'I'm fine. We should bring the hay in, cut the top field while this weather lasts, cart the bales this afternoon.'

Trask, still shouting, said, 'You're getting to be like your pa when he was young; rutting all night, then comes in all innocent and gives his orders on the farm. Have you had breakfast?'

Henry said, 'No.'

Trask restarted the tractor. 'I'll get on with the hay,' he yelled. 'You'll be wanting to watch them parasites.'

'What parasites?' Henry's farmer mind switched to his sheep. 'We are not dipping until next week,' he shouted.

'I'm meaning your lodgers,' yelled Trask. 'Matthew's taken off with your precious car.' He laughed, pleased with his bad news.

'What the hell for?' Henry was enraged. 'Was he drunk?'

Trask let the tractor idle. 'That, too,' he said, 'but Antonia's hopped it with the baby; he's looking for her. She took their car.'

Henry said, 'Bugger him.'

' 'Twas he took Margaret up to bed.' Trask roared the engine and drove off, laughing. Calamity is the spice of life for men like Trask, thought Henry resignedly; people like Trask live vicariously.

25

Crowded by her parcels, Antonia looked out from the bus at the people hurrying along the pavement. An autumn gale was playing tricks with their umbrellas. Departing, the French au pair had quoted, *'Il pleure dans mon coeur comme il pleut sur la ville.'* Had the girl been making fun of her? Literary au pairs were no good. Matthew had said, 'Get yourself a German.' How right, as always; Matthew was almost as irritating as her parents. Antonia bundled her parcels onto her lap so that a large woman in a heavy coat could crowd beside her. 'Cadogan Street?' the woman enquired, spreading her hips, squashing close. She had an A to Z map in her hand, impossible to spread in the crowded bus. 'Stop after next,' Antonia said, turning back to the window, then, 'Oh. Hi. I must get off.' Struggling free, clutching her parcels, she lurched down the bus, pushed past the conductor and leapt for the pavement, where she tripped and landed on her knees.

'Stupid cunt,' yelled the bus conductor as the bus diminished.

'What did you do that for?' Henry bent to retrieve her parcels. 'Hurt yourself?'

'Banged my knees. Saw you from the bus. Thanks.' Antonia stood upright, a little shaken, holding two parcels while Henry held the rest.

Henry said, 'Have you no umbrella?' The rain darkened her hair, streamed down her face. 'We are blocking the pavement,' he said as people pushed past.

'The bus was moving,' he said crossly. 'Whoops, I love seeing that happen,' as ahead of them a freak wind snapped an umbrella inside out and back again. 'You've torn your stockings,' he said.

Antonia laughed.

Henry took her arm. 'I'm staying near here. You can borrow a pair of Angela's stockings. It's just round the corner. Unless you want me to take you home? What about lunch?'

Antonia said: 'No, no. Who is Angela?'

Henry said, 'Friend I am staying with, she's out. I have to make a phone call, come along.'

Antonia said, 'Lunch would be lovely.'

Henry said, 'Good,' and led her round the corner to a block of flats.

In the lift Antonia said, 'I hesitate to make free with a stranger's stockings.'

Henry said, 'She won't mind,' and opened a door with a latchkey. 'You must not be squeamish,' he said. 'She's a clean girl,' he said, opening and shutting drawers in a bedroom. 'Here we are,' he said. 'Put them on while I telephone.'

Antonia took the stockings and, finding the bathroom, removed her own torn ones. Borrowing a sponge, she dabbed gingerly at her knees. In the next room Henry was telephoning, something to do with sheep; his conversation was brief.

Outside the bathroom he said, 'What lunatic impulse propelled you from that bus?'

Drying her knees with a tissue, bending with her skirt rucked up, Antonia answered through gritted teeth, 'I had a lecture this morning from my mother; the subject matter was caution versus impulse. When I saw you from the bus strolling in the rain, in your London suit, I obeyed an impulse long suppressed to ask you to make love to me.'

After a minute pause Henry said, 'Why not now, before lunch?'

Antonia pulled down her skirt.

Henry said, 'There's a nice bed.'

Antonia said, 'Your friend Angela's?'

Henry said, 'If you are going to be scrupulous, we can do it on the floor; personally, I go for comfort.'

'It was amazing,' Antonia said some years later, 'such a healing experience.' She was moved, as she had been several times before, to apologize to Calypso for her drunken visit of years ago – quite a number of years, actually. Susie, visible in the distance helping Calypso's son Hamish (who had left Oxford a year earlier), was twelve now and her sister Clio, nearly nine, was hindering, as was Hilaria, Barbara and James's daughter. Hamish was coppicing hazels. Antonia had brought the little girls from Cotteshaw to picnic in the Grants' wood; now she sat with Calypso on the terrace in front of the house. 'They are all falling in love with Hamish,' she had said and Calypso, lazing in a deck-chair, had answered, 'As you girls were with Henry,' deflecting Antonia's apology, which she had guessed was impending. She had no wish to hear it since Hector was dead and could not enjoy it with her. Antonia answered unguardedly, for with Calypso one was apt to indulge in indiscretion, she being a notoriously safe depository of secrets, 'And as some of us still are.'

Calypso tipped her hat against the sun.

'Henry saved my marriage,' Antonia persisted. 'There's no doubt about it.'

Calypso still said nothing.

'I have never talked to anyone about him,' Antonia pressed on.

So why talk now? Calypso asked herself and

234

mischievously, since a reply was expected, murmured, 'Your mother?' Antonia's mother, with her impeccable virtue, was a person she and Hector had always deplored.

'It was my mother, long-suffering and moral, who was responsible for what happened,' said Antonia and went on to relate her meeting with Henry and the lovemaking in the borrowed bed. 'It was wonderful,' she said, 'an eye-opener. I had rather wanted to sleep with Henry when I first met him. Wondered what it would be like. He has the most wonderful four-poster at Cotteshaw. It was when Matthew and I were getting engaged. I wanted to marry Matthew, of course, I had decided I would. But I wondered about Henry in the way one does. Then, the night of the June dinner party, when Margaret went bananas and killed the cockatoo, I saw Henry in his bath and I knew I absolutely must try some time.'

In spite of herself, Calypso murmured, 'But when you did, there must have been something to set you off.'

'There was,' said Antonia, 'a combination of frustrations. I had left Susie to spend the day with my mother – she loves to play the omnipotent granny – I had tried to get away but she got in her spiky oar, she always does, about my being selfish and not putting Matthew first, as she does Father. It came on top of Matthew boring on about wanting a son, which he did a lot of at that time. I was browned off and not wanting to get pregnant again – putting it off, feeling pretty bitchy. Then I saw Henry walking in the rain and jumped off the bus. Meeting Henry did me so much good,' said Antonia earnestly. 'I was taking life too seriously, you see, making a meal of it. Henry can be absolutely beastly, as we all know, but he can also be very kind; look at the way he treats Margaret

235

and how good he is to Pilar. Then he has this streak of frivolity which is so engaging, such a tonic. Once,' said Antonia laughing, 'when I felt a guilty pang and suggested that what we were doing was immoral, he said, "And all the more *fun* for that."'

Calypso said, 'You had rather a racy great-aunt.'

'Oh yes!' said Antonia. 'I think she would have approved of Henry, don't you? Did you know her well?'

Calypso shook her head. 'Before my day, pre-1914. I was born in 1920, after her heyday.'

Antonia blushed. 'How idiotic of me, sorry.' Then she said, 'I have bottled this up for years.'

'Couldn't you go on bottling?'

Antonia said, 'No, I can't. It's OK for Catholics like you; you can hiss through a grille in a confessional, get absolved and feel better. I have to tell someone or I shall start being nasty to Matthew. I've thought of converting, but Matthew would hit the roof. I can't.'

Calypso laughed.

'You don't know how lucky you were, married to Hector,' said Antonia. 'Gosh, you were fortunate.'

'I do know,' said Calypso.

Antonia said, 'I should not have said that. I just wondered whether you who have had lovely, lovely Hector can guess what it's like to be married to Matthew.'

'I am not totally devoid of imagination.'

'No, of course not. Oh, Calypso, I can say it to you, it's so disloyal but I can't help it, Matthew can be – quite often is – boring. Not always, of course.'

'He loves you a lot,' said Calypso. 'It's noticeable.'

'I know, I know, and I love him. I don't want to be married to anyone else. I've never thought of leaving him, he is jolly good to me, he is a wonderful father, he hardly ever gets drunk – not since he woke in

236

Margaret's bed and got such a fright he practically signed the pledge. But I don't suppose you knew about that.'

Calypso smiled. 'The Jonathans—'

'Oh, of course. Yes. I ended up on their doorstep after crashing in on yours. By the way, I never apologized, I—'

'Oh, do shut up about it,' said Calypso.

Antonia said, 'I'm sorry. Of course I will. I had not realized I was being a bore.'

'Time you did.'

'Oh dear, how diminishing, how—' Antonia was abashed.

'Not to worry,' said Calypso more kindly, as she watched Hamish. He was making a good job of the coppicing. It should have been done in the winter, would have been done in the winter if Hector had been alive, but it was not too late and Hamish was being patient with the little girls, more patient than she felt with Antonia, who was speaking again.

'I decided that day, when I made love with Henry,' Antonia carried on, 'that I would hang on to Matthew for dear life, keep him on the hop so to speak. I mean, he would not know I was keeping him on the hop, yet it would be for his benefit as well as mine.'

'Ah.' Calypso thought of Antonia's great-aunt and the lateral inheritance of genes.

'So, as I said just now, Henry saved my marriage.'

In spite of herself, Calypso said, 'Why did you not go with all this to your friend Barbara?'

'Well,' said Antonia, drawing out the word, 'I know we tell each other everything, or did at that time certainly, but somehow I couldn't. She had fallen tremendously in love with James; they'd been married some time. And I thought, in fact I knew, that all was not well. Then suddenly, bingo, it clicked, I have never known why. They had gone to Paris on the spur of the moment, had a super, super time and presently there she was, pregnant with Hilaria and bloody smug about it. That child over there is a true love child, in every sense.'

Calypso said, 'Isn't that nice.'

'So you see,' Antonia went on, 'with Barbara in such an exalted state, I couldn't tell her I had tricked Matthew; there was the risk she might have thought I had erred. Actually, having Hilaria rather altered Barbara; she grew more towards James, less towards me. Nor could I tell her that from time to time Henry and I did it again.'

Calypso said, 'No.'

'Somebody once said Henry is flawed,' said Antonia thoughtfully.

'Hector.'

'So it was Hector? He was right. Henry must be flawed. D'you know he says he feels safe, married to Margaret? That she represents his freedom?'

Calypso said, 'It figures.'

'Free, married to that incubus, that albatross!'

'Well—'

'He told Barbara that he uses call-girls – Oh gosh, I've just thought; d'you think that woman Angela, whose bed we used, was a call-girl?'

'I wouldn't know,' said Calypso. 'Would it matter?'

Antonia did not answer this but said, 'Poor Henry. What a disappointing life.'

Calypso said, 'Disappointed people make poor company.' She was growing tired of Antonia.

'Oh,' cried Antonia, flushing, 'I see what you mean. That's the last thing Henry is. You must think me very stupid.'

Calypso said, 'A little.'

Antonia said, 'Thanks. I'm getting better.'

'In what way?' (They come over here and I quite like it, but they always stay too long.)

'I'm better with Matthew, for one thing. When he wants to – er – well, if you must know, bugger me, I know he is remembering my brother Richard. He was in love with him at school. I can understand.'

(High time she left.) 'I have met him,' said Calypso. 'Fat man in the Board of Trade.'

'He was thin once.' Antonia laughed. 'And he was a very pretty boy.'

Calypso laughed, too. Then, because she feared a further torrent of indiscretions, she said, 'I think it's time you took your brood home.'

'Oh yes,' said Antonia. 'Yes. I hope we haven't outstayed our—'

'Here they come,' said Calypso. Hamish had obviously had enough of adoring little girls, yet he looked amiable as he came towards them. 'Why,' said Calypso, getting to her feet, 'did they call that poor child Hilaria?'

Antonia said, 'James has a rich aunt. Easy.'

'So Barbara kept one foot on the ground.'

'Barbara thought Hilaria was the goddess of pleasure.' Antonia chuckled. 'She was not undeceived until after the christening.'

'They are lovely children.' Calypso mellowed at the prospect of her guests' departure. 'Henry seems very fond of them,' she said.

'We all think it's good for him, with none of his own, to have a share in ours,' said Antonia.

Calypso drew in her breath.

'One wonders,' said Antonia, 'what Henry's life would have been like if he had not got himself lumbered with Margaret.'

Irritated, Calypso snapped, 'Should it not suffice that he has been a remarkably good friend and kindness

239

itself to your children? Henry,' she said, 'knows how to behave.'

Snubbed, Antonia said, 'Of course, he is wonderful to them, wonderful to the children.'

(The silly bitch has reservations.) 'And you never made it to the four-poster?' Calypso waved her good-bye.

Slipping her arm through her son's, Calypso said, 'Let's go in. I need a drink. Antonia has been telling me about a healing experience.'

'And was it interesting?' Hamish asked.

'Only in so far as I suspect she was trying to tell me something else.'

Part Four

1959

26

From visiting Margaret one winter afternoon, the Jonathans came down the stairs loose-limbed with laughter. In the hall they leaned against one another and gave way to an explosion of giggles more suitable to adolescents than the middle-aged. They had viewed Margaret's new décor; it had been a shock.

Gone were the gold walls and carpet; in their place red-striped wallpaper, red ceiling, carpet and furnishings. Hell, they told each other, an inferno made acute by bounced reflections from the mirrors. And they were to blame, they told one another ruefully; had they not persuaded Margaret to leave her bed and trip up to London? It was they who had taken her to Apsley House, where she had been entranced by striped wallpaper, permissible for the victor of Waterloo but anathema in a house like Cotteshaw.

If they had not worked so hard to ease Margaret from her bed, this would never have happened, they wailed. Getting her out of bed had caused a U-turn. Now she had a taste for shopping, there would be no stopping her. It would be all right if Henry cut off the money, but Henry was a pig-headed fool who felt responsible for his wife; he should make her spend her own. 'He feels responsible,' the Jonathans complained. 'What about us? It's awful to laugh,' they said. 'Awful!' And they went to find Pilar in the drawing room.

'So you see it?' she said.

'Oh, Pilar!'

'Ebro got discount for the wallpaper,' she said.

'But it's terrible,' they said. 'Terrible.'

'Is change,' said Pilar robustly. 'Is Republican Flag, is colour for bulls.'

'Gruesome,' they said.

'And red dress, see the red dress?' she asked. 'Is all red now.'

'No!'

'Red with tight waist.' Pilar pressed her hands to her middle. 'Is contrast,' she said, laughing and nodding towards the window, from which Barbara and Antonia were visible, pacing ponderous in advanced pregnancy, silhouetted against the winter sky.

'Don't tell us Margaret is jealous,' the Jonathans exclaimed.

'Of the attention. She mock their shape.'

'They do indeed look comical,' said the older man, 'like huge bells. It's hard to imagine what it must be like for girls.'

'Some men is always so.' Pilar glanced to where his waist had once been. 'And not only for a few months,' she said cruelly.

'Come on,' said John. 'We must be on our way. Crumpets for tea.'

'Perhaps I should go easy on the crumpets.'

'Wait until Lent,' said his lover.

'There go the Jonathans,' said Barbara, waving. 'Aren't they touching? Their union is so stable, it's positively enviable.'

'Not what one would expect from the children of Henry's father's randy and irresponsible friends, is it?' said Antonia.

'You have been listening to village gossip,' said Barbara. 'Mrs Watson at the post.'

'One of their mothers was French; the stabilizing

244

gene must come from her,' said Antonia, and added wistfully, 'They never seem bored.'

'Are you,' Barbara glanced sharply at her friend, 'bored?'

'Since you ask, yes,' said Antonia flatly.

'Oh,' Barbara paced slowly. 'Oh.'

'There are times when I can't think what to talk about at meals,' said Antonia.

'Oh,' said Barbara again. 'Oh. What about Matthew? Doesn't he talk?'

'I don't always listen,' said Antonia. 'But it's all right, I can manage.'

'Hidden resources?' quizzed her friend.

'You could say that.'

'Oh?'

'And it will be better when he gets into Parliament. He will be out most evenings.'

Barbara said, 'Oh,' yet again.

'Oh, oh, oh.' Antonia mocked her. 'Do you never find James tedious?'

'Never,' said Barbara, 'but then James and I are very much in love.'

It was Antonia's turn to say, Oh, but she merely mouthed it. Barbara had not been the same since she had had a migraine and cured it by rushing off to Paris. 'I have a theory,' she said, fishing, 'that you did not manage an orgasm until you had been married for some time.'

'Is that what you think?' asked Barbara sharply.

Antonia said, 'Yes,' standing firm. 'It is.'

'And what about you?' asked Barbara. 'I take it that if Matthew is so boring, he doesn't provide orgasms to counter the tedium of his chat?'

'Take it however you like,' said Antonia good-naturedly, 'but it doesn't mean you have got it right.' Bed is where there is no need for talk, she thought.

'Before we married we used to tell each other everything,' said Barbara plaintively.

'We only thought we did,' said her friend. 'There are things one hardly knows oneself; time passes and we forget them.'

Barbara said, 'Um,' and considered her love for James. 'I was not really in love with James when I married him,' she said, 'but now—'

'I am glad for you,' said Antonia. 'And I shall love Matthew more when he is an MP.'

Barbara said, 'That figures.'

'Anyway,' said Antonia, switching the subject, 'it is going to be smashing for us having babies of the same age.'

The expectant mothers meandered on, each with her thoughts. Then, in an endeavour to recapture the intimacy they had once enjoyed, Barbara ventured, 'Do you still suppose Matthew spent that night with Margaret?'

Antonia said, 'I know he did. Who told you?' she asked slyly. 'The Grants?'

'Not the Grants. Of course not.'

'Who then?'

'The Jonathans did, and Maisie and Peter did, and I dare say the people at the Post Office would have the details.' (And Matthew too, in an effort to pre-empt reproach, but she would not tell Antonia this.) 'But you cannot suppose anything happened,' said Barbara. 'Not with Margaret.'

'I can't not,' said Antonia, who would have felt better if the so-called 'something' had occurred.

'The idea's absurd,' said Barbara.

'No more absurd than your James and that woman Valerie,' snapped Antonia.

'We had not met when he had his little fling with Valerie,' said Barbara, unruffled, 'but what did Matthew *tell* you?'

'He said he fell asleep.'

Barbara laughed. 'I supposed he was pissed.'

'He comes out of it so boringly,' said Antonia, aggrieved.

'Does any of it matter now?' asked Barbara. 'Look, the Jonathans are waving. Shall we go in? I begin to feel chilly.'

Antonia and Barbara waved and the Jonathans, who had reached the point where they would lose sight of the girls, waved again.

'Those stately galleons look as though they had been squabbling,' said the younger man.

'What would they squabble about? They are engrossed in baby talk, my dear. I do see Margaret's point, they are grotesque. I can't think how James and Matthew bear it,' said his lover.

'They brought it on themselves,' said the younger man. 'I keep remembering James, when I asked him what they had seen in Paris that time, he said, Nothing much; they had concentrated on the restaurants, eaten oysters at every meal for a fortnight.'

'Rash. Wasn't he sorry? Oysters!'

'The reverse, rather smug.'

'Careful, here he comes. Hullo, James, how are you?' the Jonathans addressed James.

'Well, thanks,' said James, who had already sighted the Jonathans and half-hoped to avoid them.

'Alone and palely loitering,' said the younger man. 'Come in and share our crumpets, we have crumpets for tea.'

'Walking briskly, thank you, and in the pink,' said James. 'Loitering is not my style.'

'Spare us a few minutes all the same,' said the Jonathans. 'We have been to see Margaret's frightful colour scheme. Do us a kindness and tell us your thoughts as you walked so briskly.'

Over my dead body, thought James; catch me confiding in these old poofs. 'I was thinking about money,' he said, and saw that he had successfully irritated them. 'Did you say crumpets?' He led the way into the Jonathans' cottage. 'So tell me about Margaret's latest folly,' he said. 'I haven't yet been invited to see it.'

'I thought he'd never leave,' said the older man an hour and a half later. 'Sitting there expounding on stocks and shares. *And* he ate all the crumpets.'

'An inadvertent good turn for your figure.' His lover puffed out his moustache. 'Could he really be thinking of money and look so happy?'

'He is doing very well, and money makes Barbara happy. But don't let's be catty, you need not have described Margaret's room in such detail or at such length.'

'I thought I did it rather well!'

'But no need to bore on with tiny minutiae; you were in danger of repeating yourself.'

'I *was* repeating myself! I hoped to bore him into leaving.'

'Well, clever Dick, you did not succeed. He just sat there eating our crumpets and looking beatific.'

James had not been listening. Hungry from his walk, he had enjoyed the crumpets. While pretending to listen he had relished not the crumpets but his good fortune. The Jonathans would never understand. They would think me crazy, he thought, if I told them that when I hold Barbara in my arms at night it is like holding a wonderful flower-pod; that our baby leaps and kicks under my hand; that I can put my ear to her stomach and listen to the child. I feel such happiness, he thought, there are times when I wish her pregnancy were longer. I enjoy this time so much. How could these two understand? If I told them I get a catch in my throat when I see Barbara's lovely little navel stretched inside out by the baby, they would think me insane. They would feel disgust, not tenderness. Oh God, I am fortunate, James thought as he walked back to Cotteshaw in the winter dark; that fool in Harley Street may have been ninety per cent right but I have proved myself ten per cent righter. I never imagined I would feel a love like this.

In this mood of euphoria he overtook Henry trudging back from his farm. 'Had a good day, Henry?' he asked. The poor fellow would understand his feelings no better than the Jonathans, he thought, as they kicked off their gumboots by the back door.

Henry said, 'Yes, thanks,' and looked kindly at his friend. 'Your mouth turns up like a cat's,' he said. 'Makes you look happy.'

'But I am happy,' said James.

Henry said, 'I am glad.'

James said, 'I hope we are not too great an imposition, the way we come in increasing numbers to occupy your house. Your hospitality stretches like elastic.'

Henry said, 'My father had a quote about helping each other out, I forget how it went – but surely you know you are welcome.'

'A present help in trouble – that the one?' James offered.

'No.' Henry smothered a laugh. 'No. Forgive me, James, but I have some telephoning to do. Why don't you put in some practice and help Matthew. Antonia has left him in charge of their child while she perambulates with Barbara.'

'OK,' said James. 'I'll find him. I think Barbara is hoping to pry tips on maternity from Antonia.'

'Matthew can supply you with the paternity angle,' said Henry. 'He has the experience.'

'He does not feel as passionately as I do,' said James. 'He is almost indecently relaxed. I feel it's unsafe to let Barbara out of my sight, I have to force myself.' Then, seeing that Henry smiled, he said rather nastily, 'I come of different stock from you.'

Henry let this ambiguous swipe pass.

27

A fortnight before their child was due, Barbara persuaded James to come to Cotteshaw. She wanted to get out of London, she said. She pined for country air. The weather, bright and frosty, was too good to be hanging about in London; hanging about would not make the baby come any faster.

In point of fact James, loving and nervous, was making her twitchy, she told Antonia as they walked by the lake, their feet crunching on the frosted grass.

'I am not due for two weeks; my mother says all first babies are late. It will take his mind off me if we are with you. You have been through it; Matthew can steady James's nerve, and you,' she said, 'can steady mine.'

'I don't know about that,' said Antonia. 'If it were not for Henry, Matthew and James would be dogging us now, but he's sent them out with their guns to pot a pheasant or shoot pigeon. Matthew went because I urged him to, and your James was only persuaded by the thought of taking a brace back to London. Henry said pheasant does something special for pregnant mums, and he believed him,' she said, laughing.

Barbara said, 'Henry is a thoughtful and generous man. I am grateful.'

Antonia said, 'I suppose he is. Yes, I dare say you are right,' and grinned.

They walked slowly for Susie was with them, keeping up as best she could, stamping her miniature boots in her mother's larger footprints.

'What's it like?' Barbara questioned. 'Can you tell me what to expect? I'm not very good with pain, never have been.'

'You forget,' Antonia said. 'You are so pleased it's over, and you've got the baby, you don't think about it.'

Barbara said, 'I remember you swore never to repeat the experience.'

Antonia said, 'I am sure I said no such thing. I was so happy I forgot all about it. Anyway, you should have an easy time. You have wider hips than me.'

Barbara said, 'I don't think I have. I suppose Matthew was overjoyed? That must have been lovely.'

'To be honest,' said Antonia, glancing back at her small daughter, 'Matthew wanted a son.'

'He seemed very pleased to me,' said Barbara. 'So he was not overjoyed? Goodness!'

'Matthew's into primogeniture,' said Antonia shortly.

'You will have a boy this time,' consoled Barbara. 'And as for me,' she said a touch smugly, 'James will be ecstatic whatever I have.'

'Lucky you,' said Antonia. 'Come on, Susie, come away from the edge. Run, I am getting cold.' She held out her hand to the toddler, who responded by sitting backwards onto the frosted grass. 'And they talk of the joys of parenthood,' she exclaimed as she jerked Susie to her feet.

Susie began to cry.

Barbara said, 'Let me take her,' and picked Susie up. 'You shouldn't be cross with her,' she said. 'You will make her jealous of her little brother.'

'Put her down, she is quite able to walk,' snapped Antonia. 'If I don't have a boy this time,' she said, 'Matthew can stuff his primogeniture. Put her down,' she repeated. 'You should not be heaving weights in your condition. Matthew must learn,' she said, 'that two tots per couple is quite enough on this overcrowded planet.'

'And if it's another girl this time?' Barbara kissed Susie's plump cheek.

'He must lump it,' said Antonia robustly.

'I don't think James sees further than the bliss of one.' Barbara kissed the child again and set her down to walk between them, holding hands.

'Poor little Suez,' Antonia said more kindly. 'Susie Suez,' she teased her child. 'Thank the Lord,' she said, 'that there isn't a world crisis raging at the moment with the threat of petrol rationing there was then.'

Barbara laughed. Susie, born during the Middle East crisis of 1956, was often referred to as 'Suez'. 'It's a terrible nickname,' she said, 'you must drop it. Her friends at school will call her "Sewage".'

'The Jonathans already do.' Antonia grinned. 'Now *that's* a marriage which has lasted,' she said thoughtfully. 'No tiny sewages to aggravate, just their two sweet selves.'

'I had not thought of it as a marriage,' said Barbara, uneasy that Antonia should be thinking of marriage lasting – or not.

Antonia said, 'What else would you call it? They share a house, they share an occupation, they share a bed, they—'

'Share love?' suggested Barbara doubtfully.

Antonia said roughly, 'Well, I haven't watched through the keyhole, but it's love all right.'

Barbara said again, 'I had not thought of it that way.' And, as they walked on, each holding one of Susie's hands, she thought of the marriages she knew, shying away from her parents'; of Antonia's, which was not always straightforward, and her own to James, loving and giving, she thought gratefully. Then, noting

253

Antonia's discontent, she wondered whether Antonia in bed with Matthew ever in imagination substituted someone else in his place? Henry, for instance.

'Henry has an odd sort of marriage,' she said, 'and *that* lasts.'

'Speaking of which,' said Antonia, 'here comes Margaret dressed in red, showing off her figure to annoy us.'

'Not agoraphobic today,' remarked Barbara.

'Patently not. Hullo, Margaret,' Antonia shouted. 'Nice to see you up and about. Come and walk with us.'

'It will be nicer when you no longer blot the landscape like a couple of barrage balloons,' said Margaret equably. 'Hullo, Sewage,' she said, coming up to them. 'Like to hold my hand?'

To Antonia's annoyance Susie ran to her and Margaret, catching her by the hand, ran with her along the path by the water, making her jump with her short legs to keep up. Her own legs, long and slender, were encased in tight dark red trousers, over which she wore a heavy scarlet jacket. When the child failed to keep up, she took both her hands and swung her round and round. Susie shrieked with delight.

'You'll make her throw up,' shouted Antonia. Margaret whirled the child round again before setting her down.

'Wouldn't you like a child of your own?' Barbara asked. 'You looked so happy doing that,' she said, 'and beautiful. The sun caught your hair.'

Margaret said, 'People like me don't have children. The idea's obscene.'

Barbara swallowed. 'You say that for effect,' she said. 'Admit it, you would love to have a child.'

'If I did, I would drown it,' said Margaret.

Deciding that Margaret joked, Barbara laughed.

(Later, discussing her with James, she explained that Margaret had been so much better lately, getting up, joining a bit in life, shopping, it was possible to interpret her remarks as a form of humour – if one stretched it a bit, tried to be charitable, she said.) So, laughing, she said, 'Oh, Margaret, you desire to shock,' and smiled at Susie, who looked up at Margaret, tugged at the hem of her jacket and cried, 'Swing! Swing!'

Margaret said, 'In a moment,' pushing the child's hand away.

'You and Susie seem to get on rather well,' said Antonia, puzzled by her daughter's behaviour. (One knows, she said later to Matthew, that small children's taste is invariably bad.)

'Pilar lets her trail along when she is working for me,' said Margaret, 'when, as so often, you are taking advantage of her time. I know Sewage quite well, don't I, Sewage?'

Susie, looking up adoringly, said: 'Yes. Swing? Swing?'

'Run, then,' said Margaret, 'run,' and she chased the child along the bank until, catching her, she took her hands and began whirling her round and round, laughing as the child shrieked with terror and delight.

'It's amazing to see Margaret enjoying herself. She looks quite lovely when she laughs,' said Barbara, watching. 'D'you think she's getting better from her agoraphobia?'

'I don't think she's ever had it,' said Antonia. 'It's all pretence. She's comfortable in bed and doesn't have to work. She hasn't enough brain to get really bored, but I admit,' she said grudgingly, 'that she has the most marvellous figure. Gosh,' she said, 'I shall be glad to get my body to myself again.'

'I have thoroughly enjoyed being pregnant,' said

255

Barbara. 'James and I – Oh, should she go so near the edge? What a stupid thing to say, that she would drown a child if she had one.'

'She tries to get a rise, says things like that for effect. Oh! *Careful*, you fool!' Antonia's voice failed as Margaret, swinging Susie, slipped on the frozen ground and, staggering back to regain her balance, let go of Susie, who appeared to fly away from her to land with a splash in the lake.

Antonia and Barbara plunged into the water.

'Her hands slipped out of mine,' Margaret said from the bank.

Barbara and Antonia, waist deep in water, held Susie, silent and stunned in shock, between them.

'You should have taken your wellies off,' said Margaret.

Susie, taking a deep breath, began to scream.

'Oh well, she's obviously all right,' said Margaret, standing back from the edge.

Henry, crossing the field with his dogs, had sighted Margaret in her red coat talking with Antonia and Barbara and was amused by their contrasting shapes. When next he looked Margaret was apparently alone. He began to run.

Antonia, up to her armpits in water, was yelling when he arrived, her voice almost drowning her daughter's. Neither she nor Barbara, encumbered by their pregnancy, were finding it easy to move. Both women held tightly to the child.

Leaning from the bank, Henry took Susie from them, put her down safely, then, stepping into the lake, pulled the two out.

'It was an accident.' Barbara had never seen Henry's face white.

'She tried to drown her.' Antonia hiccuped with

cold. 'She's a murderer. Look, she's walking away.'

'She didn't want to get wet too, don't exaggerate.' Barbara's teeth began to chatter. 'It was an accident,' she repeated.

'I told you you should have taken your boots off,' Margaret called over her shoulder.

Henry said, 'Boots?' and looked at the women's feet.

Antonia said, 'They are in the water.' She began to laugh as Lysander breasted into the lake to retrieve a boot which, retaining a little air, had bobbed to the surface.'

Barbara said, 'Suction,' and began to weep. 'Mud.'

Henry said, 'My turtle doves. Quick,' he said, kissing Antonia, 'let's get you home. I don't want to lose my babies.'

Barbara whispered, 'Yours—?' as Henry kissed her in turn, and he, with his mouth on hers, said, 'James's.' And then, 'Let me wring some of the water from your skirts, it will be easier to walk. Can you manage without boots? The grass is soft. Hurry,' he said, 'or you will freeze. It's going to snow, the sky went dark as you plunged into the lake – dramatic moment – Here, let me carry the child.' He worked to keep their spirits up. 'Come on, my brave girls.'

'Margaret,' Antonia gasped. 'She—'

'Margaret is a very stupid woman,' said Henry grimly. 'The only idea in her head is herself. I once got a psychiatrist to see her, and he said, "There is nothing I can do for a brain that size." Look, Susie,' he said to the child, who was whimpering with cold, 'Hector's bringing Mummy's boot. We'll soon get you warm and dry,' he said. 'Ah, there's your pa. Matthew,' he shouted, 'James,' and waved at the distant figures strolling home with their guns. 'Over here,' he called.

They were halfway to the house and James and

Matthew were running to meet them when Antonia's pains started.

'Oh, Christ! Oh, bloody hell.' She held on to Henry. 'You wanted to know,' she said to Barbara. 'Ouch! This is what the pains are like. I am giving you a live demonstration.'

28

'Pilar?' Margaret shouted as she let herself into the house. 'Pilar,' she called, standing in the hall. 'Pilar.'

'Yes,' Pilar answered from a distance. 'What is it?'

'I am cold. I should not have gone out. I shall go to bed. Bring some tea.'

'Can't you get your own?' Pilar called back. But she went into the kitchen and set the kettle to boil. Waiting on Margaret to save argument and save herself trouble was an ingrained habit. But there was an unusual note in Margaret's voice.

Pilar went through to the hall.

Henry came hurrying in. 'Telephone,' he said. 'I must get the doctor. Please help, Pilar. Perhaps we should get an ambulance? I'd better – Here, can you cope with Susie? She's been in the lake. Get her dry,' he said, beginning to dial. 'She's sopping.'

Pilar ran forward and took the child as Matthew and James, each supporting their wives, came into the house.

Halfway up the stairs Margaret sat down to watch.

Henry was telephoning the doctor. 'He *can't* be out,' he said. 'Where can I catch him? Where? What? At the hospital? All right, I'll try there. Yes, yes, it's urgent.'

Straining to sound calm, Matthew said, 'Tell him Antonia's in labour, tell him—'

Dialling, Henry said, 'I'm trying the hospital, he's there. We—'

Antonia, doubling up, groaned, 'Aaah!'

Matthew said, 'Here, sweetie. Sit here. You should get out of those wet clothes. Let me help.'

In Pilar's arms, Susie began to shriek, 'Mummy, Mummy,' kicking out her legs and arching her back against Pilar, so that it was difficult for Pilar to hold her.

Looking through the banisters, Margaret said, 'What an extraordinary spectacle. What about that tea?'

Trask, appearing from nowhere, took Susie from Pilar and began stripping off the child's wet clothes, saying, 'Trask will get 'ee dry. Keep still, my beauty, soon have 'ee warm.' Deftly he removed the child's clothes until she was naked, then, removing his sweater, he pulled it over her head.

(In adulthood, in times of stress, Susie would recollect the comfort and warmth, how the jersey clothed her from chin to feet in scratchy, soothing Fair Isle, how it smelled of Trask, and the struggle her hands had had when he set her down in a chair to find their way out of inordinately long sleeves to pat Lysander's kindly enquiring nose.)

Margaret, watching, called down, 'And what about *me*? What a fuss you are making. What about my *tea*?'

Without looking up, Henry said, 'Fuck your tea. No, no, not you,' he said into the telephone. 'I'm trying to get through to the doctor—'

James said, 'Barbara, I must get you to bed, I must—'

Barbara snapped, 'Rubbish! Just help me out of this wet clobber and wrap me in something while you fetch some dry things. I'm quite all right,' she said. 'Don't dramatize.' She had no wish to be separated from Antonia or from the comfort of Henry who, holding the telephone in one hand, had lifted the lid of an oak chest and was pulling out rugs. 'Give me one of those,' she said. 'My top half's dry. I'm only wet from the waist down.'

Margaret remarked, 'Waist! What waist?'

While James exclaimed, 'You can't undress in the hall – all these people – the baby.'

Barbara said, 'I can,' and divested herself of skirt and knickers. 'They are too busy to admire my bush,' she said, her teeth chattering. 'This is no time to be modest.' She snatched a rug from Henry and wrapped it round herself. 'Ah, that's better,' she said more calmly.

Henry said, 'He's on his way,' and replaced the receiver. 'Won't be long.'

Barbara said, 'If you want to be useful, James, you could get me my warm slippers and some wool socks.'

James said, 'At once. You all right if I leave you?' and raced up the stairs past Margaret.

As James rushed past, Margaret shouted, 'I did ask for some tea. Won't someone—'

Henry turned to Antonia, struggling out of her wet clothes with Matthew's help. 'The doctor will be here soon,' he said. 'He asked how frequent your pains are.'

'Too bloody frequent,' Antonia grunted. 'Did you get the car back from the garage?' she asked Matthew.

Miserably Matthew said, 'No. They have to get a spare part. It never occurred to me that you – that you'd start.'

Antonia said, 'That's all we need.'

Henry said, 'Don't worry, Matthew, there's James's car and mine.'

Antonia said, 'I'd like to give birth in a vintage Bentley, it smacks of style. Ooh!' She gripped Matthew's hands. 'Ooh, Matthew, I am not enjoying this.'

James came down the stairs three at a time. He carried Barbara's fur slippers and an armful of eiderdowns.

Margaret said, 'If her waters break, it will make a mess on the carpet.'

Matthew said, 'My God! Wonderful! You have been quick. This is my wife, she's—' to a man who was coming hesitantly into the hall.

'The door was open,' the man said. 'The bell doesn't seem to function.'

'It never has,' said Matthew. 'It's my wife, doctor, she's in labour. The child's not due for at least a month.'

'I'm not a doctor.' The man stepped backwards in alarm, 'I came to see—'

'What on earth are *you* doing here?' Margaret said from the stairs. 'I imagined you dead,' she said disagreeably.

'Not yet.' The man looked up at Margaret. 'How are you?' he asked. 'You look fine,' he said, moving towards her. 'What's going on?' he asked.

'A disgusting exhibition,' said Margaret. Then she said, 'Perhaps *you* could get me some tea. I went out and got awfully cold. I need something hot to revive me.'

'I wouldn't know where to find it,' said the man, sitting down on the step below her. 'I heard you lived in bed,' he said.

Margaret said, 'Where have you sprung from?'

'Some acquaintances are putting me up for the night.'

'The Jonathans?' She narrowed her eyes.

'Yes.'

Matthew, gaping, said, 'So you are not the doctor?'

The man said, 'Afraid not.'

Margaret said, 'This is my brother Basil.'

Matthew turned back to Antonia. Henry had taken it upon himself, he noticed in sudden fury, to move her from the hall to the drawing-room sofa and was wrapping her in an eiderdown brought by James. 'Let *me* do that,' he said and pushed Henry aside.

From the stairs Margaret shouted, 'I asked for tea, for Christ's sake.'

Henry murmured, 'Good idea,' and left the room.

James, tenderly enveloping Barbara in an eiderdown, asked, 'Are you all right, darling? I love you so.'

She said, 'And I love you. Sorry I was stroppy. You know I don't mean it.'

James said, 'Of course not,' and held her hand. 'Are you sure you're all right? You gave me such a fright. What possessed you to jump into the lake?' he said, peering into her eyes as though they would divulge the secrets of her heart.

Barbara said, 'Don't worry, don't fuss, please. It's Antonia,' she whispered. 'Her baby isn't due for weeks.'

James said, 'I had not thought, I was thinking of ours. After all,' he said, 'they've got one already. We haven't.'

'Not yet,' she said, 'soon. It's going to be all right, darling.' She could see that he was shaken and was moved. 'It might be a good thing if you put some logs on the fire,' she said. (It might be a good thing, she thought, to keep him occupied. This was not the moment to tell him that she had begun to have funny pains in her back. Time enough when the doctor had come and dealt with Antonia.)

James busied himself with the fire. Barbara watched him.

Antonia groaned.

Matthew exclaimed, 'I wish that doctor would hurry.' Then he said, 'I am trying to keep calm. Giving birth is such an everyday occurrence, but when it's applied to myself I feel it's unique, not easy at all.'

Antonia, with jocularity, said, 'I shall tell your son

you endured my time of travail with true British phlegm.'

Matthew snapped, 'This is no time to make jokes. If you heap all those logs on the fire, James, you'll set fire to the chimney.'

Antonia gasped, 'If not now, when? When can I make jokes?' But she took his hand and pressed it to her cheek. 'It will be all right,' she said, 'you'll see.' Then she said, as Henry came into the room followed by Pilar, 'Oh good, hot tea, just what we need.'

Henry, carrying a loaded tray, said, 'And hot toddies for Dads. I think I hear the doctor at last.'

Matthew, remembering, said, 'Your brother-in-law, Basil, is with Margaret.'

Henry, pouring tea, said, 'I don't know that I have a brother-in-law. Trask has brought James's car round and mine, should we need it. Here, Antonia, drink this if you can,' passing her a cup. 'And Barbara,' he said, 'you look as if you could do with one. Here he comes,' in accents of relief as the doctor came into the room.

The doctor's arrival had a magical effect. Antonia and Barbara grew compliant.

'There is intensive care, if you need it,' he said to Antonia. 'The child will be fine.'

'I am afraid of incubators—' Antonia looked askance.

'Your baby won't be, he will not know he is in one.'

'How d'you know it's a he?' Antonia shouted, gripped by a strong pain. 'Sorry,' she said, 'I did not mean to shout.'

'Get your wife into my car,' the doctor told Matthew. 'We shouldn't waste time.'

'Even a new-born child would know the difference between my tum and a machine.' Antonia let Matthew lead her out. 'Matthew,' she said, 'you've stopped being jittery.'

Matthew said, 'Get into the car. I never was.'

Antonia said, 'Ho!'

'And you,' the doctor said to Barbara, 'are to follow with your husband. He tells me you are due very soon.'

Barbara said, 'I think we are neck and neck, but I don't want to frighten my husband.'

The doctor laughed.

Henry stood on the steps and watched them go.

Basil, thinking it time to introduce himself, joined Henry by the front door. He would explain his presence, arrange to come again at a more convenient time.

29

'And Margaret's brother, did you say his name is Basil? What's happened to him?' asked Antonia, propped up by pillows in the hospital bed, in the room she shared with Barbara. 'He was staying with you, that much we know. What sort of account did he bring back to you? He must have been quite surprised by the birth drama.'

'He's gone,' said John. 'I must say, Antonia, maternity suits you. You are looking beautiful as well as pale and interesting. Where's the baby?'

'Looking ugly in an incubator,' said Antonia. 'But she will be all right, I'm told, given time. Tell us about Basil.'

'James and Matthew can't tell us anything,' Barbara interjected. 'He was gone when they got back to Cotteshaw. What do you think of my achievement?' She pointed to the cot at the foot of her bed. 'Isn't she divine?'

The Jonathans stared at the scrap in the cot. 'Not as pretty as you,' they said, peering. 'A strange form of divinity,' they teased. 'Not our line of country.'

'So tell us about this Basil,' said Barbara. 'Is *he* your line of country?'

'Actually, yes,' said John. 'As Henry will have told you.' He helped himself to a grape from the bunch he had brought the girls.

'Henry has not been to see us,' said Antonia.

The older man said, 'Oh?' and he, too, took a grape. 'Oh.'

'Have a grape,' said Antonia. 'Help yourselves.'

'Thanks,' said the older man. 'Is Matthew thrilled with his new daughter?'

'If he is, he's hiding his feelings pretty successfully,' said Antonia. 'Lots of *sangfroid anglais* in my Matthew, deep wells of it,' she said. (If they say I can always try again, I shall scream, she thought.) 'Have another grape and tell us about Margaret's brother,' she said. 'Is he beautiful, like her?'

'He is, actually,' said the younger man, 'but in character I'd say chalk to her cheese.' He picked at the grapes and thought of Matthew's ridiculous desire for a son. What did its sex matter if the baby had survived and Antonia come to no harm? 'Margaret's brother,' he said, spacing his words with grapes, 'has the same hair and skin but darker eyes and a much nicer expression. I'd say, from what we've seen of him, that he is a kind man.'

'Very kind,' said his lover, putting out a hand for the grapes.

'Have some of mine,' said Barbara. 'James brought these.' She reached for a plate of fruit. 'We can't possibly eat them all. James is taking me home tomorrow.'

'Taking the baby, too?' asked the younger man.

Barbara said, 'Of course.'

Barbara looked radiant, they told one another later, so happy and proud. There had been no snide remarks about James.

'And you?' the older man asked Antonia. 'Are they letting you go?'

'In a few days,' she said. 'It's got to be worked out. The poor baby may have to wait to be on the safe side, and if she stays, I do, too. Come on,' she said. 'Tell us about the mysterious Basil. Is he really her brother? Why have we never heard of him? Is he an old friend of yours? What's all the mystery?'

'There is no mystery,' the Jonathans protested.

Antonia said, 'Then tell.'

'He is a friend of a friend who went to the States in the war. We barely know him. He is in England on business and thought he would check up on his sister. Out of duty, perhaps? That's about all,' they said.

'Bet it isn't,' said Barbara. 'Why so many years before he visits?'

'He and Margaret don't get on.'

'Then he must be all right,' said Antonia. 'You heard, I suppose, that she tried to drown Susie?'

'It was an accident,' said Barbara.

'Tell us about it,' said the Jonathans.

'No. You tell us about Basil,' said Antonia. 'If you don't I shall regale you with how the nurses come and pinch my nipples and milk me so that they can feed my baby with a pipette.'

The Jonathans rose to go.

'Sit down,' said Barbara, laughing. 'Tell us what happened when we were rushed to hospital with our distraught husbands in the advanced stages of parturition. What took place between Henry and his long-lost, new-found brother-in-law?'

Suddenly angry, the older man said, 'Very well, I shall. Basil had been watching you all with Margaret from the stairs; when you left Margaret went, as she always does, to her bed. He was alone in a strange house. He was embarrassed. He thought he'd creep away and come back on a more suitable, less fraught occasion and introduce himself properly.' Jonathan looked from Antonia to Barbara.

Barbara said, 'Go on.' Then she said, 'Please.'

Jonathan cleared his throat. He said, 'He found

Henry standing on the doorstep blinded by tears.'

Barbara said, 'Oh, my God,' and began to weep.

Antonia, leaning forward, asked quietly, 'What else did this Basil tell you?'

'Nothing.'

'There must have been—'

'Henry and he went for a walk.'

'And?'

'Basil said he and Henry talked and talked. Basil said it was like strangers meeting on a train. He talked about his sister—'

'And Henry?'

'Basil did not tell us what Henry talked about.'

'No?'

'Basil said what Henry told him was private.'

'And you are aggrieved,' said Barbara gently.

'Yes,' they said, sighing, shamefaced. 'Yes. We are.'

30

Margaret's brother Basil had had to hurry to keep up with Henry, who was at least a head taller, had long legs and walked fast. If I drop behind, he thought, I shall look ridiculous and may fall foul of one of those awful dogs. He lengthened his stride and managed to keep abreast by putting in a stride in the nature of a leap every so often. Doing this, he was aware that the dogs, trotting with ears and tails depressed, hastened too. He was reminded of the pains of childhood when, outpaced by impatient adults, he had wailed, 'Wait for me, Daddy, wait!' and forced his legs into a tired trot.

Henry had seemed unaware of him. I should catch his attention, talk. Talk about what? Talk about what I came to talk about, he chid himself, as they progressed across a couple of fields until their progress was halted by an intractable gate. While Henry wrestled with the gate, which sagged on its hinges and had to be lifted clear, Basil said, 'Your dogs are rather lugubrious.'

Henry said, 'What?'

Rather breathless, Basil said, 'I said your dogs are lugubrious. They look unhappy.' He was embarrassed to see that Henry still had tears running unchecked down his thin cheeks, splashing on to his chest as he lifted the gate to close it.

Henry said, 'It's sympathy. Poor old boys, cheer up, no need to put on your Humble and Cringe act. It's *not* your fault,' he said and leaned down to pat flanks and stroke heads. The animals' ears rose and tails lifted, they sneezed in appreciation, and the younger dog pranced away for a few paces before resuming station.

Leaning on the gate, Henry exclaimed, 'It is so awful. They were comical young creatures when they first came here, and now they are women in labour, for God's sake! Oh dear!' He pulled a handkerchief from his pocket and blew his nose. 'And I am lachrymose.' He stopped crying. 'Did you say you were Margaret's brother?' he asked, remembering his manners.

Basil said, 'Yes. But don't let it bother you.'

Henry said, 'I won't,' and resumed walking, but not as fast as before.

Basil said, 'What on earth possessed you to marry her?'

Henry had walked on without answering and Basil thought, I've lost him again, but he went on talking. 'I live in the States,' he said. 'I have not seen my sister since before the war. News of her marriage to you took time to reach me. I am an American citizen. I move around a lot.' His voice grew nasal as he reminded himself of his adoptive country.

'Margaret's a lot older than me,' he said, 'and frankly I never liked her. And she drove our parents mad. I was glad when she got off her butt and left home. She always spent all her time in bed; I gather she's not changed overmuch. Then she suddenly got a job in a beauty salon. Father was furious; he wanted her to do something "worthy". Father himself was worthy, or aspired to worthiness, actually. He was a bit of a snob, didn't think "beauty" a worthy occupation, but worthy or not it took her to Egypt and in due course she married Clovis. That didn't please Father, either; he was rabidly anti-German. Anti-semitic, too. Clovis was both, German and Jew. The marriage didn't last, of course. Margaret's devotion to bed was for sleeping solo and Clovis is like me, he – Well, let's say we are of the same persuasion.'

Basil had risked a glance at Henry. Was he listening? If I go on talking, it will give him time to recover from whatever hit him, he thought.

'So there Margaret was,' he said, 'a German national in Egypt in wartime. The only friend she had was some sort of Pasha who was pro-Nazi – a purely non-sexual relationship, of that I am sure. Anyway, when the Brits interned him, Margaret must have taken fright; actually I know she did. I heard this from your chums the Jonathans. We all know the rest. Your father was a great guy, I hear, given to acts of kindness to women in peril, but – but he seems to have committed his last act by proxy.' Basil's voice sank to a whisper.

They had reached another gate; the younger of the dogs, cheerful now and jolly, leapt it, showing off. The older dog slid through the rails.

Henry, frowning, said, 'I am not wanted at the hospital, I shall not go. Curse it. Curse it.'

It was Basil's turn to say, 'What?' Then he said, 'So why on earth did you marry Margaret?' Standing in Henry's way as he opened the gate, looking up, he had raised his voice; it had occurred to him that Henry might be deaf.

Henry said, 'I am not deaf,' and closed the gate. 'What business is it of yours?' he asked rudely. 'But of course, you said you are her brother,' he said more pleasantly. Then he smiled. 'There's a strong resemblance. I trust it's only skin deep.'

Basil said, 'I sincerely hope so.' They walked on. Basil wondered how far Henry was in the habit of walking. If only I'd known, he thought, I would have worn more suitable shoes.

He said, 'Our parents left a muddle with their wills, it's taken years to sort it out—'

Henry said, 'Jarndyce and Jarndyce.'

And Basil had said, 'Oh good, you are listening,' allowing himself a tinge of sarcasm. 'Shall I go on?'

Henry said, 'Why not?'

'I could have got the lawyers to write,' said Basil, 'but frankly I was curious to see what sort of fellow would get himself embroiled with my sister. I was even more anxious when I discovered that you were not one of us. Anyway,' he said hastily, seeing Henry look surprised, 'I came to tell Margaret that she's in for a lot more dough than she has already. She'll be well able,' he had said, chuckling, 'to have that awful red room redecorated without bothering you. I suggested blue for the next—'

'I would not dream of letting my wife spend her money on Cotteshaw,' Henry shouted. 'I never have and I never shall. I don't give a damn for her money,' he yelled. 'It would be obscene to – Oh dear,' he said, 'I apologize. Do forgive me. You are my brother-in-law. I should not be so offensive. It is just,' he said quietly, 'that you look so like her, it's, well—'

Basil said, 'I quite understand,' and wished that he did.

Henry began walking again. Basil followed.

Henry said, 'Of course it would be quite different if I liked her. I'd use it then, gladly.'

Basil laughed. 'I still would like to know why you married her,' he said.

Henry said, 'Oh – you must forgive me, I'm so – It's Barbara and Antonia. I find it difficult to think of anyone else.'

Basil said, 'Those girls will be all right, I'm sure they will. Of course they'll be all right. Their husbands were pretty fussed, that's natural, but you were splendid. So calm. So outside it all. So practical.'

Henry murmured, 'I have treated them lightly, irresponsibly, as a sort of joke. I had no right.'

Basil saw that he was again distraught. He said, 'Margaret? Marriage? Why?'

'What a gadfly you are.' Henry had stopped in his tracks to look at Basil, taking in his stocky build, wide smile, a mouth so different from Margaret's which was more like a knife wound than anything else, hazel eyes the antithesis of her cold and silver slits, a nose brave rather than elegant, good but slightly wayward teeth. His hair was the same colour, though gingery gold. Unlike Margaret, he felt he could trust him.

'If one put your face and Margaret's together,' he said, 'you would look like the masks of tragedy and comedy.'

'Except that Margaret is not tragic.' Basil smiled.

Henry said, 'You think not?'

Basil said, 'No way,' laughing. 'Come on,' he said, 'even if I am her brother I think you should tell me firstly why you married her and, more importantly, why you stay tied? That really throws me.'

'Paradoxically,' Henry said grimly, 'the situation provides me with a sort of freedom.' He resumed his walk at a pace Basil could comfortably match, and the dogs, sensing a relaxation of tension, began circling round, sniffing at feral smells and indulging in mild play.

'So the Jonathans told you of their part in my marriage,' Henry said. 'I have long suspected it, never been sure. I dare say,' he said, 'that they feel a bit funny on that score.'

Seeing no reason to protect the Jonathans, Basil said, 'Who wouldn't? The way they present their case is that they were helping your father, whom they revered, do his bit in the war effort.'

'He was dying,' Henry interposed.

'They say it was his attempt to minimize the suffering of innocents,' Basil explained.

Henry laughed.

At that Basil, laughing too, said shrewdly, 'No doubt at the time they did not realize you were such an innocent.'

Henry said, 'Not so much innocent as sorry for myself, I am ashamed to say. I had had a surprise.'

Basil hazarded, 'A disappointing surprise?'

Henry said, 'Yes. And,' he said, 'I had the idea, common to a lot of us at that time, that I would not survive the war. People were getting killed; why not me? So I thought, What the hell, and married your sister. Can't say I take any pride in it,' he said, glancing at Basil, who kept quiet, glad that he had succeeded in goading Henry into speech. 'When I found I had not been killed or even wounded,' Henry went on, 'and the chance came to get Margaret back to England, I brought her here to Cotteshaw. I was trying by then to make a go of it. I thought I must try; that if other people made unsatisfactory marriages work, it should be possible for me.' Henry sighed, then he said, 'I love Cotteshaw. Naïvely I thought she would too, that here we could start afresh—'

They had reached the top of the hill behind the house. Henry stopped and looked down across the tops of trees to the house, its gardens and fields stretching down the valley to distant hills.

'She went to bed,' Henry murmured, 'and there she stayed.' Basil bit his tongue. Henry said, 'The medical people say there is nothing wrong with her. I have tried to entice her out of it,' he gave a short laugh and said, 'with various and diverse results. She seems happiest in bed, not that so positive a word as happy can be applied to your sister. And when she does get up of her own accord – well, look at today.'

'She seemed to be enjoying herself,' said Basil, 'a bit perverse—'

Henry said, 'The Jonathans and other friends try their luck; she isn't easy. Pilar and Trask are wonderfully patient. Ebro redecorates her rooms when she wants a change. It's an odd set-up.' He resumed walking and Basil kept pace. 'I tried once,' Henry said quietly, 'I knew it was a gamble but I had to try, I suggested we sleep together. I thought it possible that she might want a child.' Henry winced at the recollection; he had thought that with an effort of will during the act he could pretend he was making love to Calypso; he shuddered and Basil wondered whether he was ill. They had come to another gate and Henry opened it to let Basil through. 'I must have a go at these gates,' he muttered. 'They are dropping on their hinges.'

Basil thought then that he had stopped talking; he watched him close the gate and latch it, then ventured, 'So?'

'She went for me with a knife,' Henry said.

Basil said, 'My God!'

'Oh,' Henry said, 'it was stupid of me.' Then he said, 'You may not know you want a thing until it is denied you,' and Basil realized he was not referring to any need of Margaret's. 'Your sister,' Henry said, 'is a prime example of the stronger sex; by doing bugger-all she has a whole household dancing attendance, indulging her whims.'

Basil said, 'How do you survive? I mean—'

And Henry, detecting a note of prurience in the other man, answered drily, 'There are other women, friendly and complaisant, and call-girls. I manage. I can't waste my time wishing your sister dead,' he said roughly.

Basil swallowed. 'You suggested earlier that she gave you a sort of freedom.'

'And a precious element of privacy,' Henry agreed,

276

and Basil thought, but could not be sure, that he had then muttered, 'but which has now gone sour.'

Henry had then suddenly increased his pace, walking as though he were alone with his dogs, or perhaps hoping to shake his companion off. Basil ran a few steps. 'So what do you do?' he asked.

'Do?'

'Yes.'

'I work. I run my farm. The Jonathans work the vegetable gardens along with their smallholding and, since Matthew and James brought their girls and became permanent features, they have paid their share. It has helped to keep the wolf at bay.'

'A commune?'

'I suppose you could call it that. It's not an appellation my father would have enjoyed. I don't know what will happen now. It started with a foolish attempt at reviving a pre-war custom, a posh dinner party. There was a bird I had given Margaret, a cockatoo, she – The party went sadly wrong. And now – I don't know.' And Basil thought he whispered, 'I am excluded,' or, 'I must exclude myself.'

Basil said, 'I am not with you.'

'You seem very much with me, to me,' said Henry rather nastily. 'Do forgive me, I am not usually so rude.'

He was looking white and miserable again, but Basil could not stop now. He said, 'So what's your bother now?'

'Antonia and Barbara, of course. Their babies.' Henry shouted, 'What a mess, what a worry.'

'You seem absurdly worked up about those women and their children.' Basil, too, raised his voice. He was losing patience, for he much disliked the thought of women pregnant, women in labour, indeed the whole gamut of women's sexual functions was repugnant –

not that I dislike women, he told himself; I have many women friends. 'It's perfectly natural,' he assured Henry, 'it happens all the time.' One just wishes it were out of sight, he thought. 'What's the fuss?' he asked loudly, rather more loudly than he intended, for it occurred to him that this man, his brother-in-law, had suggested that Margaret should go through 'all that'. Perhaps she and I have more in common than I imagined, he thought. 'It seems to me,' he said, still speaking loudly, for Henry was again beginning to outdistance him, 'that you should be grateful to your father and the Jonathans for their proxy act of kindness. It seems to me that you have been saved a helluva lot of pain.' He shouted to make sure Henry heard. 'It seems to me,' he cried, 'that you are jealous.'

Henry stopped, waited for Basil to catch up. Then he said, 'Jealous?' There was astonishment in his voice, but when he repeated the word the pain was almost palpable.

When, presently, they stood by Basil's car outside the house, Henry had asked, his tone disinterested, 'Shall you stay with the Jonathans?'

Basil said quickly, 'Only long enough to collect my bag. I don't wish to linger.'

Henry had said, 'Thank you.'

Part Five

1990

31

James Martineau and Matthew Stephenson, meeting by chance at a garage in Sloane Avenue as they filled their cars with petrol, exchanged chat.

'Off to the country?' James eyed Matthew's BMW, smarter and sleeker than his Volvo estate.

'On my way to my constituency surgery, via my father-in-law's funeral.' Matthew's tone was of vicarious importance; Lowther of Lowther's Steel was, or had been up to now, a household name.

Hastily James said, 'Of course. I'd forgotten it was today. Alas,' he said mendaciously, 'we cannot attend.' Why can't I be truthful, he asked himself? Why can't I admit I relied on Barbara to tell a wifely lie? Why can't I admit I never knew old Lowther well enough to feel I should go to his funeral?

'We sent a wreath,' he said. 'Is Antonia cut up?' He remembered as he spoke that Barbara, replying to the same question had said, She is delighted. It would be in poor taste to repeat this to Matthew, so he said again, 'Is Antonia cut up?'

'Not so that you'd notice. They were not all that close,' said Matthew guardedly.

'And her mother? She bearing up?'

'Actually,' said Matthew, giving way, 'we all think his death comes as a relief. My father-in-law could be – er – difficult.'

For difficult read fond of the bottle, thought James. 'So,' he said, 'Antonia and her brothers—' (I wonder

281

how much the old man has left? Must be a tidy sum even after death duties.)

'They will rally round,' said Matthew. 'We all will. Antonia's with her mother now. Susie and Clio will be there, of course, and Susie's boy Guy. My son-in-law's in the States; can't get back in time, he says. We all thought Clio's little girl a bit young, she won't be coming. Did we tell you that Susie's boy Guy is going to Eton? Antonia's inclined to call it a retrogressive step,' he said, laughing.

But you are pleased, thought James. 'I had heard,' he said. 'Scholarship?' It was fun to tease Matthew – Guy, a dear boy, was not scholarship material.

Matthew laughed. 'No, thick as two planks. Good at games, though. My son-in-law,' he said, 'is pro-Eton, considers it the best springboard, and so does Susie.'

A trifle out of date there, thought James, but then Matthew had scrambled and sprung in his day. 'Well, good luck to him. If you *had* had a son, would you have sent him to Eton?'

'If we could have afforded it, it's possible. I might have wanted to, but Antonia would not have stood for it. It's a hypothetical question, James. Susie and Clio—'

'Are girls,' said James, 'and jolly attractive.'

Matthew said, 'Thank you, and so is your Hilaria, a smashing girl.'

'Our lot did not do badly with state education,' James remarked, in a bid to lure his old friend away from dreams of grandeur. 'The end result can't be faulted,' he said.

'I agree,' said Matthew. 'My Clio and your Hilaria could not be nicer young women. I often wish, though, that I had not allowed old Lowther to pay Susie's fees at that boarding school. It was a mistake. All she learned were expensive tastes and bossiness and now we are expected to dig deep in our pockets to finance Guy at Eton. A comprehensive school would save a lot of bother and holidays at Cotteshaw would—'

James said, 'Times have changed, old friend. Pilar is long gone, and Trask is dead. Henry is grown old and ill. Things have altered since our young days.'

Matthew said, 'True, but how our children loved it. And whatever the changes, their kids love it now; when Clio tries to take her Katie abroad, all the child does is nag to get back to Cotteshaw.'

James laughed. 'It's the same with Hilaria's Eliza, but it can't last for ever. Well,' he said, 'I must get on. Let's meet soon.'

'I'll get Antonia to telephone,' said Matthew. 'You sailing this weekend?' he asked, having noted James's casual clothes and earlier white lie.

James said. 'I gave up sailing many years ago. Barbara never took to it. I am fishing, then joining Barbara at the cottage.' He got into his car and fastened his seat-belt.

Matthew and I are out of touch, he thought as he drove; then he thought, Matthew has aged, gone bald, doesn't keep as fit as he should, and was glad that he himself still had his head of hair, albeit white, and was pretty fit at sixty-five. Then, as he drove, reminded by his meeting with Matthew, he remembered the good times they had all had when they were young at Cotteshaw, their weekends and holidays, Henry teaching the children to ride and swim, letting them tag behind him on the farm. What fun those children had running wild in the country.

It had been good for Barbara and Antonia too, an idyllic period lasting until Pilar got it into her head to go back to Spain when Franco died. When was that – 1975? What possessed us all to let her take the three girls with her? Anything might have happened, but of course it hadn't; one could trust Pilar. She had sent them back speaking fluent Spanish and boasting that they had joined with her in spitting on Franco's grave. It was about then that one had stopped hesitating, bought the cottage and moved out of Cotteshaw.

Hilaria had never taken to the cottage, and now continually took her own child back to Cotteshaw. Had Barbara, loyal Barbara, missed the place? If she had she would not say. Had she really agreed that they had imposed on Henry for long enough, and that it was time they had a place of their own? Difficult to say. There were depths in Barbara, James thought uncomfortably. Had she agreed to please him? How can I doubt her? James asked himself. We have been so happy; we may only have the one child, but what a pearl! As great a joy to us as Barbara has always been to me. I have never loved any other woman, James assured himself.

Then he wondered, as he drove, whether Matthew still regretted his lack of a son, whether pushing his grandson into Eton was a solace? One knew from Barbara that Antonia, after the rough time she had had with Clio, had stuck in her toes, gone on strike, refused to try again. One sympathized with her, yet Matthew had so wanted a boy. It would not worry me, thought James, it never has, but Matthew is ambitious; look how he pushed when he was in business, look at him now in Parliament, it's all go!

Lucky 'thick as two planks' Guy is a grandson; Matthew will be indulgent, won't push too hard. He had pushed his elder daughter Susie all right, and she had gone along with it. Susie Stephenson should definitely have been a man, James ruminated as he drove. Susie was a woman of iron will.

Heavens, thought James, how lucky we have been with our affectionate, tactful, sweet-tempered Hilaria; family life would have been a real pain if Hilaria had had a nature like Susie Stephenson's.

I can't stand bossy women, James told himself as he headed out of London. I dare say, he thought, Susie will miss her grandfather Lowther. She doesn't drink, but in other respects she could not be more like him: bossy, interfering, and often rude. Small wonder her sister Clio has cleaved, if that is the right word, to our Hilaria rather than to her elder sister. Susie-the-know-all would know the correct use of the word or term cleave. I cleave, you cleave, he cleaved, or perhaps clove? James chuckled.

Would Eton teach Susie's Guy? Perhaps Guy was fortunate in his parents' ambition? Perhaps his mother's mania for managing other people's lives and directing their actions would be curbed by the school? Mind you, James told himself, his essential fair-mindedness reasserting itself, I should not be too hard on Susie; there have been occasions when her interfering bossiness has had the most excellent if unexpected results.

No, James thought, reverting to his old friend, Matthew's life would not suit me. Gosh, he thought, think of always having to toe the party line *and* please your constituents. No wonder Antonia – well. He checked himself. It was said, but there was no proof, that Antonia had stepped out from time to time. Maybe she found Matthew a bit boring? From the very beginning she had not hesitated to snap or speak a bit sharpish; it would be small wonder if she had not had the odd canter.

People, James thought, with less than his usual charity, would say anything or, if there was no evidence, they would invent, as Henry's ghastly wife Margaret had invented. Now *her* funeral, James's thoughts came full circle, was a funeral one had been truly glad to attend. Calypso Grant had called it a celebration.

32

Matthew, driving north out of London, was inclined to pity his old friend, whose in-laws, both still living, would not be leaving as substantial a fortune as Antonia's parent. Antonia would inherit a decent sum now and a lot more when her mother died; why should not Guy's education benefit?

Poor James was his own worst enemy, thought Matthew. He had not striven as he should have done, had lacked ambition, been content with a moderate law practice and only one child to show for his marriage, a girl at that. I dare say the old boy is more than a bit envious of my grandson, thought Matthew. I am proud of Guy and don't mind showing it. I shall play an important role in that boy's life; a grandparent's relationship can be close.

But I shall not let my closeness to Guy resemble Susie's to old Lowther, who positively fed and encouraged her bossiness. I bet, thought Matthew, that she is at this moment driving her grandmother and Antonia mad by organizing the funeral, not letting them have a say, 'knowing best', as is her way.

Susie has too much push, poor old James not enough; Guy's push must be moderate, as mine is. Even so, thought Matthew, James might have made an effort. Surely he and Barbara should be coming to the funeral? Wasn't this non-effort to attend rather insulting? Did it not belittle their long friendship, the closeness of their two wives, not to speak of the children? Our Clio and their Hilaria are thick as treacle, and their two children look like carrying the feeling on.

But there goes James, off for a day's fishing and a weekend in his grotty cottage, thought Matthew, annoyed, while I, after my father-in-law's funeral, have to work. Even when we all met every weekend at Cotteshaw I brought work with me, Matthew told himself, and it was surely I who had the bright·idea that we should pay our way, go shares, so that we should not be beholden to Henry. It had worked so well.

It was James who split the harmony, thought Matthew irritably; we should be congregating at Cotteshaw to this day if James had not taken it into his head to buy a cottage of his own. All very well for him to point out that Pilar had left; Pilar did not leave until the girls were almost grown-up and Trask, poor old Trask, had latterly been nothing but a liability, an incontinent one at that, thought Matthew, steering his BMW into the fast lane heading north.

James and Barbara came to Trask's funeral all right, thought Matthew crossly, the whole village came. People came from miles away. Calypso Grant brought Hamish, the Bullivants were there, Pilar and Ebro flew back from Spain and oh dear, thought Matthew, remembering how the children cried, not so much Susie, but Clio and Hilaria, buckets! And the Jonathans, grown men, quite old, had blubbered in the front pew. While Henry, stiff and silent, had looked bereft.

We could have found substitutes for Trask and Pilar, thought Matthew. A living-in couple. Such people exist. Antonia could certainly have found one, if only Henry had allowed. The house was his, one was aware of that, but considering how much one had contrib- uted over the years one had felt entitled to suggest, to have a say. One would gladly have contributed to their wage.

Perhaps making the suggestion so soon after the funeral had been premature. Certainly Antonia – Matthew winced in recollection of Antonia's forceful rejection of his proposal. She had not lost her talent for making herself disagreeable when so inclined. Even so, if she had helped, we could have preserved the status quo, arranged something better than Henry's present mode of life, only cared for by daily ladies and Clio and Hilaria on their infrequent visits.

I blame James, thought Matthew resentfully, James and his cottage. I was not yet in the position which I am in now to buy Henry out; that would have made sense. He has no heir, the place is a millstone. One could have sold most of the land, done the place up. Cotteshaw has sentimental attraction. I proposed to Antonia in the garden; I remember the feel of her skin, velvety as a mushroom. Clio was born there, and Susie was nearly drowned.

Cotteshaw had been home to both families. Growing up, the little girls had trailed round the farm behind Henry or Trask, watched Pilar cook, played hide-and-seek round the haystacks, been taught to swim by Henry, taught to ride by Henry. Henry had made them a toboggan when it snowed, taught them to skate; they had sat on his knee while he read them stories. Thinking about it, one owed Henry quite a lot, but small wonder that there had been moments when the children's worship of Henry had been rather irritating. At times of childish stress, a dog dying or a guinea-pig going AWOL, it had been to Henry they turned for comfort, not to oneself. One was not always there, nor was James.

Henry and Cotteshaw had been extremely useful as a base. It had been handy, when the children were small, to leave them there when taking Antonia on trips abroad; James and Barbara had done the same.

Things had gone stunningly until Susie had taken it into her head to reform Henry's wife Margaret. One would think, thought Matthew, that after the experience of Margaret letting go of her hands, letting her fall in the lake, Susie would not have wanted much to do with Henry's wife, but it had not been so. Margaret had held some sort of fascination for the child who, as she grew into her teens, had determined to succeed where everyone else had failed. Effect a transformation in Margaret's *modus vivendi*, that was what Susie had called it, flaunting the Latin from her posh school over less educated mortals such as her sister and James and Barbara's Hilaria. She would, she had said, normalize – dreadful word – Margaret's life.

So it was his own daughter Susie, nicknamed Sewage, with her innate bossiness, her passion for interference, her talent for knowing best, who had irreparably destroyed the happily-balanced set-up at Cotteshaw, not James.

Driving up the motorway to his father-in-law Lowther of Lowther's Steel's funeral, Matthew Stephenson made a mental apology to his friend James Martineau and, unable to stop himself, laughed out loud.

33

Susie Stephenson's intimacy with Henry's wife was short-lived but intense. It was in the summer of 1970, when she was fourteen, that she began visiting Margaret. Up to then she had, like the other children, kept out of Margaret's way, only meeting her on the rare occasions she put in a disruptive and surprise appearance downstairs. These occasions usually brought some unfortunate consequence; there was general relief when she went back to bed.

Susie had had a fight with her sister Clio and Hilaria who had, she thought, selfishly monopolized the ponies. A third animal was *hors de combat*, lame. Henry, who happened to be passing, hearing the shrill argument, had called out, 'For Christ's sake, shut up, girls,' and, 'You should be a little less selfish with the younger ones, Suez,' an accusation Susie took to be profoundly unjust, for Clio and Hilaria went to day school and were able to ride in term-time, which she was not.

Furious, and to demonstrate her thoughtful and caring nature, Susie had then volunteered to carry Margaret's lunch tray up and spare Trask, who had been about to do it, the trouble. Trask's legs in his old age were giving him rheumatic gyp.

Arriving outside Margaret's door, Susie knocked and was told to come in. She did so, feeling a twinge of apprehension, but buoyed by her annoyance with Henry.

Margaret, pale and beautiful, looked Susie up and down. 'You are the one they call Sewage.' Her eyes flicked from Susie's head to her feet. 'Far too pretty to be Antonia Stephenson's daughter.'

The room was now pale blue, matching its occupant's eyes. Susie, expecting angry red and stripes, was both taken aback by the décor and disgusted by Margaret's use of her nickname. Yet, flattered by the compliment, she said, 'Oh, er – mm,' and blushed as she placed the tray across Margaret's knees.

'Good legs and breasts,' said Margaret, and began picking at her lunch. 'Sit down,' she said. 'Try and amuse me. Your hair's not bad, too long of course. I gather it's the mode.'

Susie flicked the said hair over her shoulder and sat on the edge of a sofa, mute.

'Why do you dress in butter muslin?' asked Margaret, snapping at a chicken bone held in her fingers. 'Your clothes are terrible. I have seen you from my window. Are you supposed to be a "Flower Child"?' she asked contemptuously.

'No!' Hastily Susie denied her up-to-date ethnic attire. 'It's this or jeans,' she said, sliding the onus elsewhere. 'My mother—' She was tempted to say Antonia tried to dress her otherwise, but refrained.

'So you do not go to these festivals I hear about? King Arthur's Hump?' Margaret chewed the chicken.

'Glastonbury? No.' Susie shook her head. Matthew had put his foot down. ('Certainly not – no daughter of mine – far too young.') 'No.' Susie denied her interest in pop festivals.

Margaret sipped her glass of wine. 'See what you can find in those cupboards,' she said. 'Go on, help yourself.'

Willingly Susie explored the cupboards. Within minutes she was trying on Margaret's clothes.

The seduction, beginning with the lending of clothes, progressed naturally to question and answer. Where had this lovely dress come from? And this? And this? Susie was not a shy girl.

Margaret answered, 'Egypt.'

'Egypt?'

'I lived in Egypt. I was married there.'

'To Henry?'

'To someone else first. A monster.'

'Tell me.' Like the other children, Susie was only vaguely aware of Margaret's antecedents. Margaret told.

Susie's parents had been anxious to spare her young sensitivity, so the saga was fresh to her ear. She listened, goggling, to the allegations of mental and physical cruelty. The drugs, the sodomy and rape. But she was a sensible girl and when the same barbs were directed towards Henry she became less credulous, doubtful even. If she had not been angry with Henry she would not have believed any of it; as it was, she decided that there was something wrong. Henry had been neglectful, did not understand Margaret. Not a girl to let matters rest, influenced by her intellectual and breezy school, Susie suggested reasonably enough that some of Margaret's malaise might be due to boredom. If this were the case she, Susie, would volunteer to help.

There was never any explanation as to why Margaret accepted Susie's offer. Others, the Jonathans for instance, had cajoled Margaret into leaving her room without success. Henry had long since given up trying. Susie, of all people, should have known better; her trouble was that she thought she did.

The weather was warm. Susie and Margaret toured the garden. Susie taught Margaret croquet, watched at a distance by Hilaria and Clio, who giggled.

Pilar said, 'It won't last. She will go back to bed, she always does,' and brought Margaret's meals to the summer-house. Margaret returned to her room for dinner, but continued to rise every morning after breakfast. Susie felt that her sympathy and under-standing were having an effect.

The days grew hot. Clio and Hilaria spent all day by the lake, in and out of the water like frogs. From the croquet lawn Susie could see them leaping, watch the splashes. 'Margaret,' she said, for success made her bold, 'why don't we swim? You have a bikini, I've seen it.'

'My skin does not like the sun, I do not swim well,' Margaret quibbled.

Susie pressed her to try. The lake was alluring, but she would not abandon her charge. She grew insistent.

That night at supper she announced that she was going to teach Margaret to swim properly; it was a shame that nobody ever had.

Henry said, 'I would rather you didn't, Suez.'

Perhaps, he thought later, Susie would not have persisted if he had not called her Suez? If he had not been so busy on the farm. Not been preoccupied with his decision to sell the poor old Bentley to pay off the bank, a wrench he had delayed for too long. If her parents had been there, which they were not, and nor were Hilaria's. If he had not had a stinking summer cold which made his head feel stuffed with soggy cotton wool. If he had not been so sure Margaret would return to her room as she always had before, for she had never shown the slightest interest in swim-ming. If he had not, when Susie said, 'I understand Margaret, Henry. She is *quite* different with me to the rest of you. I can help her,' in that superior tone of voice, shouted at her, called her a silly interfering little bitch or words to that effect.

She had tossed her long hair, so like her mother Antonia's. She had flared up. 'You don't know how to treat her, Henry, you simply don't know. Leave us alone.'

If Clio and Hilaria had not laughed.

Neither Clio nor Hilaria had a stitch on the next day, fooling in and out of the lake.

Margaret, allowing herself to be led to the far side, out of earshot if not sight, by Susie carrying their bathing things, a rug to lie on and a parasol to protect their skin from the sun, remarked that that was how the wretched Fellaheen behaved in the Nile, a pretty disgusting sight.

'I shall speak to my mother,' said Susie, disparaging her sibling. (She would remember saying this with discomfort years later.)

Margaret said, 'You do that,' and settled on the rug which her acolyte spread for her.

Solicitously Susie smoothed suncream onto Margaret's shoulders, back and upper arms before rubbing a little onto her own shins. 'Shall we swim?' she said.

'You swim,' Margaret said, 'if that's what you want.'

'Oh no.' Susie lay back beside her, then, as Margaret did not relax, she sat up. And so they sat.

Unable after a while to endure the spectacle of her sister and Hilaria disporting themselves, Susie again suggested they swim.

Margaret said, 'You swim, show me whether you can.'

So Susie swam, showing off the crawl Henry had taught her, how she swam on her back, duck-dived and swam under water. Returning to the bank, she said, 'It is so lovely, Margaret, do come in. I will swim beside you. You can trust me. If you feel in the least uneasy, just grab hold of me.'

'We did not see her go in.'

'We were getting dressed.'

'I had one leg in my jeans—'

'My head was covered by my T-shirt – I was not looking.' Hilaria and Clio wept inconsolably; they had been too petrified to scream.

Henry was out of breath when he reached the lake and Margaret, panicking, had dragged Susie under; when he got them out Susie was unconscious and Margaret dead.

All this Matthew remembered as he drove up the motorway.

34

Antonia Stephenson picked up Barbara Martineau from her house in the street equidistant from the Brompton and King's Roads in which she and James had lived all their married lives.

'I can't imagine you living in any other street,' she said, kissing her friend as she got into the car.

'And I, just as I get used to you living in Kew, have to readjust to an address in Bayswater, Hampstead, Barnes or Westminster,' said Barbara amiably.

'Matthew accumulated a tidy bit of capital,' said Antonia. 'It was worth the nuisance. You and James should have done what we did, bought low and sold high, hard work but profitable.'

'James would not bother,' said Barbara. 'The only move he ever wanted was to our cottage. Moving is not his style.'

Antonia said, 'Nor it is,' neutrally. To her mind James lacked gumption. Then she said, 'Actually, since Father left me some lolly, I don't suppose we shall move house again. It is quite exhausting. And how,' she asked, 'is your menopause? Still sticking to Morning Glory? Susie says you should switch to HRT.'

'Morning Glory suits me,' answered Barbara. 'When Susie's hormones go astray, let her try HRT. Meanwhile—'

Antonia laughed. 'You should not let Susie get up your nose. I don't.'

Barbara, laughing too, said, 'I don't much,' and,

changing the subject, 'What are you bringing Henry?'
They were on their way to Cotteshaw.

'Caviar.'

'Gosh.'

'He once brought caviar for Margaret, do you
remember? Only the dogs profited.'

Barbara said, 'I do remember. My offering is
humbler, Gentleman's Relish.'

'Most suitable,' said Antonia, and drove in silence
until they had passed Chiswick and were heading
down the M4. Then she said, 'What's the latest news?
Is he better or worse?'

'It's always worse with emphysema,' said her friend,
'progressively.'

'Alas, that's true,' Antonia agreed. 'Such a shame, he
never smoked. It seems unfair.'

Barbara thought it would be unkind to remind her
friend that Henry only developed emphysema after the
double bronchial pneumonia he had caught from fishing two people out of the lake when suffering from a
fearsome summer cold, so she said no more.

Presently Antonia, laughing, said, 'Gentleman's
Relish; would you describe Henry as a gentleman?'

'Oh yes,' said Barbara. '*Sans peur*—'

'And no reproaches?' quizzed Antonia.

'What would Henry have to reproach himself with?'
asked Barbara.

'What indeed!' said her friend with ironic lack of
conviction.

'Oh, come on!' exclaimed Barbara hotly. 'Think of
all the things Henry has not done and weigh them
against what he has.'

'I agree,' said Antonia equably, 'The scales whizz up
in favour. It was naughty of old Calypso to say he had
pushed Margaret under when she was in difficulties.'

'She did *not* say that!' exclaimed Barbara. 'What

298

Calypso said – I was there so I know I've got it right – was that if it had been *her* she would not have pulled Margaret out. You must try to be exact. It's all at least twenty years ago, anyway.'

'You sound like your solicitor husband,' said Antonia, grinning. 'My version makes the better saga, but all right, I will try and remember.' She glanced slyly at her friend. Amazing how Barbara kept her figure, she thought enviously; from a distance she looked like a girl and the white threads in her dark hair suited her. I am glad, though, thought Antonia, that my hair is fair and white doesn't show. Glad, too, that a little extra weight suits me. I am not nearly as lined as she is. 'Did you ever sleep with Henry?' she asked idly.

'Sleep with Henry?' Barbara sounded astonished. 'Goodness, no! Did you? Why?'

'I just wondered.' Antonia ignored the question.

'He had call-girls, don't you remember? He told me – must have been on his trips to London – and "other women" – I am sure there wasn't anyone in the village. Of course, he may have been pulling my leg.'

'He wasn't. I slept with him.' Antonia watched the road ahead. There is something about conversation in cars, she thought, which leads to indiscretion. Perhaps it is because one doesn't see the other person, doesn't look them in the eye? 'I slept with Henry,' she repeated, 'from time to time. It was most agreeable.'

Barbara said, 'Gosh! Matthew?'

'Matthew strayed, too, but not with Henry. Are you positive you didn't sleep with Henry?' Antonia probed.

'Of course I did not.' Barbara sounded shocked.

Noting the use of two words, 'did not', as opposed to the less emphatic 'didn't', Antonia was certain that Barbara had slept with Henry at least once, but was for reasons best known to herself intent on forgetting it.

299

She would, anyway, being Barbara, have called the act 'making love', so out of affection for her old friend she refrained from saying, Ho, out loud, but thought it nevertheless. But when Barbara, unable to leave well alone, said, 'You *are* peculiar, Antonia. What an extraordinary suggestion,' Antonia could not resist teasing. 'Oh, darling,' she said, 'no need to be so prissy. Surely we all had our flings. Look at you and James.'

'James?' Barbara bristled.

'Yes, James and that woman.'

'What woman?'

'The one who made the bed squeak. That woman. Valerie Something. I saw her the other day, you should see what she's done to her hair—'

'That was another of Margaret's wicked inventions, a fantasy,' said Barbara.

'So you and James have always been true? Wasn't it dull?'

'Not dull,' said Barbara. 'Yes, we have.'

Ho, ho, ho, thought Antonia, and we used to tell each other everything! But all she said, pretending to change the subject, was, 'Have you noticed how Matthew, since he got into Parliament, has latched on to their jargon? Everything is Perfectly Clear or Absolutely Clear. They never give a straight answer.'

'That is how politicians survive,' said Barbara. 'I couldn't do it myself.'

This time Antonia said, 'Ho,' out loud, but as they were passing a noisy lorry Barbara did not hear. Antonia heard Barbara say, 'What is clear and absolutely true is that Henry is dying.'

Antonia said, 'Oh God, how I shall miss him! He was such an attractive man.'

'Still is, the old darling.'

'Not as old as all that; he's only in his seventies. Are

300

we supposed to stay the night? I've brought my things in case.'

'Hilaria said she and Clio thought we'd better not, he gets very tired,' said Barbara. 'We could spend the night at the cottage, if you'd like.'

'I think I'd rather get back to London,' said Antonia, 'if that's OK by you.'

'I don't think Hilaria and Clio want us to stay,' said Barbara. 'We shouldn't be hurt.'

'I am not hurt,' said Antonia. 'Their attitude is understandable. Henry has always belonged more to them than to us. It's natural, when you consider that they were practically born on his doorstep.'

'They saw Margaret drown,' said Barbara, her mind niggling back to their earlier conversation.

'Of course,' said Antonia, 'and they saw him save Susie's life. He's been their hero.'

'That's another myth,' said Barbara. 'Both Hilaria and Clio told the same story. Susie was quite recovered when she had sicked up the water she'd swallowed; she was only half-drowned.'

'Don't let's split hairs,' said Antonia. 'It was, half or whole, a terrible experience for all three girls.'

'Worse for Margaret,' said Barbara. 'One shouldn't laugh,' she said, stifling a giggle. 'Why don't you turn off here? The road's prettier, even if it's half a mile longer. It's the way James brought me the first time I came to Cotteshaw.'

'And Matthew brought me,' said Antonia, complying with her friend's suggestion.

Turning presently into the Cotteshaw drive, Antonia slowed to let an oncoming car pass. The driver, Peter Bullivant, stopped and wound down his window. 'Antonia!' he said. 'And Barbara! We have just been to visit Henry; he is very poorly, poor fellow.'

'He wouldn't see us,' said Maisie, leaning across her

301

husband, 'so he must be pretty bad. Your Clio and Hilaria seem to be in charge. I hope they know what they're doing. They said he is too tired to see anybody.'

Antonia said, 'Oh. Oh dear.'

'Come from London?' Peter asked. 'A wasted journey. You should have telephoned.'

'We will just leave our presents and a message, then,' said Antonia sweetly.

'You two might tell your grandchildren not to make such a racket,' said Maisie, leaning further past her husband. 'Sick people need quiet. They are watching *Dr Who* on TV and shrieking.'

'It frightens them,' said Antonia, 'and the television is downstairs out of Henry's earshot.'

'Henry should be in hospital,' said Maisie in an aggrieved voice. 'We told him so weeks ago.'

'What did he say?' asked Barbara, leaning across Antonia, joining in.

'Something about his father dying in that bed and he would, too. Henry can be hurtful. He told me not to talk rubbish when I told him he was looking better, one *has* to tell ill people they are looking better, it bucks them up. Henry is one of our oldest friends, it's wounding when he won't see us. He should be in hospital, well away from noisy children.'

'We are blocking the drive,' said Antonia tightly. 'We mustn't keep you.'

'Goodbye,' shouted Barbara as they drove on. 'Silly old cow,' she exclaimed, 'of course Henry doesn't want to see her.'

Antonia cried angrily, 'Noisy children, indeed, and hospitals! What's quiet about a hospital? I have never understood how Henry could find time for those bores!'

'It seems to have run out now,' said Barbara, beginning to weep. 'I knew Henry was going to die when he refused to have another dog after the last Cringe died.'

'But that was months ago, when he was still up and about,' cried Antonia. 'Oh, Barbara, don't cry, you will set me off and I'll run us into the ditch.'

'Henry was so wonderful and comforting when one was unhappy,' sobbed Barbara.

Antonia said, 'Oh, Barbara, shut up and brace up. We are nearly there. And look,' she said, 'there's Hilaria with your grandchild waiting to greet us.' And in trying to distract Barbara she forgot to hark back and puzzle as to when Henry could have comforted Barbara and she not have been aware of it.

Hilaria put her arms round her mother and hugged her, while her dark and lanky child Eliza hopped from foot to foot awaiting her turn. 'Come in,' Hilaria said. 'Henry is longing to see you. Do you want some tea? Or you, Antonia?'

'No, love,' they said. 'Later, perhaps, before we go.'

Hilaria said, 'We thought we'd leave you alone with him. He gets weary with too many people. Go and ask Katie to come away,' she told her child. The child raced off.

'How that child has grown,' said Antonia. 'How old is she now?'

'Ten, same age as Clio's Katie,' said Hilaria. 'The Bullivants tried to see him,' she said, following her mother into the house. 'We had to say no.'

'We met them,' Antonia laughed, 'bubbling with injured feelings.'

'He preserves his strength for nearest and dearest.' Hilaria led the way to Henry's room. 'He has not been downstairs for weeks.'

Henry lay propped by pillows in his tall four-poster. The two women were shocked at how gaunt he had become. His furrowed cheeks sucked in, his large nose larger, the sinews of his neck stringy, but eyes lighting at the sight of them, he said, 'Hello girls,' pleased.

They took his hands and leaned to kiss him.

Antonia said, 'I brought you caviar. Do you think you could eat it?'

Henry said, 'For my supper, thank you. Is there any vodka, Clio?'

Clio, who had been sitting by the window, said, 'Yes, and lemon. It will do you good.' She came forward and kissed Antonia. 'Hullo, Mum.' Then she said, holding out her hand, 'Come on, Katie, don't pretend you are not there. Kiss your grandmother and come with me.'

A child similar to but smaller than Eliza uncurled from where she had been lying at Henry's feet.

Henry said, 'They lie there, taking the place of all the Humbles and Cringes. Go on,' he said to the reluctant child. 'See you later.'

Antonia hugged her grandchild, then let her go.

The door closed, Barbara said, 'Gentleman's Relish,' and put her offering by his hand.

Henry said, 'You spoil me,' and ran his hand through his thick white hair. 'I shall eat it for tea,' he said. 'Please sit down.'

Barbara sat by the bed, but Antonia moved to the window. 'Do you want this open?' she asked. 'It's quite chilly.'

'Leave it, it helps me wheeze.'

Henry's breathing was painful to his visitors' ears. He said, forestalling questions, 'Hilaria and Clio are doing a great job. The nurse comes to wash me, there's a terribly hearty physiotherapist, the doctor of course, and the little girls,' he gasped, 'entertain.'

'How do they do that?' Antonia left the window and sat by the bed.

'Dance.' Henry gave a choky laugh. 'And sing.'

'Oh?'

'The old Jonathans gave them clown costumes. They chalk their faces,' Henry coughed and fought for breath, 'black crosses across their eyes, clowns' make-up to conceal pain. The children don't know.' He looked away from Barbara and Antonia, trying to breathe.

From his bed he could see across the garden to the fields and woods beyond. There was a blackbird singing, and if these two would not interrupt he might hear a mistlethrush and, ah yes, the sheep. They looked all right from here, but I wish I could get to them. No good. Can't. They are listening to my breathing. It's a free country but I wish they wouldn't, he thought.

Barbara said, 'I see the girls have brought you a television; what do you watch?'

'The news.' How old was Barbara? Fifty-five? Fifty-six? Must be. Antonia, too. Grandmothers. 'Exciting, isn't it? Who would have thought Eastern Europe, in our lifetime – And David Attenborough's animals consummating their liaisons—'

Barbara laughed. 'Anything else?' James had told her that old people watched the children's programmes, perhaps—

Henry said, 'No, I don't,' and shot her a sly glance.

Antonia asked, 'Radio?'

Henry said, 'Third programme.'

'Of course,' she said, 'music.'

Henry wheezed, 'There's a concert I want – ask one of them to bang my pillows—' It was dismissal.

Antonia exclaimed, 'Can't I?'

Henry gasped, 'They know how I like—'

Barbara caught Antonia's eye. 'We must go,' she said. 'We will come again.' She stood up, then bent to kiss his cheek. 'Goodbye, darling Henry.' She felt his

305

bony fingers grip her hand and felt inadequate.

Henry said, 'Pilar came last week. Good of her. She's frightfully fat and old, chesty like me.'

Antonia said, 'Dear Pilar.'

Henry said, 'She made me laugh,' and started a laugh which almost choked him.

Antonia, kissing him goodbye, said, 'Sh—'

Henry, wheezing, said, 'It's a bit thick when you can't even laugh.'

On their way back to London Antonia complained fretfully, 'Clio and Hilaria and their children have eased us out,' but Barbara was not listening; she was wondering what Pilar had told Henry that was so amusing.

Pilar had not intended to amuse when she confessed that she had read his father's letter all those years ago. Steamed it open, read it, then posted it. 'As I put it in I feel the box will bite my hand. I had done wrong,' she moaned, her eyes cast down in shame. 'But he save my life and Ebro,' she said more robustly. 'Who was I to refuse an old man's last wish? I was young. Now I know old man's last wish often stupid.'

'I shall bear that in mind,' Henry whispered.

Pilar said, 'I waited to get back to Spain for my spitting on Franco, as your father ordered, then I confess to priest.'

'You confessed to spitting?'

'No, no, to posting letter.'

He had laughed and almost choked on spongy phlegm. When able to speak he said, 'Dear Pilar, you did right.'

The Jonathans visited Henry several times a week. One of them would read snippets from the paper, for they thought Henry's arms too weak to hold it. Some days

Jonathan opened his bills and wrote the cheques for him to sign. John apprised him of local gossip and the state of his farm or told him long, rambling tales about their cats. Sometimes they just sat, hiding their concern.

Halfway through June they came down from Henry's room and ambled into the kitchen, as was their wont. 'We left him snoozing,' the elder man told Clio.

Clio said, 'Cup of coffee?'

They said, 'Yes, please.'

'I am not sure he is asleep.' The younger man pulled up a chair.

'He shuts his eyes and listens to the birds,' said Hilaria. 'They give him pleasure.'

'More than we do?' The old man was aggrieved.

'It is no effort listening to the birds,' said Clio. 'Sugar?' She passed the sugar.

Hilaria was sorry for the old men. They were nearly eighty, their eyes and their teeth gave trouble; they complained of rheumatism and were short of breath. One was too fat and the other too thin. They frequently mentioned that old age was no joke.

But Clio, who had inherited Antonia's briskness, maintained they were wonderful for their age and should not be pandered to, that they came not so much to see Henry as to gain sympathy themselves. 'You should not encourage them to come so often,' she told Hilaria when they left.

'They are part of Henry's life,' Hilaria protested.

Clio snapped, 'That does not give them the right to precipitate his death. I shall ask Henry what he wants.'

Hilaria said, 'He will be too kind to say.'

Clio said, 'No, he won't. I shall ask him.' Which she did that afternoon. 'Do your visitors tire you? I mean do some of them, the Jonathans for instance, stay too long?'

Henry said, 'They come for comfort, darling, you know that.'

And Clio said, 'That's why I asked. They should restrain themselves, they tire you.'

But Henry, catching his breath, said, 'They arranged with the men for the sheep to be in the top field, so that I can see them from my bed and hear them bleat.' Clio, miffed that she had not thought of this ploy herself, admitted, 'You wrong-footed me there. I shall mind my own business.'

And when Henry said, 'You do that,' felt she deserved the rebuke.

Calypso came one afternoon, bringing a sumptuous bunch of lilies of the valley, which she put in a bowl near the window where Henry could see them but not be overwhelmed by their scent. 'And how is the old widower today?' she enquired, seating herself by the bed.

'Dying,' said Henry.

'So you have reached that point?'

'Yes,' said Henry. 'It's slow work, though.'

'Clio and Hilaria stressed that I was on no account to make you laugh as it might hasten your demise.' Calypso leaned back in her chair, smiling.

Henry said, 'The dear girls,' grinning.

Calypso too said, 'The dear girls,' and they sat for a moment sharing their age and considering the young. Then she said, 'When Hector died, we were cheated. He dropped, there one minute, gone the next. I had no chance to ask what it is like. What is it like, Henry?'

'Exhausting.'

'Keeping their spirits up?'

'That's about it, and it is a bore not being able to breathe. Laughter, of course, is lethal. But I am not beefing. I only wish they did not all take it so seriously.' Then, seeing that Calypso looked distressed, he said, 'Tell me about Hector's wood; are the cherry trees in flower, and the bluebells?'

She said, 'Yes, they are, and for such a young wood, only forty-five years, it's wonderful. I wish Hector could see it now; he put his heart into that wood.'

'What was left over from you.'

Calypso said, 'M–m–m. This will please you, Henry. There are nightingales this year.'

Henry said, 'Wonderful.'

She said, 'Hilaria's child tells me you listen to the birds. Cotteshaw birds were always in a class of their own.'

Henry said, 'The dawn chorus rewards me for the nights.'

'Which are long?'

'Yes.'

'But you have owls?'

'There is no mad joy in a hoot,' he said.

'As you know, and I know, the "mad joy" is a furious "keep off my patch" – Oh! Now I have made you laugh!' Calypso waited for Henry to stop wheezing. 'What do you think about in the long night watches?' she asked.

Henry turned towards her. 'I think of friends, friends like you. I think with gratitude of the girls' generosity. They used to come at weekends with their men. It was like old times with Barbara and James, Antonia and Matthew and their babies. I have rather lost the taste, the habit, what is the word, for that lot, but now Clio and Hilaria have left their men to fend for themselves in London and here they are, looking after me. It's good of them.'

Calypso said, 'They love you, and modern husbands have been taught to cope.'

'Hilaria isn't actually married,' said Henry.

309

Calypso said, 'It's the new mode. There's some sort of cachet in not being married to your child's father.'

'Not as new as all that!' Henry, catching Calypso's eye, tried not to laugh.

She exclaimed, 'Don't laugh! I refuse to be responsible to Clio. Oh, do try not to! What else do you consider during those lonely hours?' she asked.

'I consider my little clowns. Get them to show you their costumes—'

'They have. How clever of the Jonathans! Such a good idea.'

'Apt?'

'Well, original. I take it, this was prior to the interdiction on laughter?'

'Yes.' She had not changed, he thought, watching her. She had not been sentimental as a girl; she was even less so now.

She said, 'I hope you do not waste what time is left on regrets.'

I regret never telling her that I was in love with her, he thought. Would it be in order to tell her now? 'I regret that I was something of a moral coward,' he said. 'I regret that very much.'

'It was not noticeable,' said Calypso cheerfully. 'You always, from what I saw of you, appeared rather brave. A bit on the rash side. Hector said you were flawed. I supposed it was your *joie de vivre* overcoming various hindrances and obstacles.'

Henry smiled. 'You were ever discreet. I could confess my regretful flaws to you if you'd listen.'

'Don't!' exclaimed Calypso, flushing. 'You are taking advantage of your death-bed. A confession made to anyone other than a priest would be a selfish indulgence.'

Henry said, 'I got a rise out of you, didn't I? You've gone quite pink.' Then he sighed and looked past her and out to the view of the garden and, in the distance, the sheep. She was right. Barbara had long since blocked anything that might harm James, and Antonia was strong. 'OK,' he said. 'I dare say you know it all, anyway.'

Relieved, Calypso said, 'That's possible.'

Clio, coming upstairs with the intention of a tactful hint that Henry's visitor had stayed long enough, was surprised by a burst of laughter.

35

The Jonathans could not keep away from Cotteshaw. After visiting Henry, they shuffled down to flop into armchairs in the drawing room, where Hilaria brought them coffee.

'We are a nuisance,' they told one another, watching her go, straight-backed in trim jeans and T-shirt, glossy shoulder-length brown hair held back by an Alice band. 'They are so efficient, those two. Will the little girls be the same in their thirties?'

'They are the same model, Hilaria and Clio. I can't tell one from t'other. Their kids will be the same.'

'Only because they dress alike do they look alike. That one is bossy,' said John, watching Hilaria's disappearing back.

'Less bossy than Clio. Antonia was tougher than Barbara. It's inherited,' said Jonathan. 'Are you afraid of them?' he asked slyly.

'It is their youth which alarms me.'

In their anguish the old men did what Clio and Hilaria told them, resentfully, for they had known them from birth, played with them as they now played with their daughters, Eliza and Katie, spoiling them by giving them presents.

'They make themselves useful.' Hilaria excused the Jonathans to Clio, who had let slip a remark in the nature of 'Taken root again' or 'Have they no home?', which meant no more than that she was as tired and unhappy as was Hilaria. 'They answer the telephone;

they keep the children quiet when it rains. I have asked them to keep a list of callers, so that we know – They are miserable, Clio,' she said.

'I know.' Clio tucked her T-shirt into her jeans. 'I am miserable, too.' (And all the more miserable because I wish this was over. I wish Henry could die; this inching progress is nerve-wracking.) 'I am impatient,' she said. 'I snap at the children.'

'They grow bored,' said Hilaria. 'The novelty has gone. We have told them their singing and dancing is now too much for Henry. He is too weak. They find it hard to keep quiet in his room; the novelty of lying at his feet has worn off. They are less faithful than the Humbles and Cringes were, less patient as he wheezes and dozes and struggles for breath, drowning in his phlegm.'

Clio said, 'Oh God, Hilaria, must you be so explicit?' and took a deep breath. 'I am sorry,' she said, 'sorry. Of course they must stay. It's good that the very old and the very young can be together. They understand each other.' She looked out at the clouds scudding across the sky, presaging rain. 'Perhaps,' she said, 'we should let our men come. What do you think? They could take the children on, relieve the Jonathans, do their parental duty.'

Hilaria thought of Eliza's father with a fierce longing which matched, she knew, Clio's need for her husband, but she said, 'Not yet. The Js are doing a great job with the children. It helps them endure this terrible waiting.'

'What about *us*?' snapped Clio. 'Do we not need help, too?'

Hilaria said, 'You and I have got to manage. If we let the men come, they won't cope with the little girls. They will say, Leave them with the Js. They will gobble us up. You know they will.'

313

'Nothing I'd like better,' retorted Clio, 'than to be gobbled up by my husband.'

'They will be wishing Henry to get on with it, to get it over, so that they can take us home. I wish his suffering over but I will not have him hurried,' said Hilaria.

'Nor do I wish that,' said Clio. 'Dear God, no.'

'I couldn't, if they came—' Hilaria began to speak but stopped short. I could not go to bed with my lover without wanting to make love, she thought. I could not enjoy love, knowing that Henry was in his room along the passage, dying. 'Oh, Clio!' she said. 'I—'

And Clio said, 'I know, I know, me too. We'll wait,' and put her arms round Hilaria and hugged her.

In the drawing room the Jonathans sat with the telephone between them, taking turns to answer.

'No,' they said to Barbara, to James, to Antonia. 'No change. A bit weaker. Yes, your love? Of course we will give it to him. Yes, the children are well. They are being very good. The young mothers have put us in charge, it gets us out of their hair. Yes, they watch TV, they play in the garden. We try to keep them amused when it rains—'

'We should have used the answerphone,' said John. 'We say the same every day. There it goes again. Your turn.'

'No, no change,' said Jonathan. 'A bit weaker, perhaps. Give him your love? Of course I will. Yes, do, ring tomorrow. Yes. That was Matthew. He said he's getting twitchy.'

'He foresees having to interrupt his holiday and flying home from Greece for the funeral and oh, the expense of flying back.' The old man blew out his moustache, white now but still luxuriant, and laughed.

'He wouldn't like that,' said his stout friend, smiling. 'Do you suppose he intends trying to buy Cotteshaw for his grandson Guy?'

'Perhaps he assumes Henry has left it to Susie?' The question of who would inherit Cotteshaw was a secret Henry had not divulged to either old friend.

'Henry is not all that keen on Susie or Guy, and he never had Matthew's predilection for primogeniture,' said Jonathan. 'Your turn,' he said as the telephone rang.

'No,' said John. 'No, no change. A little weaker, possibly. Oh no! No need to interrupt your trip—' ('She's in the States with her husband,' he whispered.) 'No, there would be no point. What could you do? No. He sleeps most of the time. Yes. Yes. Of course, your love and Guy's. Is he with you? I thought it was term-time. Oh, I *see*, he would send his love if he thought of it! OK. Love by proxy it is.' Replacing the receiver, he said, 'That was Sewage. Huh!'

'You hung up on her.' His old friend chuckled.

'One has to do something,' John muttered, 'or bust. I think I shall explode if Henry has left the place to Susie.'

'Don't be an idiot,' said his lover. 'He will have left it to the clowns, Eliza and Katie.'

'Wouldn't that create a terrific—' The old man's eyes lit in pleasurable anticipation.

'Why not? He won't be here. Oh, *curse* it, there it goes again!'

John lifted the receiver (the States again; must be the cheap rate or something). 'Who?' he shouted. 'Who? Basil? Heavens! We imagined you dead. You just heard? Met Susie? That figures. Yes. No. Not yet, no. No, I cannot tell you what day. Yes, of course I will give him your message. No! Not love, that's too much. How can you love him when you only met him once?

No, I cannot allow that, sorry. Goodbye! That was Basil, the brother-in-law,' he said. 'He asked what day the funeral is, wants to send flowers.'

'You can love after only one meeting,' said the other man, his voice trembling. 'You should not have been so rough with him.'

'I feel rough,' he said. 'Very rough indeed.' He caught hold of his moustache with both hands and tugged at it. 'He has not communicated for about twenty years; why butt in now?'

'Because Henry is dying,' said the older man. 'He probably thinks it's the right thing to do.'

They slumped mournfully in their chairs, eyeing the telephone with mistrust. Then, 'Here comes the rain,' the older man said. 'How shall we entertain the little girls? Come on, buck up, think of something.'

'Take the phone off the hook, for starters – Oh, I know. Let's show them all the albums, old photographs. Henry's family and all of us. They are over there in the bookshelf. I need a drink; you fetch the whisky, I'll find the albums. The little girls will love to see what we all looked like. They may even,' he said as he shambled across the room, 'come to realize that we were young once, improbable though it may seem.'

In the kitchen Hilaria and Clio stripped wet clothes off their children, rubbed their hair dry and urged them into dry jeans and warm sweaters. 'Go to the Jonathans,' they said. 'You can ring Daddy tonight. Here, take some bread and honey with you. Be careful not to make the furniture sticky. No, you can't ring Daddy now, he won't be in. No, you can't see Henry, the nurse is with him. Go to the old Jonathans. Yes, yes, you can see Henry for a minute before you go to bed.'

'Is Henry dying?' the children asked.

'Yes,' said Clio, who believed in the minimum of lies.

In his office in the City, Hilaria's lover Patrick picked up the telephone and put in a call to Clio's husband Richard. He said, 'I am fed up with this situation, Richard. I shall go down to Cotteshaw tonight. Are you game to come with me?'

Richard replied that he was indeed game; he would be glad to keep Patrick company.

'In spite of what Hilaria says, I have a feeling that I am needed,' said Patrick.

'Clio tells me not to come,' said Richard, 'but her voice betrays her need.'

'It is not only Clio's and Hilaria's need,' said Patrick. 'Willy-nilly it becomes ours, too.'

They arranged to drive down that night in Patrick's car.

In the drawing room Katie and Eliza laughed themselves into fits. The photographs were a great success. They crouched on the floor, surrounded by albums and loose photographs of bygone times. Chiefly they were fascinated by the women's clothes, their hair piled up and later shingled or bobbed and their jewellery. 'Who is this?' they asked the Jonathans. 'Look at her hat!'

'That's my mother,' said John. 'She was French, a governess.'

'Not when that was taken,' said his friend. 'When that was taken she was expecting you.'

'Such funny clothes!' The little girls giggled.

'She had style,' said the old man, 'style.'

The little girls felt rebuked.

Outside the windows it grew dark. Jonathan drew the curtains against the persistent rain tapping on the panes. 'Filthy evening.' He helped himself to whisky and resumed his armchair. His lover made a thumbs-up sign; the children were absorbed, they could drink their whisky in peace.

At their feet the children discovered Ebro as a baby, Pilar as a young woman, a young Trask and pictures of an adolescent Henry, grouped sometimes with his parents, sometimes alone with early versions of Hector and Lysander. There were loose photographs pushed higgledy-piggledy into albums which they brought to the old men for identification.

Margaret, strange and beautiful, had to be explained; they had been unaware that Henry had once had a wife. They were not as much interested as they had been in snaps of Henry's mother with friends in intriguing clothes and strange hats. They riffled through the snapshots until they found photographs of their own mothers, holding themselves as infants in christening robes grouped in a church porch. 'Look, look,' they squeaked, 'that's me and Grandpa and Grandma. That's *us* as babies, do look.'

'I took that photograph,' said the older man. 'I remember it well. It's good of your mums and dads. Why don't you try and put all these loose photographs in order?' That will keep them busy, he thought, and got up to go to the lavatory.

On his way back he stood in the hall and listened, cocking his head to hear sounds from upstairs. All was quiet, he thought. Time for another drink, then surely it's time for the kids to go to bed. They are beginning to squabble.

In the drawing room there was dissension as Eliza and Katie fought over a studio portrait of a young woman. His lover, who had dozed in his chair, woke with a jerk as Eliza, who had gained possession, pushed the photograph under his nose. 'It's *my*

318

mummy, isn't it?' she squeaked, as he blearily put on his glasses. 'Katie says it's *hers*.'

Katie snatched at the photograph and, holding it out of Eliza's reach, thrust it at John, crying, 'You tell her, John. That's *my* mother, it's *my* mother, not hers, tell Eliza.'

The old man took the photograph from the child and turned it over. He said, 'This was taken in 1930, darling, before your mothers were thought of. That's Henry's mother.' Then, as his eyes met his lover's over the children's heads, he said, clearing his throat, 'Of course, there's a look—'

Some time in the early hours the rain stopped. Henry stirred and tried to say something.

Hilaria held a feeding cup to his lips. He sipped and whispered, 'Air.'

Clio went to the window, pulled back the curtains and opened it wide. Together Hilaria and Clio heaved the old man up, plumped his pillows and laid him gently back.

In chairs once occupied by generations of dogs, Clio's and Hilaria's daughters who, creeping in in the night, had not been turned away, slept.

Henry whispered, 'Don't wake them.'

The young women stood on either side of the bed and held Henry's cold hands as they grew colder.

Presently Henry said quite clearly, 'Is it light?'

Hilaria said, 'Nearly.'

A blackbird began to sing in the garden, but Henry Tillotson had died a moment before.

THE END

www.vintage-books.co.uk